The Assassin

by

Suzanne Rossi

The Assassin

Cover Art by *Kim Mendoza*

The Wild Rose Press, Inc.
PO Box 708
Adams Basin, NY 14410-0708
Visit us at www.thewildrosepress.com

Publishing History
First Crimson Rose Edition, 2016
Print ISBN 978-1-5092-0601-8
Digital ISBN 978-1-5092-0602-5

Published in the United States of America

Pausing, I listened. Silence reigned.

Surely the thief still wasn't here. I took a chance and crept into the living room. The desk drawers and those of the secretary also showed signs of having been searched.

I stopped at the foot of the stairs, licked my lips, and wondered if I was being a fool. Get out and call the cops. The silence got on my nerves. My breaths quickened. I hustled back to the desk and looked for my letter opener. It was ornate and sharp—a perfect weapon for self-defense, assuming that if the thief was still here, he didn't have a gun.

Of course, the thief isn't here. He's long gone. Still, better safe than sorry.

Unfortunately, I couldn't find the opener, so I grabbed a pair of scissors instead and tiptoed up the steps. No one jumped from a doorway to halt my progress. I tiptoed down the hall to my bedroom door. It stood half closed. I pushed it open and entered. My gaze never made it to the jewelry box.

Instead, I stared at the body of Don Merrick on the bedroom floor, his sightless eyes staring at the ceiling—with my letter opener sticking out of his chest.

Dedications

On several occasions I've dedicated my books to my editors, especially, Johanna Melaragno. She guided me through eleven of my twelve previous releases. Now, however, she has moved on to greener pastures. Thank you for all you've done. I'll miss you, Jo.

~*~

My new editor is Anne DelSignore and this novel, The Assassin, is our first together. Needless to say, I'm looking forward to many more. So, thank you, Annie, for guiding this sometimes-lost author onto the right track. And another big thanks to my readers. I hope you enjoy reading the story as much as I enjoyed writing it.

Prologue

The great Ross Patterson was dead. He lay slumped across his desk, his head a bloody mess. The killer stared, flooded with the sense of a job well done.

Patterson groaned. His hand made a feeble movement toward a cell phone just inches away.

Not so dead after all.

The cast iron frying pan once again descended on the man's head. Finally, he lay still.

There! Now, the son of a bitch is dead.

The killer dropped the skillet and wiped fingerprints from the handle. A silly weapon, but effective.

How does it feel to be on the receiving end for a change, Mr. Big-Time-Lawyer? No more screwing innocent people for the Almighty dollar. No big tell-all book deal that may or may not make former clients nervous. Are you burning in Hell yet? I hope so. You deserve to be and—

The grandfather clock in the hall chimed the hour interrupting the rage-filled thoughts. *Time to leave.*

Swallowing the anger, the assassin exited the room and closed the door. The guilty could keep their secrets a while longer. Their problems had been solved.

Chapter One

I groaned, jammed the pillow over my head, and prayed whoever pounded on my front door would just *go away*. At least I hoped the obnoxious noise emanated from that source and not from within my head.

Cracking an eyelid open, I tried to focus on the nightstand clock.

Nine o'clock? You've got to be kidding! I'd just crawled into bed four hours ago.

The pounding ceased for a moment before resuming. *Persistent asshole!*

"Damn it to hell," I cursed sitting up and throwing the pillow across the room. It bounced off my vanity table, rattling the assorted perfume bottles.

I swung my legs to the floor, then groaned again. My head felt like it was going to fall off and roll across the carpet.

Amidst great pain, I leaned over, grabbed my dress from where I'd tossed it next to the bed, and then pulled the silver sequined mini-garment over my head.

"Can't answer the door naked," I muttered out loud.

I rose and staggered toward the stairs, praying I wouldn't tumble head over heels and break my neck. Or maybe praying I would. I wasn't sure at this stage. I clung to the banister anyway.

"I'm coming! Knock off that goddamned noise!"

In the foyer, I peeked through the peephole. Two uniformed cops—one male, one female—stood on my front stoop.

Cops? *What the hell have I done now?*

I hadn't driven to either Ross's party or Beale Street the night before. Jim had, or maybe Wyatt, or Krissy. Perhaps, I'd taken a cab. Shit, I couldn't remember.

Unlocking the deadbolt, I left the safety chain in place, opened the door, and peered through the six inch gap.

Cop number one, the guy, smiled. "Hilary Watson?"

"Yes."

"I'm Officer Larson. This is Officer Bellows. May we come in?"

Not a trusting sort, I asked for identification. They both flashed authentic looking credentials.

"May we come in?" Bellows asked.

The sooner I let them in, the sooner they'd be gone.

"Yeah, I guess so." I closed the door, removed the chain, and re-opened it. "What's this all about?"

They entered, stopped, and stared. I guess the sight of a five foot, ten inch woman with ratty blonde hair, bloodshot blue eyes, and smudged make-up sporting a skimpy cocktail dress in the morning was unusual.

I led them into the living room where I plopped onto the sofa. With elbows anchored on my knees, I held my head. They stood.

Officer Larson flipped open a small notebook. "Miss Watson, we got your name and address from Ephemia Tollivar."

My head hurt like hell and my mind was slow on the uptake. "Who?"

"Mrs. Ephemia Tollivar, your stepfather's housekeeper," Bellows said.

"Oh! You mean Effie. Yeah, okay. Effie gave you my name and address? Why? What's going on?"

Larson's face grew grim. "Miss Watson, I'm sorry to tell you your stepfather, Ross Patterson, was found dead in his study this morning."

Good thing I was already seated. Shock rolled through me. I trembled and felt sick to my stomach.

"Dead? But I just saw him last night! What happened? Was it a heart attack?"

Ross wasn't big on eating healthy or exercise, but he'd looked fine when I'd said goodnight.

"No, ma'am, he was murdered."

I gasped. "He…he was murdered? How?"

"He was bludgeoned to death with a cast iron skillet."

"What? You've got to be kidding!"

My voice rose several octaves. At the same time I had the most absurd desire to giggle like a teenager. Ross? Nailed with a frying pan? How mundane, how plebian. The least the killer could have done was use one of the man's golf trophies.

"I'm afraid not," Bellows replied. "Would you mind coming down to the station? The detectives need to ask you some questions."

"Yeah, sure, no problem. Let me shower and change. When did this happen? Who found him?" My fogged mind still had trouble grasping the news.

"I don't know when, but the body was discovered by Ms. Tollivar this morning when she came to work."

Poor Effie! A quiet, religious woman who never had a bad thing to say about anybody, she did her job with little fuss. Ross had hired her five years ago when his previous housekeeper moved away.

"Uh, do you need me to hurry? Because I really need a cup of coffee right now." A cup? Try a dozen. "Has Ian Rogers been notified? He's Ross's nephew."

"Ms. Tollivar called 9-1-1 immediately, and then Mr. Rogers," Bellows said. "And no, we don't need to wait for you. Just please come in as soon as possible. I understand how coffee comes first."

"Thank you, I'll be there as soon as possible."

Rising, I led them back to the foyer. They left and I leaned against the door. It came as no surprise that Effie hadn't contacted me. I was Ross's stepdaughter and didn't live in the house. I wondered if Mother had heard yet. She didn't live in the house anymore either.

My head throbbed. I made my way to the kitchen of my townhouse and started a large pot of coffee.

As the water burbled, the enticing aroma of Colombia's finest tickled my nose. I swallowed several aspirins and thought about Ross.

He was a self-centered bastard who loved watching people squirm, and not necessarily clients. His favorite sport was calling various family members who needed a loan into his study to question them like common criminals about their activities, friends, and of course, money. I'd spent my fair share of time standing before his desk like a penitent, explaining why I needed an extension on my allowance.

My mother had married him ten years ago when I was a freshman at Ole Miss, but they had recently separated. He'd continued paying my bills after Mother had left. Of course, he only did that so he could retain control of my life. If I were a stronger person, I'd have told him to stuff it long ago and found even a low-wage job. But over the years, I'd gotten used to the good life. The step up was easy. The step down would be a lot harder. Now that he was dead, I would have trouble coming up with the bucks for recent charges at local boutiques and jewelry stores.

The coffeemaker beeped. I shook my head, ceasing the reverie, and poured a large mug of the strong brew.

Still, I couldn't help but think. *Roswell Patterson's sins finally caught up with him.*

****

Three hours and numerous cups of coffee later, I emerged from my townhouse. More aspirin helped reduce my headache to a mild annoyance. A glance at my cell showed two unanswered calls, both from Mother. I'd deal with her later.

Instead of heading for the police station, I gave in to impulse and drove by Ross's home. I don't know why. Mother wasn't there, but I wanted to make sure Effie was all right. Finding what I assumed was a bloody body must have upset her beyond belief.

I live on the western edge of Moreland, a rapidly expanding, upscale suburb just east of Memphis. Ross lived on the east side of town where two acres and six thousand square foot houses are called estates. Recognizing me, the guard at the gate waved as I used my swipe card to gain entrance. I drove up the circular drive and parked behind three other cars. No police cruisers, ambulances, or other official vehicles were in sight.

I climbed the porch steps of the pseudo-antebellum

house and walked in, then followed the voices I heard coming from the den. En route, I passed the closed study door crisscrossed with yellow crime scene tape. I paused, staring for a moment, and then shivered before continuing on.

Ian Rogers, Ross's nephew, stood near the fireplace talking with a man and a woman I didn't recognize. My attention, however, focused on the man sitting in a wing chair, his long legs crossed. Colin Blackwood, another nephew, eyed me with raised eyebrows, but said nothing before returning his gaze to the notebook in his hand. In his mid-thirties, his dark hair showed a few strands of gray threading their way along the temples. His gray eyes could change from soft to hard as stone in an instant. He was a private investigator.

Conversation stopped. Ian looked surprised to see me.

"Hilary, what are you doing here?"

"Two cops pounded on my door at nine o'clock with the news."

"And I'm sure you were already up and at 'em," Colin murmured.

I didn't much care for Colin Blackwood nor did he like me. His sarcasm and obvious dislike of my partying lifestyle sent my blood pressure soaring. It was none of his business, and for the life of me, I couldn't figure out why I let that disdain bother me.

I ignored the barbed comment and shifted my gaze back to the group by the fireplace.

"I'm so sorry, Ian. Do the cops have any idea who killed him? And with a frying pan, no less."

"And how do you know that?" the unidentified

man asked.

"The cops who showed up told me."

"I can see I'll have to have a discussion with certain officers regarding the dissemination of information." He shot a glance at the woman.

"I doubt it could be kept secret anyway," Colin said. "Effie found the body and saw the weapon."

"Why should it be kept a secret, and who are you?" I asked staring at the man.

"Hilary, these are Detectives Brad Parker and Claudia Hamilton," Ian replied nodding toward the strangers. "Detectives, this is my uncle's stepdaughter, Hilary Watson."

I stepped forward to shake hands.

Detective Hamilton smiled. "A pleasure, Ms. Watson."

Detective Parker didn't smile, but shook my hand anyway. "I'm glad you stopped by. We'd like to talk to you informally."

"Make it formal if you like," I said with a shrug.

"Have a seat, Hilary," Ian said.

I chose the sofa. From his winged chair, Colin stared. The amused expression on his face made me run a nervous hand through my short, spiky hair. I didn't find anything amusing about this. My attention was pulled away when Detective Parker spoke.

"You were here at the party last night, I believe."

I sat back. "Yes, I was. Ross announced his retirement a few of months ago and wanted to celebrate a book deal for his memoirs."

"Can you give us a brief rundown of the evening from your perspective?"

"I arrived somewhere around seven forty-five,

maybe eight, greeted people I knew, introduced myself to those I didn't, had a few drinks, some hors d'oeuvres, chatted for a while, and then left. It was really very ordinary."

"Did you speak with your stepfather?" he asked.

"Sure, he circulated among his guests, too."

Detective Hamilton's smile never wavered. "What did you talk about?"

I shifted my weight and crossed my legs. "With Ross? Just the usual—hello, how are you, it's been a long time since I've seen you—that kind of thing. With the other guests? I don't remember. Social chit-chat, the kind you get at any cocktail party."

"When did you leave?" Detective Parker asked.

"Around ten, I think."

"Did you drive straight home?"

A soft snort from the winged chair had me glancing at Colin. His amusement increased. I wanted to slap him silly.

"No, I had plans to meet friends on Beale Street, and since I knew we'd be drinking, I took a cab."

I don't know why I volunteered this information. Maybe to show Colin Blackwood I had some sense of responsibility, and then immediately gave myself a mental kick in the butt. Why on earth did I care what he thought? I sneaked another glance at him. He didn't look impressed.

"When did you get home?" Detective Hamilton asked.

When indeed? The bars closed at four in the morning. I vaguely recalled a bouncer shoving my friends and me onto the sidewalk.

"I really don't know."

"Did you take a cab home?" she continued.

I licked my lips. "I…I'm not sure. I think I did, although one of my friends may have driven." Four pairs of eyes stared at me. I became defensive, my voice taking on a belligerent tone. "Look, it was a long night and I had a lot to drink. All right?"

"In other words, a routine evening," Colin commented while writing in that damned notebook.

Hot words bubbled to my lips, but before I could spit them out, Ian intervened.

"Colin, that wasn't necessary."

Colin shrugged, but offered no apology.

Detective Parker closed his notebook. "Thank you, Ms. Watson. Would you mind coming down to the station to make a formal statement, say about two o'clock this afternoon?"

"Not at all. The officers this morning requested the same thing. In fact, I was on my way when I decided to drive by here."

"Why?" Detective Hamilton asked.

I shrugged. "I wanted to check in on Effie. Finding Ross's body must have upset her. It was just an impulse."

"Do you have a phone number where we can reach you?"

I gave her my cell number, rose, and asked, "Is that all?"

"For now," Parker replied.

The detectives thanked everyone and left. The minute the front door closed, I stood glaring at Colin.

"Thanks a lot for making me look ridiculous."

"You do a good job of that all by yourself."

"Oh, go cram it up your…"

"Please, you two," Ian said holding up his hand. "Let's check the animosity at the door. Ross is dead. Murdered. And I think we need to focus on who did it."

"Grab the phone book and pick a name," I snapped, resuming my seat.

"Uncle Ross rubbed a lot of people the wrong way," Ian said with a frown. "But a frying pan is a weird weapon choice."

"He was a high-profile, self-aggrandizing defense attorney," Colin replied. "He garnered numerous threats from victims' families and friends, and I know a couple of former prosecutors who weren't too fond of him either."

"And don't forget some of his clients," I added. "They were scum. Ross was planning a memoir. Maybe one of them didn't like that idea."

"If that was the case, he'd have been shot. Those people don't mess around with frying pans. Besides, the attorney/client privilege still applies. He'd have merely changed the names," Colin said, sending me a bored glance. "But he did have four ex-wives floating around, including your mother."

"She's not an ex yet." My voice rose. "Are you suggesting my mother strolled in, rummaged in a kitchen she never entered while living here, grabbed a frying pan, and whacked him?"

He smirked. "Their upcoming divorce had the potential of being bitter and protracted."

"Oh, go to hell, Blackwood. Mother would probably have gotten a huge settlement and collected alimony. Why kill the golden goose?"

"Alimony isn't forever. Maybe they argued over how much and for how long. It turned nasty, and she nailed him."

"That's ridiculous," I sputtered. "Mother has no money issues."

"Your mother always has money issues. So do you."

That one cut a little too close to home. "You arrogant jerk! Maybe *I* should find a frying pan."

"Colin, Hilary, stop it now!" Ian ordered. "This is getting us nowhere. I couldn't make the party last night. How about you, Colin? Were you here?"

Colin shook his head. "I was meeting a new client for dinner. After that, I went home and reviewed notes on an old case that just went to trial. I'm due to testify in the next couple of days."

"Can you prove it?" I challenged just to piss him off.

"I don't need to," he replied with raised eyebrows and that damned amused expression again. "I'd have no reason to see Ross dead. I rarely saw the man."

I should have known he wouldn't take the verbal bait. He was the coolest cucumber in town and always had been. A sharp pain slashed through my head reminding me of last night's binge. I rummaged in my purse for the aspirin bottle I always carry, popped two into my mouth swallowing them dry, and then rose.

Colin's amused expression widened into a grin. "Must have been one hell of a night."

"Go take a flying leap," I muttered before turning to Ian. "The cops have no clues at all?"

Ian shook his head. "None that they're sharing at the moment. I've already told them Colin will be working for the family on this. He can do things and go places the police can't legally."

"Things like breaking and entering, stealing papers or files, threatening people? Good choice. Colin's a whiz at all those endeavors."

"I'm good at my job. Why don't I start my investigation with you? Who were you with last night and where?"

"I'm sure you know what you can do with that." I turned toward the doorway. "I have a two o'clock appointment with those detectives, but first I'm going to have lunch. I'll talk to you when I feel like it."

"In that case, you'd better consider a fast food joint. Ross's death means no more money. You might actually have to get a job," Colin said.

I ignored the comment. "Goodbye, Ian."

I walked from the room. Unfortunately, he was right. My money source had just dried up courtesy of a frying pan. I was almost to the front door when the sound of sobs stopped me. Someone was crying in the living room. I peeked around the doorjamb. Effie sat on the edge of the sofa wiping her eyes with a tissue. In my irritation with Colin, I'd forgotten why I'd dropped by in the first place.

Without pausing, I entered the room and sat next to her. "Oh, Effie, I'm so sorry. It must have been horrible finding Ross like that."

She raised her washed out blue eyes toward me. "Oh Miss Watson, it was the worst thing in my life."

"Tell me what happened."

"Well, miss, I came to work at six just like usual. Your stepfather was very particular about his breakfast—sausage, scrambled eggs, two pieces of toast heavily buttered, no jelly, tomato juice, and coffee—every day. And all precisely at seven o'clock."

She didn't have to tell me about Ross's eating habits. My guess was they hadn't changed in thirty years. He was anal in that respect.

"Yes, I know. Then what happened? Did you make his breakfast?"

"Yes, miss. But when I went to serve him in the dining room, he wasn't there. I thought maybe he'd slept in because of the party, so I went upstairs to his room, but his bed wasn't disturbed at all. Then, I thought he might be working on his book. That's when I went into the study and…and…" She sobbed again.

I hugged the woman. "Try not to think about it, Effie."

"How? There was blood everywhere and my frying pan on the floor next to him! The police asked me all kinds of questions about it. I know they think I killed him!"

I squeezed her shoulders again. "Of course they don't suspect you. Did you use that pan a lot?"

"Quite often if I fried something. Your stepfather liked my chicken and catfish. Said it was the best in the South." She wiped her eyes. "I just know they're going to arrest me."

"Don't be silly. What kind of motive would you have?"

"Motive?"

"Yes, why on earth would you kill Ross?"

She hiccupped and stared at me with a look of understanding on her face. "That's right. Why would I kill him? He paid me a very generous salary. Now I'm out of a job, and I need the money. What am I going to do?"

"The family will see to it you don't go without,"

Colin said from the doorway.

I looked up. His smile was genuine and kind. *Guess he isn't a horse's ass all the time.*

He strode into the room and crouched in front of the housekeeper. "I'll be moving into the house for a while, so you can continue your duties until we find you another position."

"Why are you moving in?" I asked.

"Ian doesn't want the house empty. Might become a magnet for thieves."

Effie dried her eyes and smiled. "That's very kind of you, Mr. Blackwood."

I glanced at my watch. Crap, it was after one. If I wanted to eat and be on time at the police station, I needed to leave now.

I rose. "Don't worry, Effie. Everything will be all right. I promise."

"Me, too," Colin said also rising. "Wait up, Hilary. I want to talk to you. Goodbye, Effie. I'll see you tonight."

"Is there anything special you'd like for dinner?" she asked.

He smiled. "Keep it simple. Is seven o'clock all right?"

"Yes, sir."

On the front porch, I slapped a pair of sunglasses over my eyes. My head still hurt. I needed food.

"I'll drive you down to the police station," Colin said.

"I have my own car."

"I know, but I want to talk to you."

"Well, I don't want to talk to you."

He cupped my elbow in his hand and steered me

down the steps. "Too bad."

I glared at him as we walked. Colin topped out several inches above six feet. I looked up to meet his gaze.

He yanked open the passenger side door and shoved me inside before slamming it again. He slid behind the wheel, started the engine, and drove down the driveway. Neither of us spoke for several blocks.

Unable to stand the silence, I said, "So, what is it you want to talk about?"

He pulled into a side street and stopped, then turned to me with a worried expression.

"I have to know, Hilary—did you kill Ross?"

Chapter Two

Astonished by the question, I stared into Colin's steel gray eyes in total disbelief.

"Are you nuts? Of course, I didn't kill him. I was with friends on Beale Street the entire freaking night."

"And after a few hours of drinking, you all were likely hammered. It wouldn't be hard to grab a cab, go to Ross's, kill him, and return. Who'd be the wiser?"

"Oh, give me a break. That would take an hour or longer. Someone I was with would have missed me. Besides, the cops would find the cabbie. He'd remember a trip with a drunken female passenger out to Moreland and back. Plus, the gate guard would see me."

"And maybe you were too drunk to think of that. Do you and your friends stick together while on these little excursions?"

I squirmed and looked away. "Most of the time."

"But not all."

"All right, we split up. I'm not a big fan of Jazz It Up, so I went to listen to the street singers in Handy Park."

"Alone?"

"Yes, dammit, alone!"

"Where and when did you meet up with your friends again?"

"I don't know. Basic Blues, I think. I didn't keep

track of my time. You know, you've got a lot of nerve."

"The cops are going to ask you the same thing, and you'd better hope your friends can tell them what you want to hear."

"I did not kill Ross, although I'd like to take a crack at you."

He laughed and swung the car around in a U-turn. "Okay, just don't use a frying pan."

His reference to the murder weapon brought my mind off of his comments and onto Effie.

"Poor Effie. She's really afraid. I mean, I'm sure her fingerprints are on the murder weapon."

"I overheard part of your conversation. It's not likely any fingerprints would be on the pan. It doesn't have a smooth surface. It's textured. Fingerprints wouldn't adhere. Besides, soap and water would erase any latent prints Effie would have left."

I sighed. "So, the killer was an amateur?"

"Probably. Or just being careful."

Colin pulled into a fast food burger joint and parked. "I'm hungry. Could do with some lunch myself."

"Lotta Burger? You're kidding."

"Get used to it, honey. It's going to be your restaurant of choice for a while." His eyebrows rose. "Hey, maybe you can apply for a job while we're here."

I sent him what I hoped was a scathing look and exited the car, slamming the door on his chuckles. I was pissed. His suggestion wasn't that far off the mark, although with the upcoming divorce from Mother, Ross would have cut me off sooner or later. Either way, I was screwed.

****

After checking in at the reception desk, Detective Parker came to escort me into the bowels of the Moreland Police Station. A quick glance over my shoulder as I followed him showed Colin giving me the thumbs up sign.

The interrogation room was a lot smaller than those on TV. A mirror hung on the wall opposite a table and chairs. It didn't take a genius to understand it had two-way glass.

"Please have a seat, Ms. Watson. This won't take long. It's just routine," Detective Parker said, closing the door to the room.

His craggy face reminded me a bit of one of the faces on Mount Rushmore. I wondered if he ever smiled. His partner, on the other hand, smiled a lot.

I nodded and pulled out a utilitarian, armless, plastic chair, sat, and rested my arms on an equally utilitarian Formica topped table. Cigarette burn marks scarred the surface. He sat opposite me and was joined by his partner, Detective Hamilton. Her smile was still in place from earlier at Ross's. For some reason it gave me the creeps. Now, I was nervous. She was too damned cheerful.

"For your information, we will video and audio tape this session," he said. "Just routine."

I glanced up at a camera in the corner of the tiny, airless room.

"Sure, no problem," I replied taking a deep breath to calm my nerves. *Right, just routine.* I'd never done this before and didn't want to admit I was intimidated.

"Now, Ms. Watson, for the record can you describe the scene at the party last night? When did you arrive? Who did you talk to? Did you talk to your stepfather?"

I gave them the same information I had at the house a few hours earlier.

"Did you notice anyone who seemed out of place?" Detective Hamilton asked.

"Out of place? How do you mean?"

"Someone who was attending but wasn't what you'd call a friend of Mr. Patterson's."

"Ross's parties didn't follow a specific guest list. He invited whoever he thought would be the most beneficial to him."

"Beneficial? In what way?"

"Ross contributed to charities and political campaigns. I guess he thought having friends in high places might one day be beneficial to him."

Ross never passed up an opportunity that could help him down the road. It gave him leverage when he wanted something. But I wasn't about to tell the detectives that, nor did I want to indicate how much I disliked my stepfather. I had to tread carefully. After all, the man had been murdered, and thanks to Colin's heads-up regarding my alibi, I wasn't about to reveal too much.

"You said you introduced yourself to people you didn't know at the party. Did anyone in particular stand out?" Detective Parker asked.

I rubbed my temples and shrugged. My headache had subsided, but not by much. "I met a few people in the publishing business. That made sense since Ross had signed a deal for his memoirs. I know one of them was a literary agent and another an attorney specializing in contracts. We had a rather long conversation about the upcoming book. She seemed to think it would be a bestseller. Other than that, no one had 'killer' tattooed on their foreheads."

"Did Mr. Patterson leave the party at any time?" he asked.

"Not that I noticed." I paused. "No, wait, he must have because I saw him coming out of his study at some point."

"Was anyone else with him?"

"Yes. A guy—medium height and weight with dark hair—followed him into the hallway. The dude didn't look happy."

Detective Hamilton raised an eyebrow. "Can you identify this man?"

I shook my head. "Sorry. Never saw him before."

Detective Parker took over the questioning again. "And you say you left the house around ten?"

"Approximately. I was joining friends on Beale and called a cab."

"Did you speak to your stepfather before leaving?"

"I think I said goodbye. He was talking to the literary lawyer and just nodded."

"Other than the party, when was the last time you'd seen Mr. Patterson?" the woman asked.

I shifted my eyes to the tabletop. "I'm...I'm not sure. Maybe two or three weeks ago."

She made a notation on a pad of paper in front of her. "I see. You don't live at the house, do you?"

"No, I have a townhouse a few miles away."

"A townhouse bought for you by Mr. Patterson, is that correct?" Parker added.

"Yes. It was a gift from him and my mother when I graduated from college."

"According to bank records, he also wrote you checks on a regular basis."

"That's true. He gave me an allowance."

"You don't have a job, Ms Watson?"

I squirmed. At twenty-eight, I knew my life had no direction or purpose. Colin knew it, and now these detectives saw the light clearly, too. I wanted to change that, but had no idea how to go about it.

"No, and what does it matter?"

"Just trying to get a picture of things, that's all," Hamilton said with that damned smile still slapped on her face.

"It's also apparently no secret your stepfather paid your bills. And you had a lot of bills." She consulted a sheet of paper in a file folder. "Fashion Forever, Holland Jewelers, The Shoe Boutique, The Ultimate Hair Salon and Spa, not to mention several credit cards. I won't even go into the expensive, trendy restaurants you frequented."

"That's right. Ross paid my bills. Why not? I was his stepdaughter. If he didn't care, then why the hell should you?" I hated being on the defensive.

The smile vanished and her brown eyes turned hard. She leaned forward. "We have a statement from one of the maids at the house. She says you paid your stepfather a visit around one o'clock the afternoon of the party. She also claims to have heard an ensuing argument through the closed door of the study, and that you stormed out a few minutes later. Care to revise that comment about when you last saw Ross Patterson prior to the party?"

My heart nearly stopped and my stomach turned over. It never occurred to me that someone had been around to see me with Ross. I'd assumed most of the staff would be busy in the kitchen preparing for the evening's affair.

I stared her straight in the eyes. "I'm sorry, I misinterpreted your question. I thought you referred to prior to the day of the party. Yes, I saw Ross earlier that afternoon. He asked me to come in. He wanted to discuss my finances."

"In what way, Ms. Watson?" Detective Parker asked.

"It was the usual. He often bitched me out about my spending. He'd shout, I'd promise to do better, and that would be the end of it. And I did not storm out of the house. The maid is mistaken or exaggerating. I was late for a luncheon appointment and in a hurry."

"With whom?" he said unsmiling.

"Jan de Witt. We ate at La Parisienne on Moreland Parkway. Afterwards, we stopped off at a boutique, tried on some clothes, then left."

"Was she one of the people with you last night on Beale Street?"

"Yes!"

Detective Hamilton wrote on the pad before skewering me with a glance. "Can you give us the names of the people with you and where you went?"

I drew in an angry breath and counted to ten. Colin had nailed this one. I rattled off the names of my companions. "I don't remember which bars and nightclubs we went to, but we hit a lot of them. You'll have to take my word on that."

"Don't worry, we'll pull credit card receipts," Detective Parker said.

Both cops stood, the smile back on Hamilton's face. "That's all for now, Ms. Watson," she said. "I'll have this typed up and you can sign it. Won't take but a few minutes. Oh, and we'd appreciate it if you wouldn't leave town for a while."

"I had no plans to go anywhere."

They left the room. Fear gnawed at my stomach. *We'd appreciate it if you wouldn't leave town for a while.* Didn't they say that to all suspects right before they slapped the cuffs on them? Was I officially a suspect?

The minutes ticked by slowly while I stewed. I tried to maintain a calm demeanor for the camera in the corner. Finally, Detective Parker returned with my statement.

I signed, stood on only slightly trembling legs, and swept from the room stalking down the hallway toward the station lobby.

Colin rose from a seat near the front door. "So, how did it go? They ready to slap the cuffs on you?"

Funny he would use the same words I'd just thought. The fear gnawed harder, but I tried to stay calm.

"I basically told them the same thing I did earlier."

"Basically?" he asked with a raised eyebrow.

I fished in my purse for the aspirin bottle, shook another two into my hand, and headed for the water cooler in the corner. I swallowed them before answering. I may not have liked Colin much, but respected that he had a keen mind. He was good at his job.

"I just remembered a few more details."

"Details? Like what?"

"What do you care?"

"Ian hired me to help with the investigation, remember?"

"I'm sure Detectives Parker and Smiley-Face will appreciate that."

He grinned. "Yeah, she does smile a lot, doesn't she? It works. Puts people at ease. Then she lowers the hammer. I've known her several years. And for the record, the police and private investigators often cooperate. Don't believe everything you see on TV. Now, what details?"

I wasn't about to tell him I'd been to the house earlier in the day. He'd ask questions and I wasn't sure I could gloss over my answers to him like I had with the police.

"I just remembered more of the conversations I had with people, especially the publishing crowd. What'll happen to Ross's book now that he's dead?"

"I doubt it'll get published."

"Why not? According to the agent I talked to, it'll be a bestseller. Bound to make money."

"Because one of his former clients will likely get an injunction citing attorney/client privilege. Publishers won't want to deal with that, even if Ross did change the names."

"Yet a controversial tell-all book from an author who turns up murdered might be worth it."

"Possibly. What does your mother have to say about all of this?"

I shrugged. "Haven't a clue. I haven't talked to her yet."

His eyebrows rose almost to his hairline. "Her husband is murdered and neither of you make a call to the other?"

"I talked to Mother yesterday morning. She was on her way to Jackson for the weekend to visit a college roommate or sorority sister or something."

"Jackson, Tennessee or Mississippi?"

"Mississippi. Are you back on giving my mother a hard time?"

"Jackson's only a three hour drive from Memphis. She could have returned, nailed Ross, and been back in Jackson before dawn."

"Oh, get real. Can we get out of here?"

He pushed the door open and held it. "Sure. What's on your agenda for the night?"

"I have no idea." The merits of a quiet evening at home along with pizza and a bottle of wine sounded pretty damned good.

"I talked with Ian a while ago. He said the family lawyer, Jim Price, wants to talk to us tomorrow morning."

"What about?" I asked as I slid into the passenger seat.

"The will, I imagine."

The will. Holy crap. Had Ross made any changes yet? He and mother had separated less than a month ago. The conversation we'd had yesterday afternoon about my bills led me to believe he hadn't.

Swell. Another motive for me or Mother to kill him.

"What time?"

"Ten. Think you'll be awake by then?"

"Don't start. I'll be there."

The drive back to Ross's was silent. He pulled up behind my car. Several other cars had come since we'd left.

"Looks like Sam and Bonnie are here," he said naming Ross's younger brother.

"I thought he and Bonnie got divorced last year."

"They did, but recently reconciled."

The Patterson family dynamics didn't interest me. Sam and Bonnie had four kids between the ages of brat and smart-ass high schooler. Bonnie and her two daughters, the smart-asses, hated my mother and me. The feeling was mutual.

"If you don't mind, I think I'll skip the condolences." I slid out of the car. "I'll see you tomorrow."

Without another word, I walked to my car, got in, and drove off. Two blocks later my cell rang. It was Mother.

"Oh my God, Hilary, what the hell happened?"

"Where are you?"

"Near Batesville. I'm on my way home. Ian called me around ten with the news and the police around eleven. I tried calling you, but got your voice mail. Where have you been?"

"Probably in the shower. My phone was downstairs this morning."

"What *happened*?"

I gave her the basics as I knew them.

"A frying pan? You've got to be kidding!"

"Yeah, I know. I had the same reaction. It's almost four. If Ian called you at ten, why are you only at Batesville?"

"I had to make a show of grief for Chynna. God bless sorority sisters. She contacted the others and they came by to comfort me, too. I didn't get away until a while ago."

"When will you be home?"

"In a couple of hours. I'm going straight to the house."

"Bonnie's there."

"I don't give a rat's ass if she is. Ross and I were separated, not divorced. It's still my house."

"Jim Price wants to meet with everyone tomorrow morning at ten. I think it has to do with the will."

Mother drew in an audible breath. "The will? Had Ross made a new one in the last week?"

"I have no idea."

Silence hammered in my ear. I could almost see the wheels turning in her mind.

"Well, until I learn differently, I'm going to assume he didn't. That ought to burn Bonnie's ass good."

"At least until tomorrow morning."

"I'll talk to you when I get in. I'm not even sure I have a black dress to wear."

"Isn't that a little hypocritical considering the circumstances?"

"Hey, for all anybody else knows, Ross and I were trying to work out our differences."

"Were you?"

She snorted. "Fat chance. I hope the son of a bitch rots in hell. Gotta go now, sweetie. I'll see you soon."

I dumped the phone back in my purse and continued on my way home. Mother had never told me why she had thrown in the towel on the marriage, but knowing Ross, it probably had to do with another woman. That was Mom's role ten years ago.

As I drove, Colin's words about driving from Jackson to Memphis and back again before dawn, rattled through my head. I wondered if Mother *could* have killed Ross.

Chapter Three

I sat on the sofa in Ross's living room surrounded by unfriendly relatives. Ross's younger brother, Sam, nursed a glass of orange juice I was pretty sure also contained vodka. Bonnie, his not so better half, sat next to him on the loveseat, legs crossed with her foot jiggling in mid-air, glaring first at me, then Mother. Empty coffee cups dotted the tables. Ian paced aimlessly; stopping every once in a while to inspect bric-a-brac he'd seen a hundred times before and didn't care about. His wife, Elaine, perched on the edge of a chair tearing a tissue into shreds with shaking fingers.

"Ian, will you please sit down?" she demanded. "You're driving me crazy."

Ian sent her a surprised glance. "What? Oh, sorry, but I wonder what's keeping Jim. He's late."

"Relax, Ian. It's only ten-fifteen. He'll be here," Colin said from another chair.

"Must be important if he's getting up this early on a Sunday morning just to talk to us," Mother said from her seat next to me on the sofa.

She'd never called back last night, so I hadn't had a chance to talk to her yet. We weren't what you'd call close and not hearing from her didn't surprise me. This morning, she wore an expensive black silk suit. Knowing Mother, she'd probably stopped at a boutique to buy it before coming to the house.

Ross's murder had been the leadoff story on last night's evening news report, and the banner headline this morning in the *Commercial Appeal*.

"And where is your mother, Colin?" Mother asked.

"On safari in Kenya with her latest husband. I called with the news yesterday. She sends condolences, but won't be attending the funeral."

Colin's mother was a lot like Ross, her older brother, in the marriage aspect. Husbands came and went on a regular basis. Nor did it surprise me she wouldn't come to the funeral. She and Ross had had a falling out thirty years ago and hadn't spoken since. No love lost there.

Ian's mother was Ross's eldest sister and had died several years before Mother even came into the picture. His father had since remarried and lived in New York City. I'd never met him either.

"I'm sure he must have changed his will," Bonnie declared. "Most likely left everything to Sam, isn't that right, dear? Which means you'll need to find new digs, Priscilla."

Mother smiled her patented Southern sweet but insincere smile. "I doubt I'll need them. Ross and I were discussing reconciliation."

"Nonsense. He told me on Thursday he was glad to be rid of you and your offspring."

"You talked to him the day before the murder? What about?" Colin asked.

Bonnie waved a hand in the air. "Nothing important. I simply dropped by to see how he was doing now that he'd been abandoned by his wife, and to tell him Sam and I wouldn't be able to attend the party."

"Yes, I was surprised you weren't here," I added. "After all, it was free booze and food. You never turn down anything free. Right, Sam?"

Sam looked up from the orange liquid in his glass. "Huh? Oh, yeah, the party. We already had plans."

"Doing what?" I challenged.

"None of your business," Bonnie snapped. "And you should talk. You've been living off Ross for years. I happen to know he paid your bills all over town."

"I was his stepdaughter. Maybe he felt an obligation to keep me debt free. I didn't question it."

Mother laughed softly while Bonnie glared at both of us.

"Can we dispense with the snide remarks?" Ian asked, finally settling in front the fireplace with his hands clasped behind his back. "After all, Ross has been murdered. Let's have at least a hint of decorum."

"And besides, I'm sure the police will want to talk to all of us about the last time we saw Ross," Colin added, sending a glance my way.

Everyone stared at him without speaking. I read concern in five other pairs of eyes.

The police always look to family first in a murder like this. I wonder if one of us did it.

A car swept up the driveway.

"Jim's here," Ian said.

A minute later the doorbell rang and a few seconds after that, Effie showed him into the room. Ross's attorney and former law partner wore golf clothes, which suggested he had other things on his agenda today.

"Good morning, everyone. Sorry, I'm late. Don't go, Effie. You need to hear this, too."

"Yes, sir," Effie answered with a surprised look. "May I get you a cup of coffee, Mr. Price?"

"No, thank you. This won't take long."

She stood near the doorway, her hands folded in front of her.

Jim sat in a chair next to the sofa and settled his briefcase on the coffee table. He opened it and extracted a large sheaf of papers with "Last Will and Testament" in big letters on the top sheet.

Mother drew in a sharp breath. Ian tensed. Elaine stopped shredding the tissue and stared. Sam drained the contents of his glass, while his wife leaned forward, an eager look on her face. Only Colin remained impassive and apparently disinterested. We resembled a scene worthy of Agatha Christie.

"First of all, I want to offer my condolences on Ross's untimely death. I'm sure the police will find the killer soon. In the meantime, I need to bring you up to date on his financial affairs and how they affect each of you."

"He changed his will, didn't he?" Bonnie declared. "Sam inherits, not his soon-to-be ex-wife!"

"Drop dead, Bonnie," Mother said with a smile. "As I told you, Ross and I were discussing reconciliation. You ought to know about that. You and Sam decided to do that a few months ago."

"But Sam and I love each other."

"What you love is ready access to all those amenities like the weekly treatments at Forever Young Day Spa. And let's not forget the Moreland Country Club along with the South American tennis instructor. How many lessons have you had? You should be ready for the pro tour by now."

Bonnie's jaw clenched. "You, on the other hand, are a greedy, money grubbing bimbo who broke up Ross's marriage."

"Ross and his third wife were well on the way to divorce court before I came along."

The animosity between Mother and Bonnie had escalated. I squirmed with embarrassment. What would Jim think of us? My first instinct was to defend my mother, but she didn't need defending. She did a good job of that on her own. I decided to shut up.

"Ladies!" Jim held up his hand. "Can we dispense with this for now? Yes, Bonnie, Ross made a new will two weeks ago."

"Ah-ha!" she crowed.

"Unfortunately, he didn't sign it. He called me a few days later and said he had more changes to make. He gave me the changes, the will was re-written again, and I was supposed to bring it by Friday for his signature. However, because of the party, he called and put off the appointment until Monday."

"So, what exactly does that mean? Surely there was a prenup," Elaine said.

"There was not," Mother snapped.

"Are you kidding me?" Bonnie said with a gasp.

Jim sighed. "There was until two months ago."

"Why? What happened?" Ian asked.

"Ross and Priscilla nullified it."

All eyes focused on Mother. "Ross and I had come to an agreement that the one made ten years ago was inadequate. He was retiring, the book deal was coming through, and he wanted to make sure I was taken care of properly if something should happen to him. We hadn't quite finalized things yet."

I shot a quick glance at Mother. Something didn't sound right. Whose idea had it been to rewrite the thing?

"So you walked out on him knowing full well you'd get a damned sight more than any prenup would bring you," Bonnie replied.

"The lack of an agreement also gave Ross the opportunity to slash Priscilla's share to bare minimum in a new will. I'm sure the prenup was more generous," Colin told her. "The knife cuts both ways."

"But he did make a new will," Bonnie insisted.

Jim sighed again looking like he'd rather be any place but here. I didn't blame him.

"Neither Ross nor Priscilla had officially filed for divorce. The new will was null and void until that occurred and he signed it. It means his old will is still in effect."

I'm sure Mother sighed in relief. So did I. Sam looked at Jim in surprise. Bonnie's face was so red, I feared she'd stroke out.

"What does it say?" Ian, always the practical one, inquired.

"The estate is extensive as I'm sure you're aware and the probate process will take time, but other than a few charities, the bulk of the estate goes to family. Priscilla, by law as Ross's widow, you get half, including the house and all that's in it. Hilary, you are down for a modest percentage, too. If invested judiciously, it should keep you afloat for several years."

"But not in the style she's become accustomed to," Bonnie murmured. "What about the rest of us?"

"And you called me greedy," Mother said.

Jim hurried on. "Effie, Ross has remembered you

and your loyal service. He apportioned fifty thousand dollars to you."

Effie gasped. Her eyes opened wide. "Oh my goodness! That was so generous of him. I never expected..." she covered her mouth with her hand.

"Fifty thousand dollars for a servant?" Bonnie yelped. She exchanged glances with Elaine who shrugged.

"Congratulations, Effie," I said. "You worked for him five years. I'm sure you more than earned it."

"I...I guess," she stammered casting her gaze on Price. "Do you need me for anything else, sir? I have things to do in the kitchen."

He waved a hand. "No, that's all, Effie."

She nodded and left the room.

"Let's get it over with," Sam said. "What about the rest of us?"

"The balance of the estate is divided evenly between Sam, Ian, and Colin. I'm not sure of the dollar figures as of yet, but it should be somewhere just under a million apiece."

"A million? That's all?" Elaine burst out. "I thought Ross was worth much more than that."

"Ross's investments took a hit with the recession."

"And I'd have thought flesh and blood would count for more," Bonnie muttered sending Mother an evil glance.

Jim dropped the will back into his briefcase and snapped it shut. "Bonnie, Sam owns several gins in both Tennessee and Mississippi. He's also part owner of a couple of cotton farms not to mention his investments in commercial real estate in downtown Memphis."

Sam squirmed and tapped the bottom of his empty glass on the heel of his hand making me wonder how hard the recession had hit him, too. I remembered Ross once saying his brother had the brains of an ox, which suggested slow and not too bright.

Jim continued. "Ian, you're a developer. You've made a lot of money over the last fifteen years, and while things have been slow lately, the economy is bound to pick up soon." He turned his gaze onto Colin. "Colin, Ross admired that you didn't give a damn about money."

"Why would my uncle admire that? He loved money and the power it could bring," Colin said.

"To my knowledge, you're the only person in this room who didn't come to him for a handout at one time or another. You generally snubbed his invites. That pissed him off, but at the same time showed you had integrity."

Integrity? That was something Ross seriously lacked.

"I'm curious," Sam said. "How did the will he didn't sign compare to this one?"

"I wondered when you'd get around to that," Jim said. "Effie's portion was upped to a hundred grand, Hilary received fifty thousand—no doubt to pay her immediate debts with a nest egg left over—and since a divorce was imminent complete with a generous settlement, Priscilla got nothing."

"Told you so," Bonnie said with a grin. "What about us?"

Jim sighed. "Sam and Ian each received two hundred fifty thousand dollars. The remainder of the estate went to Colin."

"What!" Sam, Bonnie, and Elaine all yelled at the same time. Ian merely raised his eyebrows. Mother laughed. For the first time since I'd known him, Colin looked stunned.

"That can't be right!" Bonnie exclaimed.

"Ross was tired of all of you," Jim answered. "Sam and Ian had both asked for money—a lot of it—in the last few months. And not just once, but several times." He rose, stuffing the will back into his briefcase. "That's all for the moment. I'll be in touch. No need to get up. I'll see myself out."

He hurried through the foyer and out the door as though fleeing for his life. I didn't blame him since I wanted to do the same.

"I don't believe he all but cut us out," Bonnie muttered.

"And we all know Ross would have told us the terms of this new will just to watch us squirm," Ian said. "Then he'd write a new one putting us back in. That's how Uncle Ross operated."

"He'd poke and jab, dangle the bait until we danced to his tune, and then smile saying all was forgiven," Elaine replied in a hard voice.

Sam set his glass on a table with an audible click and rose. "I think it's time we left. After all, we have a funeral to arrange. I'm assuming you don't mind if Ian, Colin, and I take over that responsibility do you, Priscilla?"

Mother stared before raising a perfectly penciled eyebrow. "I have no objections provided Hanson's Funeral Home is the site. It's nearby, has ample parking, and is only a few blocks from the cemetery."

Bonnie also stood. "Naturally. It's convenient for

you."

"That's how it should be, dear. I'm his widow. Have a nice day, Bonnie."

"I suppose we should be leaving, too," Ian commented. "Sam, let's get together at our house and discuss the arrangements now. It's only a few miles away. You coming, Colin?"

"What? Oh no, the two of you do what you think is best," he answered in a distracted tone.

Ian nodded toward Mother. "We'll be in touch, Priscilla."

They all swept from the room and out the front door.

"Well, that was interesting, wasn't it?" Mother said. "Excuse me while I go change into something less somber. Are the two of you staying for lunch?"

I glanced at Colin who said nothing, but stared, frowning, at the fireplace.

"Yes, I guess so," I replied.

"Good. Why don't you move in for a while, Hilary? Being alone in a house where a murder has been committed is kind of spooky. I could use the company."

Her request surprised me. I shot a quick glance at Colin. Had he stayed here last night as he'd intended or had Mother's presence sent him packing?

"Yeah, sure if you need me. I'll go home and pack a few things."

She nodded and left. I turned back to Colin.

"Did you stay here last night?"

"Yeah. Your mother breezed in just before dinner, but asked me to stay. If you're here, I don't need to be."

"Kind of a surprise about the new will's contents,

isn't it?"

"Can't imagine why Ross would do it, but Ian may have been right. Ross loved to dangle his money in front of us every once in a while. I think I may have more to investigate than I first suspected."

"Meaning?"

"I find it interesting that nobody had actually filed for divorce. That usually takes place within a couple of weeks if both parties are determined to end a marriage."

"In other words, it lends credence to Mother's statement about a possible reconciliation. Might also explain why he put off signing the new will."

"And I find Jim's comments about Ian and Sam hounding Ross for money strange, too. Both are supposedly well off."

"Looks like your list of suspects is growing."

Colin rose. "I need to talk to Effie about the days leading up to the party."

I had to admit to rampant curiosity. "Mind if I tag along?"

He shrugged. "Can't very well stop you."

We found Effie in the kitchen. She looked up from the stove in surprise as we entered.

"Effie, do have a few minutes? I'd like to talk to you."

"Of course, Mr. Blackwood," she answered, wiping her hands on a towel.

Colin gestured toward the large kitchen table. "Please, have a seat."

Effie sat at one end, her hands folded on the placemat while Colin and I flanked her. He extracted a notebook from his slacks pocket along with a small pen.

"Effie, I need to know about the two or three days

preceding the party. Did Uncle Ross have any visitors?"

"He's received quite a few guests since he retired, but the last few days did see a lot of people come and go."

"Like who?"

"Well, there was that lady from the book place. I think her name was Matthews."

"The literary agent. She was at the party," I informed Colin. "I talked to her for a while."

He scribbled the information into the notebook. "Who else, Effie?"

Her brow knitted into deep furrows as she thought. "A man came on Tuesday, I think it was. I'm not sure of the name—Lazlo, or Laser—something like that. Gave me the willies, he did. Had a sharp, ferret-like face. He came and had a long talk with Mr. Ross in the study. I remember he left as I was finishing up dusting in the living room. He seemed angry."

I remembered the man I'd seen coming out of the study the night of the party.

"Was he kind of short, on the thin side, with dark hair?"

"Yes."

"I saw him the night of the party, too. He and Ross had been in the study. He wasn't happy then either."

Colin frowned and ceased writing. "Hair slicked back and on the shiny side?"

"Yes," we both answered together.

"Joey Lazarus."

"You know him?" I asked.

"Not personally, but I've seen his photos. He's a small time hood into prostitution, drug dealing, and extortion. Five'll get you ten, he was one of Ross's clients."

"Or ex-clients about to be exposed in a memoir?" I added.

"Could be. Anybody else, Effie?"

"Mr. Price, was here off and on over the past couple of weeks. Mrs. Priscilla was here on Monday. Had quite an argument with Mr. Ross."

"Hear what they argued about?" Colin asked resuming his writing and shooting me a glance.

I held my breath as Effie also looked at me, and then away again quickly.

"It was money, Mr. Blackwood. The study door wasn't closed all the way. I was tidying up in the library and couldn't help but overhear. Mrs. Priscilla said she had the goods on him and if he didn't pay up, she'd take it to the judge."

And the prenup had been voided before a new one put in place. This just didn't sound right. *Unless, Ross was planning on dumping my mother for another woman.* But why would Mother agree?

"Just blew the reconciliation theory out of the water," Colin said to me. "Effie, did any other family members come to the house this week?"

"Mrs. Bonnie and Mrs. Elaine were both here. Mrs. Elaine on Tuesday or Wednesday, I think, and Mrs. Bonnie on Thursday. I didn't hear any of those conversations." She paused. "Of course, Mr. Ian and Mr. Sam stopped by week before last. They each looked worried and upset when they left."

"Looks like you'll have your hands full with family investigations," I commented.

He ignored me. "Let's get to the day of the party. Can you walk me through it?"

Effie sighed and stared at her folded hands. "I had hired in extra help as usual. After breakfast, I put two of the women to work on making hors d'oeuvres while I had the other two helping me clean the downstairs. Keisha took care of the upstairs."

Keisha was the only other servant in the house on a regular basis. She'd been at Mother's beck and call for the most part. She probably found cleaning preferable to Mother's demands.

"Lunch was a simple affair and Mr. Patterson ate in his study. When I took him his tray, he was on the phone. I don't know who he was talking to."

"I'm sure the police will pull his phone records," Colin said. "What did you do after lunch?"

"I tended to supervising the work in the kitchen. Desserts had to be made along with more hors d'oeuvres. I popped into the living areas several times to make sure the hires were setting up the dining room for the buffet properly."

"Effie," I interrupted. "Why were you doing all this work? I mean, why not hire a caterer? Mother always did for these affairs."

"Mr. Patterson told me he'd invited thirty to forty people. I could handle that. In fact, I enjoy working parties. No offense, but your mother could never make do with a guest list of less than seventy-five."

Effie didn't say it directly, but I caught the criticism. Mother thought the household staff incompetent to deal with a large number of people.

"Did you see my uncle during this time?"

"Other than when I took him his lunch? No sir, he was in his study the entire day or most of it. I think he went out sometime later. One of the maids brought his empty tray back to the kitchen around one before returning to her duties." She looked at me, and then down at her hands again.

I held my breath. Would Effie say anything about me being here? I had to assume this was the maid who'd seen me and heard Ross and me arguing. And I had been pissed when I left. So pissed I never noticed another person nearby.

"How about the night of the party?" Colin asked.

"It was a full house. Mr. Patterson had told me to hire a bartender. He was set up in the living room. The food was in the dining room, but the maids circulated with some on trays."

"Who was answering the door?" Colin inquired.

"I did at first, but then I had to make sure things were running smoothly in the kitchen. I left it open so people could just walk right in."

"When did the party end?"

"I think the last guest left around eleven. Clean up took another couple of hours. I sent the maids home, and stopped in the study before leaving to tell Mr. Patterson good night."

"What did he say?" I asked.

"He thanked me and said to go home, he'd see me in the morning. That was the last time I saw him alive." She choked and placed a hand over her mouth.

"And you were sure you were the last one to leave?" Colin said.

"Yes…at least, I think so. I suppose someone could have been hiding upstairs—or in that little closet under the stairs."

"Did you lock the doors?" I asked.

"Yes."

"So, my uncle could have let his killer in. What was he doing when you left?"

"He was at his desk reading some papers and having a nightcap."

"I can't understand why he just sat at the desk. If the killer had hidden and walked in surprising him, you'd think he'd at least try to defend himself."

Effie shivered. "The whole back of his head was smashed in, covered with blood. Is there anything else, sir?"

Colin closed his notebook and smiled. "No thank you, Effie. You've been very helpful."

We left the kitchen and headed for the living room meeting Mother coming down the staircase. She'd changed from the black silk suit into a pair of white Capri pants and a lime green silk blouse. Bronze colored sandals adorned her feet. The mourning period was over. Then I noted the fear in her eyes.

"I've just gotten off the phone with the police. They want to talk to me at the police station. Immediately!"

Chapter Four

The panic in Mother's voice didn't go unnoticed. Colin raised his right eyebrow in that irritating manner as though questioning why she should be surprised. In spite of her faults, I didn't honestly think she had killed her husband.

Trying to be casual, I shrugged. "They talked to me right off the bat, too, so I wouldn't worry."

"The family is always questioned first," Colin said.

Once again, I tried to be reassuring. "They'll simply ask about the separation, and where you were the night of the murder. That's all."

"You're sure? I mean, they can't suspect me. I was in Jackson," she said.

"And Jackson is only a three hour drive from here. You could have killed him and been back before the sun came up," Colin told her.

Her eyes widened. "That's insane! I spent the night at Chynna Delaney's house."

"Let's go into the living room." We trooped in. Mother and I chose the sofa while Colin sat in a chair. "What time did you arrive in Jackson?" he asked.

"Around four in the afternoon, I suppose. I ran a bunch of errands here in the morning, ate lunch at Le Bistro, and took off."

He pulled the notebook from his pocket again. "And what did you do in Jackson?"

"Why are you asking?" Mother said.

"Because Ian hired Colin to do his own investigation into Ross's death," I told her.

"Doesn't sound like Ian or you think much of the police solving the case," she replied with a sniff.

"The Moreland Police Department is competent at catching speeders and burglars, but I can't remember the last time a murder was committed in this town," he said. "I'm sure they're doing their best. Detectives Parker and Hamilton are good. I'm helping at Ian's request. Now, what did you do that night?"

Mother sighed. "Chynna and I met two other sorority sisters for dinner. We had a few drinks, talked, ate a fine meal, had a few more drinks, and made plans for a shopping spree the next day."

"Who were the other two women and where did you eat?"

"Oh for crying out loud, is this really necessary?" I asked.

"It is if this Delaney woman is helping your mother with an alibi."

"What?" Mother sputtered.

Colin shrugged. "Wouldn't be the first time a friend helped—or thought they were helping. Now, who were you with and where did you eat?"

She rolled her eyes. "I have no idea the name of the restaurant. Carrie Starks and Moira Jenson met us there. Chynna drove from the house. We chatted in the car and I didn't pay attention to where we went."

"When did you get back to the house?" Colin asked.

"Around ten, I think. We had some wine, and then went to bed."

"Were the two of you alone?"

"Yes. Chynna's husband, Derek, was out of town at some golf event or something."

He wrote quickly before looking up. "Where did you sleep?"

"What?"

"Priscilla, I just want to know how close your room was to Ms. Delaney's."

"The master bedroom takes up most of the one side of the second floor. Guest rooms are on the other, separated by a large space at the top of the stairs. Why?"

"By your own admission, you and your hostess had a lot to drink. If she slept soundly, then it isn't a stretch to believe you could have sneaked down the stairs, out the back door, and driven to Memphis where you killed your husband, then sneaked back in."

Mother's face went white, her eyes opened wider, and her breathing increased.

"But I didn't do that!"

"Of course you didn't," I exclaimed. "Really, Colin!"

"Like I said, the police will ask the same questions. They did with you, didn't they?"

I reluctantly nodded. "Yes, more or less."

By now I was too scared to admit to them I'd been at the house in the afternoon. Besides, I'd lied to the cops about why.

Mother stood and squared her shoulders. "Then I suppose I should go the police station and get this over with. Hilary, will you drive? We can stop by your place and pick up a few things. I just can't stay alone in a house where a murder took place."

I also rose. "Sure, no problem. Do you want a lawyer?"

"No, why should I? I'm telling the truth." She sent me a curious glance. "Did you call one?"

"No. As you said, why bother? I told the truth."

Colin stared at both of us. "This is just preliminary. Call an attorney if they want to talk a second time." He glanced at his watch. "I have to be someplace. I'll talk to you later."

"You're welcome to stay for dinner, Colin," Mother said.

"Thanks, Priscilla. I'd like that."

He left and Mother went upstairs to change clothes yet again. I paced in the living room. In spite of my reassurances to Mother, I could see where Colin was going with his questions. Jackson was close enough for a round trip with a murder thrown in to be believable.

I'd met Chynna Delaney on several occasions. She'd married well just out of college. Her husband, Derek, was not only an attorney, but sat on the Jackson city council as well. She also had a habit of popping a sleeping pill before bedtime. Had she done so that night in spite of the number of drinks they'd had? If she had, she wouldn't have heard a nuclear explosion outside her window.

Mother came down the stairs, this time dressed in what I assumed she considered proper talking-to-the-police attire. She wore a black skirt with a pale pink silk blouse and a black bolero jacket. Black high heels sealed the outfit. She had returned to semi-mourning.

"Exactly what did the police ask you?" she said as I exited the driveway.

"Oh, nothing too terrible. Where was I after the

party, who was I with, when did I last talk to Ross—other than at the party. When did you last see Ross?"

She smoothed her skirt. "I really can't remember. Early in the week, I believe. He called while I was driving to Jackson. Said he wanted to talk to me. I told him I was on the road, so he said to call him when I got back."

He'd called while she was driving? That would have been after he and I had talked.

"Mother, did he say anything about me?"

"No. Why?"

"Just wondered, that's all. He seemed perfectly fine at the party." I stopped at a traffic light and turned my gaze on her. She fidgeted and stared out the windshield. "If you don't mind me asking, why did you separate?"

She lifted her chin. "It would have all come out anyway. Ross had a thing—a sweet, young thing—on the side. Little bitch couldn't have been any more than twenty. Since he was retiring in a few months, I bought his excuses of finishing up old files and organizing his memoirs for the book. Then I noticed his absences always occurred during the middle of the week."

A horn honked behind me. The light had turned green. I rolled forward.

"Go on."

"Ross was a man of routine. He never deviated from his self-imposed schedule if he could help it. I recognized the middle of the week thing as the same excuse he gave his wife, Darcy, when he was seeing me. I put two and two together, hired a private investigator—not Colin—who tailed the two of them to a condo on Riverside, and got some damned fine photos. When the time was right, I was going to nail him with the evidence."

When the time was right. "So you initiated the new prenup."

"Yes. If we split, I wanted to make sure I didn't come out on the short end of the stick. I was surprised he didn't put up an argument. He called Jim who came by a few days later. We signed the nullification and informed him we'd be in touch with the new document as soon as possible."

This still didn't sound right to me. "What was his reaction?"

"Jim's? He advised against nullifying one before the replacement was written and signed."

"And as soon as the ink was dry you walked out?"

"Not quite. Ross got busy with the book or whatever and we never discussed the new terms. I hit him with the news about a week later."

"And?"

"He was stunned I beat him to the punch of asking for a divorce. Son of a bitch didn't even try to deny he was seeing this Carlotta."

"Carlotta?"

"Carlotta Lake or Lash or something. Apparently, she was the sister of one of his sleazier clients. I never met her face to face, but if she shows up at the funeral, I swear…"

I tuned Mother out. The sister of a client? Lash? Lazarus maybe? Could the man both Effie and I had seen been the brother? Perhaps he wasn't so keen on the idea of his little sister dating a man old enough to be her grandfather.

"How old was Ross?" I interrupted.

"Fifty-eight last March. Why?"

"No reason. Just curious." I pulled into the police station parking lot. "If you don't mind, I think I'll go throw a few things into a suitcase while you're here. Call me when you're done and I'll come get you."

She turned frightened eyes on me. "You're just dumping me off?"

"I can't go in the room with you. It's no big deal. They'll ask simple questions like they did me. Unless, you confess to the crime, you'll be out in less than an hour."

"If you say so." She exited my car and walked into the station, the picture of a demure Southern widow.

I drove home, tossed a few things into a suitcase, and then searched for a jump drive Ross had given me on Friday afternoon. I found it next to my desktop computer.

Biting my lip, I picked it up. Ross's instructions echoed in my mind. He'd hit me with the usual tirade about my lack of self-control regarding money, then had threatened to let me twist in the wind by not paying. We'd argued until I was reduced to begging. Then he'd given me the jump drive.

"Do not read what's on it, Hilary, is that clear? It's none of your business."

"It is if you're asking me to hide it for you."

"Just keep it until I tell you otherwise. If you want me to pay off your bills, you'll do as I say."

Keeping the jump drive seemed like such a small thing to do. I'd put it in a safe place and my debts would be paid.

Now, I stared at it like it was a live snake. Ross was dead—murdered—and this little object could have the motive on it. Was there something on it that could incriminate me? Or Mother? Taking a deep breath, I removed the cover, shoved it into the USB port, and turned on the machine. A minute later the information showed up.

I'm not sure what I expected, but Ross's old case files weren't it. What could be duller?

This one was about some guy named Brutus Alden who'd been arrested on drug trafficking charges four years ago. Ross's notes said it all. The little shit was guilty as hell, but bribe money had been spread around by the scumbag's organization and the witnesses against him disappeared. I knew attorney-client confidentiality was almost sacred, but if my stepfather knew about the bribes, how close did that come to being illegal?

I guess as long as he didn't bribe someone, he was in the clear.

Ross's defense planted the seed of reasonable doubt in the mind of at least one juror. Alden got off. I suspected some of that bribe money might have found its way into the jury box.

I scrolled down to the next entry. Another case file, this time on a woman named Sally Ransom and dated eight years ago. The name was vaguely familiar. As I read, the incident came back to me.

Sally Ransom had been a housewife in the very upscale neighborhood of Webster, a suburb just east of Moreland. Her husband was a CPA, and the lady of the house did all the usual civic-minded duties from sitting on improvement councils to chairing a fundraiser for a local politician.

Lady, however, was not quite accurate. Madam was more to the point. She and her husband were accused of running a high-end call girl service out of their home. To avoid jail time, she turned on her husband declaring it was all his idea and that she was forced to go along with it.

Ross, of course, painted the husband as a sex-crazed abuser and poor Sally as his ultimate victim. I don't know how or why, but it worked. She got off with a reprimand along with community service, while her spouse was convicted and did time. His last words as he was taken from the courtroom were, "I'll get you for this. And your lawyer, too."

I wonder if he's gotten out of jail yet? And if he has, would Ross have let him in the house? Or could he have sneaked in during the party and hidden upstairs as Effie suggested? It was something to think about.

I was about to scroll further when a knock on my door startled me. I wasn't expecting anyone, but the thought that it might be a reporter flitted through my mind. So far, they'd been absent, but I figured they just hadn't yet tracked me down. The funeral would bring them out in droves.

A quick peek through the peephole surprised me. I opened the door to Don Merrick. Even though he hadn't had the money, Don had been a regular with our crowd of friends a couple of years ago.

"Don, this is a surprise."

"Hello, Hilary, may I come in?"

"Sure." I led him into the living room. "Have a seat. What brings you here?"

He perched on the edge of a chair and gazed around the room with an uncomfortable expression on his face. "I read about Ross this morning and just wanted to express my condolences."

I sat on the sofa. "Thank you. It was a shock."

"Yes, I can imagine. How are you holding up?"

"Uh, fine." An uneasy silence spread between us. Don's departure from our group of merrymakers had not been cordial.

He looked at my suitcase standing next to the stairs. "Going somewhere?"

"I'm moving into Ross's for a while to be with Mother. She's very upset."

"Nice place you have here." His gaze darted around the room again pausing on my desk, a painting, the bookcase—anywhere except my face. Suddenly, he looked me in the eye. "Look, Hilary, I don't think I ever told you how sorry I was about that night two years ago. I shouldn't have been driving. I'd had too much to drink, and I swear to God, I don't know how those drugs got into my trunk. I loaned the car to several friends for a trip to New Orleans a few weeks before. I mean, you got in trouble, and I got arrested."

His babbling got on my nerves. I saw no reason to rehash the incident.

"That was a long time ago, Don. Ross dealt with it. You didn't even do jail time."

"It sure taught me a lesson, though. Thank God, I was only declared impaired, not drunk."

"What have you been doing the last couple of years?" I'm not sure why I kept the conversation going. I didn't care, but it seemed rude to ask him to leave. None of my other friends had so much as called with condolences.

"I manage my father's stores. He's about to retire."

"Oh, that's right, your father owns several furniture stores, doesn't he?"

"Yes, Merrick Furniture. I moved back to Holly Springs after what happened and all. Hilary, I was wondering if you'd like to go out to dinner one night this week. Nothing fancy, just two old friends getting together."

A date with Don was not on my agenda. "How sweet of you to ask, but I don't think that's possible. I'm going to have my hands full with Mother and the aftermath of Ross's death. I'm sure you must understand."

"Oh yeah…sure…of course…I understand."

My phone ringing interrupted the awkward moment. I walked into the foyer and snatched it from my purse. Caller ID identified Mother.

"Hello, Mother. Are you done?"

"Yes. Come and get me out of this hellhole. I swear to you, Hilary, I have never been subjected to such rude treatment in such miserable surroundings in my life. I am appalled at the…"

"I understand. I'll be right there."

"Make it snappy. If I'm here much longer, I'll explode. I have never been so insulted and demeaned in all my born years. Those detectives have no manners, no breeding, and no sense of decorum on how to treat a grieving widow."

"Mother, you're not grieving."

"That's not the point. Just come get me out of here!"

"All right, I'm on my way."

I hung up and faced Don who had also risen and was strolling about my living room. He stopped near my desk. "I'm sorry, Don, but I have to pick Mother up."

He headed for the front door, nodded his head and smiled. "No problem. If you ever need to talk, I'll be there. Okay?"

"Um, sure. Thank you for dropping by."

He left and I returned to the living room relieved he'd finally gone. His appearance was just another bizarre event in a weekend of bizarre events.

I stared at my computer convinced the key to Ross's murder lay in that jump drive. Why else would he have me keep it? Something had to be on it that made the great Roswell Patterson nervous, maybe even a little bit afraid.

I turned it off and slid the jump drive into my pocket, then packed my laptop in its case. I'd work on the rest of the files later. I also wanted to make sure I wasn't mentioned anywhere.

The fact the jump drive should have been turned over to the police entered my mind, but I ignored it—not until I was sure.

****

"And you wouldn't believe the look she gave me! Like I had hated Ross all these years! I didn't hate him until the last three months!" Mother ranted, her cheeks pink with anger. "Colin was absolutely right about what they'd ask. I'm humiliated that Chynna and my friends will be questioned like common criminals. Why, the very idea! And that woman detective smiled the whole time. I never considered a smile intimidating before."

"Well, it's all over now, so forget about it," I said in a soothing tone as I maneuvered through the late afternoon traffic. "We'll go home, have a couple of drinks, dinner, and then an early night."

She shifted in her seat and ran a hand through her

once perfectly coiffed hair.

"That sounds wonderful. I wonder what Effie made for dinner. I never got around to consulting her today."

"Whatever it is, it'll be good."

Mother leaned her head against the headrest and closed her eyes. "God, I'm so damned tired."

I didn't answer. My thoughts were on the jump drive and its contents. I'd expected the subject matter to be dry and uninteresting. Boy, was I ever wrong. I couldn't wait to read more. Legalese was boring and Ross's annotations in his usual sarcastic and snide manner livened up the prose.

I wondered if Colin would come to dinner as he'd said. For some reason I had this absurd desire to see him. It irked me. He was opinionated, snide, sarcastic—family traits no doubt—and didn't like me one iota.

And the feeling is mutual.

Only it wasn't. In a strange way, I liked the man. Why, I didn't know. His verbal jabs ripped the lid from my temper and the resulting explosion inevitably brought an amused expression to his face. I didn't want to be a source of amusement. Yet, in the long run, I knew I could count on him if I needed help. The fact I'd never turned to him for anything, even advice, was immaterial and confusing.

I pulled into the driveway. Mother exited the car and stood staring at the house.

"How long does probate take?" she asked.

"I don't know. Ask Jim Price. Why?"

"I don't think I want to live here anymore. I mean, I doubt I could stand being alone in a house of murder."

"You plan to sell?"

"Well, I'm certainly not going to give it away."

"Suppose Bonnie buys it?" I said in jest.

"Bonnie can go to hell," she replied climbing the steps to the front porch. "Of course, if she has the money, it's hers."

I grabbed my suitcase and computer, then followed her into the foyer. Colin walked in from the living room.

"So, how did it go at police headquarters?"

Mother rolled her eyes. "A nightmare pure and simple. They as much as said, don't leave town, you're a suspect. Honestly, Colin, I did not drive back to Memphis from Jackson just to hit Ross over the head with a frying pan. If I wanted to kill him, I'd have shot the sumbitch."

I suppressed a chuckle at Mother's terminology. She hadn't always had money, and her Mississippi redneck roots sometimes slipped through.

"Do you own a gun?" he asked.

"Of course I do. I'm a Southerner. But the point is I didn't use it." She rubbed her forehead and walked to the foot of the stairs. "I'm getting a headache. Any word yet on the funeral arrangements?"

"Given Ross's high profile life, the medical examiner did the autopsy immediately. I haven't seen the report, but I'd say the cause of death was blunt force trauma to the head. Toxicology will take a while longer. As soon as the body is released, Ian and Sam will call the funeral home."

"Thank you, Colin. By the way, I was meaning to ask if you wouldn't mind staying in the house for a while. Just until things are more settled. Having Hilary here helps, but I like the presence of a man on the property."

He threw me a look, his eyebrows raised. "If it makes you more comfortable, then yes, I can stay."

I had been reduced to the role of chaperone, which is probably what Mother had in mind in the first place. Made sense. Until the killer was arrested, the old safety in numbers thing had a sound basis.

"If the two of you will excuse me, I'm going to take a long hot bath and a couple of aspirins. I may have dinner in my room."

She headed upstairs and I grabbed my suitcase to follow. Colin beat me to it.

"Here, I'll take it if you can manage the laptop."

Surprised at the offer, I stared for a moment. "Thanks."

"Which room?" he asked as we climbed.

"To the right, first door on the right."

"Overlooking the front of the house?"

"Yes, that was the room I had whenever I visited from college."

I'd stuffed a lot of things into the suitcase, but he carried it into the room with ease and set it next to the queen-sized bed.

"Looks like a college girl's room," he commented, giving it the once-over.

Shades of pink and the white French provincial furniture dated it, but it had suited me at the time.

"Ross let me decorate it. Back then, pastels were my favorite color scheme. Now, I'm more into neutrals." I walked across the room and set the laptop case on the desk. "Where are you staying?"

"Across the hall and down one." He turned to leave. "It's almost five. Why don't you freshen up and join me for a drink?"

Another wave of surprise rolled over me. "Sure. What's for dinner?"

He shrugged. "Something to do with chicken, I think."

Colin left, closing the door behind him. I unpacked and contemplated his civil attitude. It was out of character for the two of us to get along, but then murder has a way of cutting personal problems down to size.

Chapter Five

I strolled into the den half an hour later. Colin sat in a chair reading a sheet of paper, a box full of folders sat on the floor next to him. He glanced up as I entered.

"Took you long enough," he said.

"A man's idea of freshening up and a woman's are not the same," I answered as I wandered over to the small bar set up in the corner. "Ross insisted on what he called 'decent clothes' at the dinner table. No t-shirts or jeans allowed."

"I guess he must have been okay with the wild kingdom."

I'd taken the time to change into a pair of gray slacks and a zebra print tunic. I didn't rise to the bait. Instead I poured a shot of Grey Goose on the rocks and sipped.

"What's that you're reading?"

"A file."

"I can see that. What file?" I ambled over to the sofa, sat, leaned back crossing my legs, and stretched an arm along the top cushion in a deliberately semi-sexy pose. If Colin noticed, he didn't let on.

"The police confiscated Ross's laptop. He kept a lot of things on it—some personal, some business—but he also insisted on hard copy backups. So, I called his secretary and asked where they might be stored. She told me he'd asked her to hang onto them for a while.

Since Ross is dead, I offered to take them off her hands. She agreed, and I picked them up this afternoon."

"So, the cops have Ross's computer? Is his book on it?"

"Probably."

I wondered if the files in the box were the same as the ones on the jump drive. If nothing else, my stepfather was a meticulous bastard. I could see him having more than one back up plan in place.

"So, exactly what are you reading?"

Colin closed the folder and dropped it into the box. "Letters from his clients' victims' families for the most part. None are sweet and sentimental. Most are of the 'I'm gonna get you' category."

"I can understand that. Ross defended a lot of drug, murder, and DUI manslaughter cases." I sipped from my glass. "I can remember an irate man showing up at the house one night with a shotgun. He let loose a couple of rounds before the cops hauled him away. Scared Mother and me half to death. Ross seemed to take it in stride—like an occupational hazard."

"He may have appeared unconcerned, but he had me investigate some of the more violent threats."

"You? Not the police?"

Colin shook his head. "He preferred to handle things like that privately, but he did take precautions. Did you know his car had bulletproof glass? And that his parking space in the office garage was right next to the elevator? That way he could enter and exit fast before anyone could get to him."

"Had no idea. Wonder if Mother did. Did you come across any other revenge-minded victims?"

"Several."

I abandoned my slightly provocative pose and leaned forward. "Do you think one of them bided his or her time?"

"Could be, but would my uncle let someone like that into the house late at night? I don't think so."

"But suppose Effie is right and someone used the party and the open front door to just wander in, hide, and waited to strike until everyone was gone?"

Colin rose, walked to the bar, and poured a scotch on the rocks. "It's possible, but too coincidental for my taste. I have the feeling this was not a spur of the moment murder."

"You mean it was planned? As in the killer knew about the party and decided this was a golden opportunity?"

He shrugged and sipped. "Maybe. May have even been invited to the shindig."

"Ross wouldn't invite someone who sent him hate mail."

"The killer may or may not have written him a letter. And as you said, Ross used people he thought could help him with things down the road."

"Like a judge or a prosecutor? People in high places often have secrets. I'm not sure I'd recognize either if they attended the party, so I guess it's possible. Ross invites him…"

"…or her," Colin interrupted.

"Or her…and that gives him or her the opportunity to plot. Maybe Ross had even blackmailed the person into doing whatever it was he wanted."

"Perhaps. And that person could have feared a repeat request."

"Which means someone, a judge, another lawyer,

took a chance to make sure that didn't happen."

I liked hashing out these details with Colin. Made me feel useful. Also made me wonder if he considered me fairly intelligent—not just a party girl. His next words brought me back to reality.

"How far in advance did you know about the party?"

I finished my vodka in a single gulp and leaned back again hoping I didn't look like a liar.

"He called me sometime last week. Said he needed someone to play hostess for a couple of hours. I was kind of surprised given the fact Mother had walked out on him a few weeks before."

Colin stared at me with those piercing gray eyes. I felt like a specimen under a microscope and lowered my gaze to stare at the ice cubes in the glass. Ross hadn't mentioned the party until the afternoon I'd seen him. And mentioned wasn't the right word. Ross had demanded my presence. *Colin knows.*

"Oh well, I'm sure the police are pulling his cell and land line phone records. The times of when he called various people will come to light."

Crap. I hadn't considered that angle. Ross's call to me on Friday would show up. The lack of a call from the week before would, too. *Can they examine my calls? Is that legal? And what about Mother's?*

Effie appeared in the doorway. "Dinner's all ready, Mr. Colin."

"Thanks, Effie." He turned to me as she nodded and left. "Shall we?"

We walked down the hallway to the dining room. With only two place settings, the large table looked bare and lonely. Colin took the seat at the head of the table while I settled on his right.

Effie brought in two salad plates and put them before us. "You said to keep it simple, sir, so I did."

"That's fine, Effie. I take it Mrs. Patterson will not be joining us. Has she eaten?"

"Yes, sir, I already took a tray up."

We ate in silence and made fast work of the salad.

Effie appeared as Colin's fork hit the plate to clear the dishes. A few moments later, she reentered with the main course—chicken in a mushroom cream sauce, rice, and green beans.

I leaned over and inhaled savoring the hint of garlic in the sauce. "Effie, this smells wonderful."

"Thank you, Miss Hilary. If you need anything, just ring the bell." She indicated a small silver bell near Colin's wine glass.

"Where's Keshia tonight?" I asked.

"She quit this morning. Said she couldn't work in a 'house of death' as she put it."

"I'm sorry. Won't that mean extra work for you?" I thought about Mother's demands and how long Effie would put up with them.

She shrugged as she opened a bottle of wine and set it next to Colin. "I like being busy."

As Effie left again, I cut into a perfectly cooked chicken breast. The sauce was fantastic, but I'd expected no less. This woman could cook. Colin poured some chilled Chardonnay into our glasses.

"So, Hilary, what do we talk about? Murder? Police interrogations? Lying?"

"None of the above."

"I find the subject of lying interesting. Everyone does it at some point in time. And certainly the killer will when the police start asking questions of him—or her." He smiled and sipped his wine.

My fingers tightened on my fork. "I don't find it interesting at all. Talk about something else."

"You know the problem with lying? Sooner or later, the liar forgets what he or she has said. That makes for contradictions in alibis. No doubt about it. Lying is hazardous to your health."

I lifted my wine glass and gulped. "My health is fine, thank you. I'm not lying."

"Oh, I think you are. So's your mother. Neither of you is very good at it."

"I don't give a rat's ass what you think and if you don't shut up, I'm eating in the kitchen."

To my amazement, Colin laughed. "Relax, Hilary. You're lying about something, but I don't believe you killed Ross. The jury's still out on Priscilla."

"Mother didn't do it either. Tell me about private investigating. How did you stumble into that line of work?"

"Funny you should use that word because I did literally stumble into the job." He ate for a moment and sipped more wine before continuing. "I came home one night after being out with friends when I saw a strange car parked not far from my house. I was in my first year of law school and to…"

"Law school? You?" I interrupted with my fork poised halfway to my mouth. I'd had no idea.

That quirky right eyebrow of his rose. "Didn't think I had the brains, huh?"

I put my fork down. "You may be a royal pain in the ass, but dumb isn't on your list of faults. How did Ross feel about another lawyer in the family?"

"He dangled the carrot of a partnership with him under my nose. At twenty-two it sounded like a good idea."

I had resumed eating and now almost choked. Ross and Colin? In partnership? *Patterson & Blackwood, Attorneys-at-Law* emblazoned on the front of a building just didn't compute.

"So, what happened? How did private investigating come into the picture?"

"If you'll quit interrupting, I'll tell you."

"Sorry. Do continue."

He topped off our wine glasses. "Now where was I? Oh, yes, the strange car. I didn't think too much about it at first, but I was unlocking the front door when I saw someone in the bushes in front of a neighbor's house. I went inside and called the cops. A few minutes later, the guy headed back toward his car. Since the cops hadn't arrived yet, I confronted him."

"Good God, he could have been armed! What were you thinking?"

He shrugged. "I wasn't. I'd been out with the guys, had a few beers, and just did it."

"What happened?" I ceased eating. This was ten times more interesting than chicken in cream sauce.

"I asked him what the hell he thought he was doing, he told me take a hike, I grabbed him, we scuffled, something hit the ground—a camera, I found out later—and then the police arrived. Turned out the guy was a P. I. hired by the neighbor to keep an eye on his wife while he was out of town. Seems he suspected her of cheating."

"Was she?"

He grinned again. "Yep. My actions told her the

you-know-what was about to hit the fan. They divorced a few months later."

"So, how did this lead to private investigation?"

"The concept of the work fascinated me. About a week later, I went to the guy's office, apologized, and asked for a job."

"That was ballsy. And he gave it to you? Just like that?"

"Said he needed an extra pair of eyes. Business was good. Lot's of cheating husbands and wives. I quit law school and never looked back."

"What was Ross's reaction?"

"Pissed as hell at first. Eventually, he used me for quite a few of his cases."

"You mean you spied on his clients' associates?"

"And witnesses for the prosecution. A good lawyer needs an edge in the courtroom."

"Yes, but…"

"Hilary, the chicken is getting cold and the wine warm. Enough about me. Let's finish eating."

He picked up his fork and stabbed a piece of chicken. I had no choice but to do the same. We finished the meal in silence. Once again Effie appeared just as before. She cleared away the plates and brought in the dessert.

My mind was still absorbing the information. I tried picturing Colin in a suit standing in front of a jury arguing a case. I failed. Not that he wouldn't have been successful, but I just couldn't see him dealing with the scum my stepfather had. Nor did I see him and Ross as partners. They'd have killed each other.

I laid my napkin next to the remains of my apple pie, and pushed back my chair. Time to get upstairs to that jump drive.

"If you'll excuse me, Colin, I have…"

This time he interrupted. "Wait a minute, Hilary. I'd like to talk to you."

"What about?" I asked as he also stood.

"Let's go into the den."

I followed him down the hall. If he planned on questioning me again, he was in for a disappointment. I didn't have the stamina to discuss my lies tonight.

In the den he poured two small glasses of Drambuie and handed me one. I sat on the sofa and sipped. The warm scotch-based liqueur slid easily down my throat.

"Hilary, what are you going to do with the rest of your life?"

The question not only caught me off guard, but stunned me as well. He'd never shown any interest in what I did, other than to disapprove.

"What do you mean?"

"How old are you?"

"Twenty-eight."

"You shop all day, and party all night. Are you going to be doing this when you're fifty? You have no direction. You're wasting your life."

I sipped from the tiny glass again. *How does he know? How does he know I've been thinking the same thing?*

Tears threatened to choke me. Nobody, not even my mother, had ever cared enough to ask.

"And what do you see as the solution? Find a nice guy, have kids, buy a house in the 'burbs, and drive a minivan?"

"If that's what you want."

I looked up and met his gaze. In a way, it *was* what I wanted. I just didn't know how to get it.

"Where do I find this marriage material? Certainly not from the crowd…" I halted abruptly.

"Not from the bozos you run around with? They're all cut from the same cloth. Aimless with too much money to spend and too much unproductive time on their hands. You're smart. You graduated from college. Did you get a degree?"

"Yes, in Art."

"Ah, one of those degrees that doesn't have a lot of job opportunities attached to it. What did you plan to do with it? Teach?"

"Oh, right. Can you see me with a room full of kids?"

"So, what did you plan to do?"

I drained my glass and set it on the end table. "I wasn't sure. I toyed with the idea of interior design and decorating. I had a few courses in that field and loved it."

"So, why didn't you pursue it?"

"I don't know," I said, my voice rising. I lowered my gaze to my fingers nervously stroking my slacks. "It was just easier to keep putting it off."

He came over, sat next to me, and took my hand. It was the first time he'd ever touched me in a friendly way. I liked the warmth, the feeling of intimacy, the awareness that suddenly existed. What I didn't like was the sense of pity I was sure he held. I didn't want him to feel sorry for me. I wanted him to like me. I raised my glance to his face. There was no answering sardonic look, no disdain or contempt. Just kindness. Like he cared. I wanted to cry again.

"You kept putting it off because you were scared— scared of failing. Right?"

"I...I don't know. It's a tough business dealing with the likes and dislikes of people, especially when it comes to their homes."

"Yet you said Ross let you decorate the bedroom upstairs. You did a nice job. I'm sure it would appeal to a lot of young women." He paused and looked down at our hands. The warmth increased. "I remember when he had his study redone. Did you do that, too?"

I nodded. "About five years ago. I had overspent really bad one month. Ross saw it as a way of getting some cheap labor. My outstanding bills were only a pittance of what a legitimate interior decorator would charge."

"You did a great job with that room, too." He released my hand and stood, ambling back to the bar to refill his glass. "I think you have talent."

"You do? I don't even know how to start." I wished he'd come back and hold my hand again. He'd taken the warmth with him.

"Enroll in a design school. Refresh your education. I'm sure design concepts have changed in the past few years."

"And then what? Make up a bunch of business cards and hand them out on the street corner?" I knew I sounded edgy, but couldn't help it. He was right. I was scared.

He took a drink. "Tonight probably isn't the best time to plot out a business plan, but you have friends with money. There's a start."

His cell phone rang, and as he answered, I thought. I did like the idea of actually having a full time job.

And Mother had a slew of friends who might consider me to re-do their dens or master bedrooms.

I wonder if it's possible. Can I do it? But what if I failed? What if nobody liked what I'd done? Would I be able to deal with that?

Colin hung up, and turned to me. "Look, Hilary, I don't mean to butt in, but just think about your future. Okay? Now, I think I'm going to take this box of hate mail upstairs and read. I'll see you in the morning. Goodnight."

He hefted the box and disappeared out the door. His abrupt departure after his kind words bordered on rude. Was he regretting being nice to me? I hoped not. Maybe his demeanor had something to do with the phone call. *Wonder who called. I guess if he wanted me to know he'd have told me.*

I sat staring at the enormous fireplace across the room for several minutes, my mind whirling about our conversation. *Don't think about the future now.* I was procrastinating again, but pushed it from my thoughts. I rose and headed upstairs to scan more of that jump drive.

I nestled in a chaise lounge with my laptop and picked up where I'd left off earlier. The scroll indicator on the right side of the screen had barely moved, showing a lot of files to follow. I sighed and opened the next one.

Three hours later, I rubbed my eyes and yawned. The cases were depressingly alike—all thieves and drug dealers with a few murderers thrown in for good measure. Only Ross's sarcastic and often malicious comments kept me awake. Even he referred to most of his clients as scum, trash, and degenerates. But they all had one thing in common—the money to pay my stepfather's enormous fees.

I scrolled down to read one last file before going to bed. The name slapped me wide awake. Don Merrick.

I remembered the night he and I were arrested. I'd called Ross immediately. He'd come down to the Tunica County Jail and convinced the sheriff I was an innocent—though slightly drunken—bystander. While there he talked to Don and agreed to represent him. I never knew too many details, mainly because I was pissed at Don for driving drunk and for having a couple of baggies of marijuana and cocaine in the trunk. I didn't do drugs. Never had. I was also pissed at myself for believing him when he said he could drive. I'd ridden down to the casinos with someone else who hooked up with a guy and decided to stay the night.

I read with growing consternation. Apparently, Don's case had been a bit more complicated than I thought and he admitted. According to Ross's investigative notes, that wasn't the first scrape Don had been in concerning drugs. He'd been busted on several occasions for possession and once on intent to distribute. The latter was a serious charge that could have landed him jail time. He'd been stopped with his girlfriend in *her* car. She took the rap because the registration had her name on it and she was driving. My stepfather was not the attorney for that one. Shortly after the incident, he'd begun hanging with my crowd.

Ross was thorough when it came to sniffing out the truth. I'd always wondered where some of my friends had gotten their drugs. Now I knew—through Don Merrick. Ross knew, too, and made him pay—literally. Don had coughed up a small fortune in what my stepfather called "monthly fees." I called it blackmail.

And Don Merrick just happened to drop by my place this afternoon.

A chill ran up my spine. *Why?*

Chapter Six

I didn't sleep worth a damn. Crazy, disjointed dreams of Ross and Don Merrick interrupted the night. I awoke at eight more tired then when I'd gone to bed, but a quick shower cleared the cobwebs from my mind. Now, I needed caffeine to get my heart pumping.

I peeked in on Mother before descending the staircase. The slight snoring told me she was sound asleep. Rather than disturb her, I closed the door softly and hurried downstairs. The eerie silence of the house gave me the creeps. Conversation would be a pleasant addition with my coffee. I hoped Colin was up, however, the dining room was empty. I guess with Ross's death, Effie saw no reason to set up. I breezed on and pushed open the door to the kitchen.

The room smelled of coffee, bacon, and cinnamon. Effie was unloading dishes from the dishwasher. She looked up as I entered.

"Oh, good morning, Miss Hilary."

"Good morning, Effie. What smells so good?"

She smiled. "I imagine that would be the cinnamon buns, miss. Can I get you something? I fried up some bacon for Mr. Blackwood earlier. Would you like eggs with that? Shall I set a place in the dining room?"

I waved my hand. "No need. I can eat here in the kitchen. You say Mr. Blackwood has already eaten?"

"Yes, miss. About an hour ago. Said he had to see

some people, but would be back in time for dinner. Have a seat, miss, and I'll fry a couple of eggs for you. Sunny side up or over easy?"

I sat at the large farm table. "Up and staring at me. And coffee. Lots of coffee."

She poured a mug and brought it to me before returning to the sink where she scoured a small frying pan, and then set it on the burner. She added a glob of butter and cranked up the heat. Unable to prevent myself, I glanced up at the enormous pot rack hanging over the island in the center of the room. One hook was noticeably empty.

I blew on the hot brew and cautiously sipped. "I take it that was where you kept the pan that killed Ross."

She looked up and shivered. "Yes, miss. And to think I never noticed it was missing that morning. I always use this pan for breakfast."

"What a strange choice of weapons," I murmured.

"Cinnamon bun, Miss Hilary?"

I dragged my gaze back to the stove. "Yes, please and you don't have to call me 'miss.' Just Hilary will do."

I wanted to thank her for not mentioning I'd been in the house last Friday, but decided not to stir the pot. *Some things are better left unsaid.*

The housekeeper smiled, nodded, and cracked two eggs, adding them to the sizzling butter. "Will you be in for lunch?"

"I don't know. Did Ross and my mother require a full luncheon?"

"Not often. Mrs. Patterson generally ate out with friends or by herself. I didn't usually make lunch. Mr.

Patterson's retirement and your mother's leaving upset the routine. He preferred soup and a salad or sandwich in the study."

"In that case, a salad or sandwich will do for me, too. Don't go to any fuss. What's for dinner?"

She hesitated. "Mrs. Patterson used to consult with me, but lately Mr. Patterson requested the meal."

"I guess since Mother's back in the house, she'll do it again."

Effie placed the plate of food in front of me, and then resumed her tasks. As I ate, my thoughts ran back to Ross's files and Don Merrick. His sudden appearance at my place yesterday hiked my suspicious nature.

Why did he show up only a couple of days after the murder? Had he intended to pump me for information? And why would he assume I knew anything about Ross's affairs?

Nothing made sense—except Ross's murder. That I could understand. He wasn't the most pleasant of people.

Effie had disappeared into the laundry room. Finished with my meal, I rinsed off the dishes and put them in the dishwasher before wandering back to my room.

I was at loose ends and wished Colin was here. Mother would sleep until at least ten, and then most likely eat out with a friend. On impulse, I turned on my laptop and pulled up interior design and decorating schools.

An hour later, I leaned back in the chair. Memphis didn't have a lot to offer, although one, Lighthouse Designs, sounded interesting. I'd investigate more later.

"Good morning, sweetheart," Mother said from my doorway.

She was dressed in a pair of skinny jeans and a long-sleeved, multi-colored, silk designer t-shirt. Bronze ballet flats graced her feet, and a slim designer handbag hung from her shoulder. Naturally, her hair was perfectly coiffed. It was ten-thirty and she was obviously ready for action.

"Good morning, Mother. Where are you off to?"

"Doreen Lindum called and suggested lunch at Quinn's. She just wants a first-hand glimpse into Ross's murder, but I don't care. I'm not about to rattle around in this house today. However, first I'm going to do a little shopping at the boutiques. I want something elegant and stylish for the funeral. The press will no doubt attend. Should I let the cameras see my face? Do you think a hat with a black veil would be too much?"

I wanted to roll my eyes. She was serious. Even at a funeral, she had to be the center of attention. Wasn't it some old-time politician who'd claimed his opponent had to be the bride at every wedding and the corpse at every funeral? Fit Mother to a 'T'.

"Considering you were about to dump his ass, I think a hat is over the top. And don't go black. Navy blue is better. More dignified. Keep it subdued. After all, Ross didn't just die. He was murdered."

"Hmmm, I suppose you're right. Want to come along? Doreen won't mind."

Doreen Lindum came from old Memphis money and Mother had spent years cultivating her. I thought she was a stuck up bitch.

"No thanks, I've got things to do." I turned back to the desk with a wave of my hand. "Have a good time."

Mother left and I stared at my screen saver of a virtual aquarium. I didn't have a damned thing to do other than continue reading Ross's files. *Says a lot about my life, doesn't it?* Sighing, I pulled one up.

At noon, Effie informed me lunch was ready. I'd read more of the same as I had yesterday. Drug dealers, murderers, and assorted scumbags were the norm. Ross's annotations revealed he had no respect for either his clients or his clients' victims.

All he cared about was the money. He was the biggest scumbag of all. My loathing of my stepfather deepened. Yet I had taken his money for years. What did that make me?

I ate in the kitchen where Effie served chicken salad over greens and fruit.

"Effie, I don't know how you do it. This is fabulous. I can't wait for dinner. What's on the menu?"

"Thank you, miss. Mrs. Patterson has requested seafood Newberg tonight. I just placed the order with our fishmonger."

"Isn't that a rather complicated, time consuming dish to make?"

"Yes, miss. Sounds like I'll be busy all afternoon."

"I'm sorry, Effie. Why on earth can't Mother keep things simple for a change?"

"Miss Hilary, I don't think your mother understands simple."

I had to laugh. She so had Mother's number.

I finished lunch and returned upstairs to read Don Merrick's file again. Why had Don showed up at my place? Considering Ross was blackmailing him, I didn't buy the condolences bit. He was probably relieved Ross was dead. Still the question of why he'd shown up at all bugged me.

Maybe I was too hasty in brushing him off. Maybe I should *go out to dinner with him. I can pump him for information and he'd never suspect.* After all, I was Ross Patterson's flighty, fun-loving stepdaughter—not to be taken seriously.

My heartbeat increased at the thought of doing my own investigating. Why not? I could do this. All I had to do was call him and say I changed my mind—that I was bored and wanted to get out. He'd believe that in a New York minute.

Unfortunately, I didn't have his phone number—at least not in my current cell phone. I changed cell phones like some people changed shoes—as often as possible. Had to have the latest gadgets and apps. And the numbers I stored also changed frequently. People came and went in my life. People like Don Merrick.

It was also my good fortune to be a bit of a hoarder when it came to phones. I had several dating back four or five years. Who knew when I'd want a number again? Don wasn't in my newest. It had been at least two years since I'd seen him, which meant that phone was stuffed into a desk drawer at my place.

I shut off my computer and grabbed my purse. A quick trip home was in order.

****

I spotted a TV news van parked across the street from my townhouse. So they'd finally tracked me down. I drove past, turned the next corner, and parked out of sight. I dashed across the lawns to the back garage door and slipped inside. Breathing a sigh of relief, I entered the kitchen. Maybe staying at Ross's was a good idea after all. Reporters weren't likely to get past the gatekeeper in the subdivision.

I entered the dining room and stopped short. The drawers to the sideboard were open—not a lot, but just enough to let me know someone had been here. I didn't have many expensive items downstairs, but my jewelry box in the bedroom was crammed with several nice pieces.

Pausing, I listened. Silence reigned. Surely the thief still wasn't here. I took a chance and crept into the living room. The desk drawers and those of the secretary also showed signs of having been searched.

I stopped at the foot of the stairs, licked my lips, and wondered if I was being a fool. Get out and call the cops. The silence got on my nerves. My breaths quickened. I hustled back to the desk and looked for my letter opener. It was ornate and sharp—a perfect weapon for self-defense, assuming that if the thief was still here, he didn't have a gun.

Of course, the thief isn't here. He's long gone. Still, better safe than sorry.

Unfortunately, I couldn't find the opener, so I grabbed a pair of scissors instead and tiptoed up the steps. No one jumped from a doorway to halt my progress. I tiptoed down the hall to my bedroom door. It stood half closed. I pushed it open and entered. My gaze never made it to the jewelry box.

Instead, I stared at the body of Don Merrick on the bedroom floor, his sightless eyes staring at the ceiling—with my letter opener sticking out of his chest.

Chapter Seven

Don Merrick! Dead on my bedroom floor! My heart squeezed tightly and my breath refused to budge from my throat. For a moment, I couldn't do anything but stare. Then the paralysis broke and panic set in.

I screamed, then whirled and ran from the room bouncing off the walls of the hallway in my haste to get the hell out. I grasped the banister with both hands as I stumbled down the stairs. Two-thirds of the way down, my heel caught on a tread. I fell the rest of the way, my body banging off the steps. I felt no pain, but sprang to my feet in the foyer and raced for the door.

Out! I need to get out now! I knew I was being irrational. Don was dead and the killer long gone, but I couldn't help it.

I fumbled with the deadbolt then jerked the door open and fled toward the street.

The reporters erupted from the news vans. They met me on the sidewalk. Microphones were shoved in my face.

"Miss Watson, any comments on the death of your stepfather?"

"Do the police have any idea who killed him?"

"Is it true he and your mother were divorcing?"

Finally, someone asked a sensible question. "What's wrong?"

I couldn't speak intelligently. Instead, I pointed and

gasped, "He...bedroom...dead!"

They ceased questioning me and stared, then like a herd of lemmings ran for my front door. One man had the presence of mind to call 9-1-1.

I stumbled across the street and leaned against one of the vans. My knees gave out. I slid down until my butt made contact with the pavement in a hard thump. My heart still hammered at ramming speed. The clog in my throat lessened, but I wasn't sure I could utter a coherent sentence.

Please God, don't let this be real! It was like I existed in a nightmare.

Within minutes, the herd returned with more questions.

"Do you know him?"

"When did you get home?"

"Did you catch a thief in the act?"

"Did you kill him?"

That last question brought me back to reality. "No, goddammit, I didn't kill him! And get those fucking microphones out of my face!"

In the distance sirens wailed getting louder as they approached before stopping at the curb. Six cops bailed out of three cruisers.

"What happened here?" one of them asked.

"There's a dead guy on the upstairs bedroom floor with a knife sticking out of his chest," a reporter replied.

The policeman glanced at the front door, a scowl on his face. "And you've all been inside?"

"Of course. This lady came running out terrified, told us there was a dead man inside. Naturally, we investigated."

"But we didn't touch anything," another said. "Just shot some footage, that's all"

The cop cursed loudly. "You may have compromised forensic evidence! All of you; get out of here. Now!"

"Hey, we have a right…"

"This is a crime scene. You have no rights!" The officer glanced down at me as the news-hungry hoard moved a few steps away, but not so far as to lose camera contact. "Who are you?"

I swallowed and took a deep breath. "I'm Hilary Watson. I live here."

"Are you all right? Do you need an ambulance?"

I struggled to my feet. "No, but Don sure as hell does."

"Don?"

"The guy inside."

"You know him?"

I nodded. "His name is Don Merrick."

"Did you kill him?"

"No! I came home, found the place ransacked and him on the bedroom floor." It occurred to me that maybe I shouldn't be talking to anyone. Suddenly nauseated, I clutched my stomach. "Oh Jeez, I'm gonna be sick."

I moved several yards away. No one stopped me. Taking deep breaths, I paused to let my stomach settle. I glanced back at my home. Already, police swarmed in and out. Yellow crime scene tape was strung from the wrought iron railings around my stoop to a couple of small trees in the swale by the street.

My mind started to function again and I realized I could be in a whole world of hurt. I might need a lawyer. Unfortunately, Ross had been my attorney and he was just as dead as Don. I could call Mother, but she was useless in crisis situations. Oddly enough, that left only one person—Colin Blackwood—and I didn't have his phone number either.

Throughout this whole ordeal, I'd held on to my purse. Now, I snatched my cell and called Effie.

"Patterson residence."

"Effie, it's Hilary. Do...do me a favor. Call Colin. I'm...I'm in trouble."

"Trouble, miss?"

"There's...been a little accident. I can't go into it right now. Just please get a hold of him and have him meet me at my place."

"Yes, of course, right away. Are you all right? What's..."

I hung up, unwilling to explain what had happened. I didn't want to upset the poor woman with news that I was now in the same position as she a few days ago.

Another car rolled up to the curb. Detectives Parker and Hamilton emerged. For once Claudia Hamilton wasn't smiling.

Swell, just who I need to see.

They approached me with firm steps. "Miss Watson, what's going on?" Parker asked.

"I...I found a dead guy in my townhouse. Should I be talking to you?"

Hamilton gave me a one-shoulder shrug. "Up to you. Stick around for a while. Why don't you have a seat in one of the squad cars while we go inside?"

That didn't sound good. I wasn't about to put myself inside the back of a cop car—the kind with no door handles to get out again.

They turned and entered my house. I remained standing next to a tree. A quick glance at my watch showed that less than an hour had passed. Seemed like a lifetime.

I folded my arms across my chest and waited impatiently for Colin to arrive. An ambulance rolled up, along with a car marked "Coroner." They, too, trooped through the front door. No one approached or paid any attention to me. Long minutes ticked by as I stood wondering what was going to happen next.

How long had it been since I'd called Effie? Fifteen minutes? Twenty? Had she been able to reach Colin? What if he blew me off? No, something told me he wouldn't do that. I just wished he'd get here. *Hurry!*

The thought had barely left my mind when his car pulled up. Colin jumped out and trotted toward me.

His hand gripped my shoulders. "Are you all right? What happened?"

I gulped. "There's a dead guy on my bedroom floor."

I gave in to that last shred of panic and burst into tears. Colin pulled me into his arms and held me close to his chest.

Instant warmth flooded through me. For the first time in over an hour, I felt safe as I bawled like a five-year-old against the shoulder of his polo shirt. His hands rubbed up and down my back in a comforting gesture.

Finally, I stepped away. "Thanks for coming."

"What happened?"

I gave him the details of finding poor Don.

"You knew the guy?"

"Yeah, he ran with us for a while a few years ago.

He stopped by yesterday to offer condolences on Ross. And before you ask, no, I don't know why he would return to rob me."

"What were you doing here?"

"I came back for something I forgot yesterday." I didn't think now was the time to confess to anything else. "Do I need a lawyer?"

"Not unless they arrest you or start asking questions you can't answer. And speaking of the devil, here come Parker and Hamilton."

"Miss Watson, would you mind coming down to the station for a few minutes? We need to get your statement."

I shot a quick glance at Colin who nodded. "Yeah, I guess I can do that. Do you want me there now?"

Detective Hamilton nodded. "If you don't mind. Brad will stay here while you talk to me."

I'd rather talk to Parker. Anything to avoid her smiling face in that interrogation room.

Hamilton looked around. "Where's your car?"

"I saw the news hounds when I got here, so I parked around the corner and came in the back garage door."

"How did this Merrick person get in?" Colin asked.

"Through the sliding glass door on the patio. Jimmied the lock and lifted it right off the track," Parker answered shooting me a look. "You didn't notice it when you arrived, Miss Watson?"

I inhaled a deep breath and shook my head. "No. I was concentrating of avoiding those reporters and never looked toward the patio at all."

"I see."

I didn't like the way he said that. Made it sound

like he didn't believe me. I shivered. I glanced again at Colin, who frowned. This wasn't looking good at all.

"In that case, Miss Watson, why don't you head on down to the police station? I'll be along in a few minutes," Hamilton said.

I had no choice. I nodded and turned toward Colin.

"I'll drive," he said in a tight voice.

"I'm in deep shit here, aren't I?" I asked as we drove away.

"Could be. You knew the guy. Did you notice if he had a pillow case or a bag of some kind stuffed with things?"

"I…I don't know. I mean, I took one look and ran like hell."

"Why the hell did you even go upstairs when you knew the place was tossed?"

His angry tone made me feel guilty and too stupid to live.

"It wasn't really ransacked, but I could tell someone had searched the place. And I heard no one moving around, so I figured whoever had done it was long gone."

"Still a dumb thing to do. Confronting an intruder unarmed is dangerous."

"I wasn't unarmed," I protested remembering the scissors. I told him about them.

"So you looked for the letter opener, couldn't find it, and settled on a pair of scissors. And where are they now?"

"The scissors? I guess I must have dropped them somewhere. How the hell should I know? All I wanted was to get out!" I paused and heaved a deep breath. "Oh God, my fingerprints will be all over the murder weapon."

"Actually, they should be. It's yours and you used it often. You've got trouble if no prints are found. And any forensic evidence from you can also be explained. You live there."

"The reporters went inside."

"What! How did that happen?"

I told him of my panicked flight and how they had rushed me.

"I said the first thing that popped into my mind—'there's a dead guy on the floor.'"

"If they were in there before the scene was secure, they could have compromised any forensic evidence. A good lawyer will bring that up."

"The first officers who came mentioned that, too."

"Anything else you're not telling me?"

There was plenty, but I didn't want to dig a deeper hole. Instead, I just shook my head and murmured a short no.

The rest of the drive was silent.

****

I sat in the same hard plastic, armless chair staring at the same, scarred tabletop in the same airless interrogation room as a few days ago. I refused to look at the camera in the corner of the ceiling. I'd been here in solitary for close to an hour about to get grilled like a pig during the Memphis in May Barbeque Contest. Colin waited in the lobby—at least, I hoped he did.

Keep your statement simple and as close to the truth as possible. I figured the reporters were in more trouble than me at the moment. Just in case they weren't, I'd asked Colin to contact Jim Price. I might need a lawyer after all. So far, he hadn't shown up.

Finally, the door opened and Detective Hamilton, complete with her smile in place, entered.

"Sorry to keep you waiting, Miss Watson."

"No problem. I'm waiting for my attorney, too."

She waved a hand in the air as she took a seat. "No need for that. We just want your statement and to ask a few clarifying questions, that's all."

Yeah right, and I'm the next Miss Tennessee.

She opened a manila folder and shuffled through the papers inside, then set a tape recorder on the table. She pushed the button and a soft whirring noise filled the room. Maybe she had no confidence in the police department's audio taping.

I folded my trembling hands in front of me and stared at a cigarette burn near the edge of the Formica.

"Now, Miss Watson, please tell me again how you discovered the body."

Did this qualify as an interrogation? I wasn't sure, but not cooperating sounded like I had something to hide concerning Don's death. Besides, I'd already spoken with the policemen at the scene.

Come on, Price, you asshole. I need advice.

"I already told the police at my place what happened."

"I know, but we need to make it formal. Now that you're calmer, you might remember something that can help us find the killer."

Her smile never wavered. It sent shivers up my spine.

Someone knocked on the door. A second later, Jim Price entered.

"Don't say anything, Hilary." He turned to Detective Hamilton. "I'm James Price, the Patterson family attorney."

"Please be seated, Mr. Price. This is just a simple statement. Your client hasn't been charged with anything."

He pulled up a second plastic chair and sat next to me. "Very well, ask your questions."

"Now, Miss Watson, please tell me how you found the body of Donald Merrick starting from when you left your stepfather's house this afternoon."

I glanced at Price who nodded. Taking a deep breath, I gave them the facts.

"And why were you at the townhouse?" she asked.

"I'd forgotten something when I'd packed the day before and went back for it."

"What did you forget?"

"Some...some jewelry. I'd forgotten to toss it into the suitcase."

She shuffled through the papers. "Earlier you stated that you didn't notice the patio door had been broken, yet it's only twenty feet from the back garage door."

"That's right, but I had those reporters on my mind and didn't bother to look. Why should I? I wasn't expecting to see anything wrong."

I shot a glance at Price who sat with his arms folded across his chest and staring at the detective. Since he hadn't spoken, I assumed this was normal.

"Yet you did once you got inside. Why didn't you call the police immediately? After all, you knew someone had been there."

"I...I don't know. I didn't think the thief or thieves were still around, so I ran upstairs to see if they'd taken my jewelry."

"What made you think that no one was there?"

"Because it was quiet as a tomb."

"Did you take anything upstairs with you?"

"Like what?" Price asked.

"We found a pair of scissors on the floor not far from the doorway. Did you bring them?" Her smile slipped slightly.

Price turned to me with a questioning look. "You don't have to answer that, Hilary."

"Mr. Price, I'm just trying to understand why if your client didn't think the thief or thieves were still in the house, she felt it necessary to go upstairs with a weapon."

"I admit I was nervous, so I opened one of the desk drawers and found the scissors. They weren't all that large, but I'd rather be safe than sorry."

"And you still didn't call the police?"

"I just wanted to get upstairs and see if my jewelry was still there. I have several very nice pieces and would be upset if they'd been stolen."

Detective Hamilton leaned back in her chair, the smile back on full beam.

"The murder weapon was very ornate, but looked more like a letter opener than a knife. It is yours, isn't it?"

I looked at Price again who nodded. "Yes."

"And where did you keep it?"

I hesitated before answering. "In the desk downstairs."

"Did you notice it was missing when you searched for a weapon before going upstairs?"

"Hilary…" Price began.

I waved him silent. "When I couldn't find it

immediately, I grabbed the first thing I found. I didn't think of it as missing, merely misplaced."

"Detective Hamilton, Miss Watson has given you her statement. This is now an interrogation. I wish to consult with my client before she answers any more questions," my attorney said in a firm tone. "By the way, were there any fingerprints on the murder weapon?"

"No, the hilt had been wiped clean."

"Which means somebody found the opener, used it, and wiped his or her prints from it."

"Your client could have done the same."

"But I didn't!"

"Oh, there's something else I need clarification on," she said turning her attention back to me. "How well did you know the deceased?"

I kept my answer brief. "Casually. He used to run with my crowd."

"And how long since you'd seen him?"

"A couple of years, I guess—up until yesterday. He stopped by to offer condolences on Ross."

"And you have no idea why he'd return to your townhouse and break in?"

"None whatsoever."

"By the way, can you tell me where you were at approximately four o'clock this morning?"

"Don't answer that one, Hilary!" Jim barked.

Detective Hamilton sighed. "Mr. Price, that is simply a routine question. We'll be asking it of everybody we interview."

"Oh for God's sake, I was at Ross's, in bed, sound asleep, and nowhere near my home. Is that good enough for you?" I was tired of answering questions and looking at upturned lips.

The smile finally left her face. "Records show you and Mr. Merrick were arrested in Tunica County, Mississippi about two and a half years ago. The charge against Mr. Merrick was DUI. The arresting officer also found several small bags of marijuana and cocaine in the trunk. Your stepfather defended him. Mr. Merrick got off with a very light sentence. You were released with no charges filed. It also seems that Mr. Merrick was arrested about five years ago on a possession with intent to distribute charge. He pleaded guilty and received probation."

Not quite accurate. According to the file I'd read, Don's girlfriend had taken the rap.

Jim's head swiveled sharply toward me. He stared for a moment before turning back to the detective.

"This interview is over. Mr. Merrick's past indiscretions are irrelevant. Simply means anyone could have followed him to Miss Watson's townhouse and killed him. My client has made her statement. Have it typed up and she'll sign it."

Hamilton and Price stared at each other, both frowning. Finally, the detective closed the folder and rose.

"I'll get this done and back to you shortly. Thank you for coming in, Miss Watson. We'll be in touch."

We'll be in touch. Didn't sound encouraging. I breathed easier when the door closed behind her.

"Did you know about Merrick's past?" Jim demanded when we were alone.

I glanced up at the camera in the corner.

He waved his hand. "Doesn't matter what they record visually or audibly, attorney client privilege is in force. What did you know about Merrick?"

"Ross took care of the DUI thing. He convinced the cops in Tunica County that I was an innocent bystander who was offered a ride home by a friend—which was the truth. Don said he had loaned his car to some friends a few weeks before for a trip to New Orleans."

"And the other charges from five years earlier?"

I knew I shouldn't lie to my attorney, but neither did I want to tell him about the jump drive or how I got it.

"It's the first I've heard about it."

"You're sure?"

I was irritated by his tone. "Of course, I'm sure. Admitting to a drug charge isn't something you do during casual conversation or a night out on the town."

"Oh boy, this could get interesting. Look, Hilary, I'm not much of a defense attorney. Ross handled that end of the firm when we were partners. I deal in wills and trusts. You may need someone better than me to represent you."

"Why did you and Ross split?"

"Ross and I didn't see eye to eye on how things were done. It just seemed easier for both of us to go our separate ways."

I could believe that. From what I'd read on the jump drive, Ross was a greedy son of a bitch who wasn't above gouging his clients with enormous fees. On the other hand, he was damned good at what he did. Price had always struck me as a straight arrow. A lawyer with ethics. Go figure.

For the next twenty minutes, we waited in silence until Detective Hamilton returned. She laid three sheets of paper in front of me. I read them through, and then handed them to Price who also looked them over. He nodded and I signed.

We both rose and left without saying another word.

If the police found out about that jump drive, I knew I'd be on the wrong side of a jail cell.

Chapter Eight

Colin rose from a chair in the police station waiting room as Jim and I approached.

"Well, you're walking out. That's always a good sign."

"God, I hate Detective Hamilton and her smile," I muttered.

"Thanks for coming on such short notice, Jim," he said.

"I'm glad I could help, but like I told Hilary, she needs someone with an expertise in criminal law. Let me have your e-mail address. As soon as I get back to the office, I'll send you a few names—just in case."

"Thank you, Jim." I gave him the information. He nodded and left as I turned to Colin. "God, let's get out of here. This has been one helluva day."

"I'll take you back to get your car," Colin said in a calm tone.

I'd forgotten about my car. "Thanks."

"So, tell me exactly what happened this afternoon at the townhouse."

I groaned. "Oh Jeez, not you, too. I've had it. Besides, I already told you."

"I need to hear it again from you."

"Why?"

"Because you might have remembered something that you didn't earlier. Plus, Ian asked me to help with

Ross's murder. I need to know if the two deaths are connected."

"Colin, not now. I'm exhausted."

The rest of the ten minute drive to my place was mercifully silent.

Back in my own car, I rested my forehead on my hands as they gripped the steering wheel and sucked in several deep breaths. I wondered how long it would be before I could get back into my house. And did I really want to? The image of Don on my bedroom floor with the letter opener sticking out of his chest would remain burned in my retinas for a long time.

But what also lingered was my reaction to finding his body. I'd always thought of myself as a cool personality—someone who could roll with the punches and, if necessary, lie my way out of trouble. It had worked in the past. And I thought I'd exhibited some of that by going upstairs when I should have gotten the hell out.

One look at Don had sent me into total panic mode. I barely remembered my near hysterical run from the house. This did not bode well for someone who had not been truthful with the police. I needed that cool personality to come forth, especially if I found any more bodies. I shuddered at that last thought.

Girl, you aren't nearly as calm and composed as you think you are.

I gradually brought my thoughts under control and started the car.

Since it was rush hour, the traffic was horrendous. Finally turning into the subdivision, I paused at the gate, and then using my swipe card, moved on through. The guard waved as I passed. In the driveway, I exited the car and staggered up the porch steps. God, I was tired. I fumbled with the door latch before lurching into the foyer. Mother was just coming down the staircase.

"Good heavens, where have you been? You look like hell."

I gave her the *Reader's Digest* version of events. Her perfectly penciled eyebrows almost rose off her forehead.

"You found a body in your house?" she squeaked in a horrified tone. "Whose?"

"A man named Don Merrick."

"Who's that and why was he in your place?"

"Don used to pal around with us a few years ago, and I assume he was robbing me. I've been at the police station all afternoon answering questions and giving a statement. Mother, can we talk about this at another time? I need a long, hot bath, and a good stiff drink."

"The police station? Did you call a lawyer?"

"I called Jim Price," Colin answered as he entered the foyer from the hallway.

"Oh, thank goodness. Are you sure you're all right?"

"I'm fine," I answered slowly climbing the stairs. "Just tired. Like I said: a hot bath, a stiff drink, and dinner."

I filled the tub with the hottest water I could stand, peeled off my clothes, and sighed as the warmth encased my body.

Colin's comments about the two murders being connected had wound through my mind, too. Ross had defended and later blackmailed Don. If he did it with one client, why not with others? I decided the best course of action was to give Colin most of what he wanted, including the part about Don's past. He'd have discovered it anyway if he investigated.

But the one question for which I had no answer was why Don Merrick was in my house.

"If he was looking for jewelry, why would he search through the drawers downstairs?" I muttered out loud. "No keeps jewelry there. It's kept in the bedroom."

But what if I had this all wrong? What if Don had interrupted someone else robbing the joint? I stopped to think about this for a moment.

"But that still doesn't answer how he got in. If he came to see me, why would he come to the patio door? And why would he return when he knew I wasn't going to be home?" I shook my head. I was beginning to think logically, like a cop, or worse yet, a private investigator.

Then the truth hit me like a shot between the eyes. I sat upright with a gasp. Taking a deep breath, I closed my eyes and remembered yesterday.

Don and I had chatted, he asked me out, I'd refused, and then Mother had called for me to pick her up at the police station. When I'd hung up, Don had been near my desk, and the computer on it had displayed the contents of the jump drive. Did he suspect his case along with Ross's blackmail of him were also on it?

"Holy shit! That's what he wanted!"

I couldn't recall if the screen saver had been on or not, or if I'd minimized the screen when I answered the door. A quick movement of the mouse would bring everything into full view. And of course later, in the dead of night, he'd have been looking for the jump drive at the house, not realizing I'd taken it to Ross's along with my laptop.

I pulled the plug on the cooling water, hurriedly dried off, and dressed. That jump had dozens of cases on it. And that made for dozens of motives for murder. Could Don have been killed by another one of Ross's client-victims?

Downstairs I headed for the den. Mother and Colin were already there, both with glasses of liquor. I poured a hefty shot of Grey Goose into a tumbler and joined Mother on the sofa.

"Feeling better, sweetie?" Mother asked.

"A bit, but finding a body isn't something I'd wish on my worst enemy. Oh, that reminds me, I need to apologize to Effie for hanging up on her earlier. I wasn't thinking straight. I'll be right back."

I hurried into the kitchen and told Effie about the events of this afternoon.

"Oh, Miss Hilary, that's awful. I know exactly how you feel. Are you sure you don't want a tray in your room tonight?"

"No, I'm fine." I hesitated. "How…how did you cope with the shock of finding Ross?"

"Well, it's not the first time I found a body. My dear sainted mother died in her sleep. Found her when I went to cook her lunch. Death comes in many forms. The good and the righteous die peacefully, in a state of grace with no pain. The evil die violently and rot in hell. Hell is where all evil goes." She stared straight ahead a far away look in her eyes. Her fingers stroked the small golden cross hanging from a delicate chain around her neck.

Then she blinked. "No, miss, finding a body is not

pleasant at all. Especially one that's been murdered. That kind of thing tends to stay with you. Would you please tell the others that dinner will be ready in a few minutes?"

I nodded and left.

"The evil die violently and rot in hell." *Her words should be etched on Ross's tombstone.*

Effie outdid herself on the seafood Newburg, but I tasted very little. Mother babbled on about her shopping trip and lunch with Doreen. I didn't care, but made the appropriate comments at all the proper times. Colin was unusually quiet. However, he watched me with a measured gaze throughout most of the meal. It was unnerving and I tried to ignore him. I was not successful. Eventually, the tense meal ended.

"Well, I have to make some phone calls," Mother stated as we exited the dining room. "I'll be in my room if you want to talk, dear. Oh, and Colin, thank Effie for me. That was delicious. She is such a treasure."

"That she is," I agreed. "I wonder how Ross found her or did you?"

"It wasn't me. Our old housekeeper and cook, Rosie, suddenly left, and before I could even call the agency, Effie was on the doorstep saying Rosie had suggested she apply for the job. One meal was all it took."

Mother headed upstairs while Colin and I drifted toward the den. I wanted to follow her in the worst way, but knew I couldn't postpone answering Colin's questions forever. I just wasn't sure what I planned to tell him now.

He poured us each a glass of wine. "Now, tell me again exactly what happened at the townhouse."

Refusing to explain was not an option. Evasion was, however, so I told him the same as I'd told the police.

"I told you last night that you aren't a very good liar. Now give me the full truth."

"That is the full truth! You think I killed Don?"

"No, because the police let you go. If they thought you had, you would be spending the night at the Shelby County Women's Lock-up. Besides, while you're smart, you aren't likely to kill a guy in your own home, and then pretend semi-hysteria when you find the body. You're not that good an actress."

"Well, I'm not lying," I answered in a surly tone.

"Yes, you are. We both know that you never forgot a piece of jewelry or clothing in your life. You plan your attire down to the last shoelace. So, cut out the bullshit and tell me why you went back to the townhouse."

Great—I was getting grilled for the second time today. In the long run, it was simpler to just tell him the truth. I caved.

"When Don stopped by yesterday, he asked me out to dinner. I brushed him off. This afternoon, I was sorry I did, but his phone number was in an old cell. I went back to get it. Okay?"

"That's better. Why didn't you tell that to the police instead of the jewelry nonsense?"

I sighed. "I don't know. Maybe because I didn't want to admit I knew Don that well." I told him about Price's theory of someone following Don to my place.

"Entirely possible. The big question is what the hell was he doing in your house?"

"I assume he was robbing me. For all I know,

that's how he made a living. I have no idea, and frankly, at this point, don't care."

Colin settled into the opposite corner of the sofa from me. His gray eyes, dark and wary, stared. I wondered if he could see right through me.

"What did you and Ross talk about Friday afternoon?"

"What? How did..." I shut up.

"Effie let it slip this morning that you'd been here, and had had an argument with Ross. Kinda forgot to tell me that when we discussed visitors, didn't you?"

I licked my lips and looked away. Damnation, I knew I should have told Effie not to say anything. The jig was up. I had no choice but to tell him everything.

"It...it didn't seem important. Ross called me in to discuss my bills, as usual. And it wasn't really an argument. It was just Ross being Ross. He was giving me a hard time and I did what I do best—I yelled some. So sue me."

"I won't have to. That argument makes you a prime suspect. The police may arrest you."

"Don't you think I didn't think of that from the moment I heard he had been murdered? That's why I lied!"

"Did he agree to pay off your shopping habit?"

"Yes," I replied in a sharp tone.

I didn't like myself much at the moment. I sponged off Ross like everyone else in the family, yet loathed the man. I should have grown a backbone years ago, gotten a legitimate job, and paid my own way. But I didn't. *And what does that say about my character—or lack thereof?*

"At what price?"

Colin's voice brought me out of my thoughts. "What?"

"What did he want from you in return? Yesterday, I believe we all discussed Uncle Ross's proclivity for demanding tribute. He wouldn't have let you off the hook with just a stern warning, especially since your Mother had flown the coop. Now, what did he want?"

Since he knew about my meeting with Ross, keeping the knowledge of the jump drive a secret didn't make a lot of sense. Besides, the burden of my suspicions needed another pair of shoulders and a head that understood what do to with the information.

"Oh, all right, he did demand something."

"What, Hilary?"

I told him about our conversation and his insistence I keep the jump drive for a short time.

He frowned and leaned forward. "Have you seen what's on it?"

"After Ross's murder, I plugged it in. It's a bunch of case files on the slimiest of his slimy clients." I also unloaded my theory of why Don was in my house.

"So, you and Merrick were arrested and Ross handled the case. Got you off scot-free and your friend with a slap on the wrist. And you had no idea this guy was a drug dealer?"

"Not until I read the information on the computer. And I have no evidence Don was still dealing drugs. It happened quite a while ago. Ross wasn't his attorney for that. When I talked to Don on Sunday, he seemed to have been walking a straight line for the last couple of years."

Colin inhaled a deep breath, and then blew it out again.

"I think it's safe to say, you didn't close the screen on the computer. Merrick saw what was on it and probably suspected his file was included, hence, he had to come back and get it. Give me the drive."

I stiffened my spine and straightened my shoulders. "Why?"

"For starters, I'm curious. If Merrick knew of its existence, then so could someone else."

"I suppose the police need to see it."

"It may be covered by the attorney/client privilege. I'm not sure. If it had been a client who'd died, then the privilege might be revoked. But since it was Ross..."

"Somehow, I don't think Detective Smiles-A-Lot will like that I didn't come clean sooner."

"I think she and Parker are going to be damned unhappy about it. But in order to see it, they'll have to find a judge willing to issue a court order permitting it. This is a sticky situation."

"What if I hand it over to them with tears, a contrite look, and a reasonable explanation—like I'm scared, which I am."

"Finally, the truth."

"Don't be nasty."

He stroked his chin. "If you hand it over, then they'll have to deal with the possible legal aspects—including the blackmail—but you're still not off the hook for withholding evidence."

"We could burn everything onto a CD. Should we?"

"Like I said, I'm curious."

"Is...is there any way I can help? I mean, I'm up to my neck in this."

"You mean do I need a loyal sidekick?"

"Something like that. Look, Colin, Ross is dead—murdered by someone who had a lot to lose by him publishing that book. Now, Don Merrick, whose case is on that jump drive along with Ross's blackmail of him, is stabbed to death on my bedroom floor. The two are connected. Ross put me in this position. I want to find out who did what to whom."

He drained his glass and rose, walking over to the bar where he refilled it. He sipped without answering. The silence stretched, getting on my nerves. Finally, he turned and heaved a sigh.

"Let's go burn a CD."

"Do you have one?"

He nodded. "In my briefcase. I have several, in fact. Never know when I might need one."

I rose and joined him by the bar, poured another glass for myself, and stared him straight in the eye.

"Let's make two. One for you and one for me."

"Makes sense. If Merrick was listed, then maybe another of your friends was, too. If nothing else, you might see a familiar name."

As we climbed the stairs, I didn't really think any of my other friends had fallen into Ross's clutches. They all had their own lawyers and as far as I knew the worst transgression for any of them was a massive accumulation of moving violations.

While Colin retrieved the CDs from his room, I plugged the jump drive into the USB port and fired up the computer.

He entered my room and closed the door behind him. Without speaking, he sat, slid a disc into the slot, then pulled up the contents of the jump drive, transferring the files. A few minutes later, he repeated the action with the second CD.

"There," he said, rising and handing one to me. "We're covered. Don't take this out of the house. And stay away from your place for a while. There's no telling who Merrick told about what he saw on your computer."

"You mean he could have told the wrong person, met that person there, and they killed him?" This was an angle I hadn't contemplated.

"Could be."

"I'll have to stop by to get my mail, pack a few more things, and report the door damage to the association so they can fix it."

"All right, but do it in broad daylight and try not to go inside alone."

"Do you really think someone's going to take another shot at searching my home?"

Colin shrugged. "I don't know. What I do know is I want you safe."

Warmth glowed from the pit of my stomach. He wanted me safe. That must have meant he cared. And having him care made me happy.

"Thank you for caring," I whispered.

"My pleasure." His gaze traveled from my eyes to my mouth. Suddenly, he leaned down and brushed his lips over mine.

The warmth turned into a furnace on full blast. We stood close to each other near the desk, my bed just a couple of steps away. Without thinking, I closed my eyes and leaned into his body. His arms wrapped around me, and his lips once again found mine, this time with hard determination.

Heat raced along every nerve ending. Even my toes

burned. I parted my lips. Our tongues twined and explored. One of us groaned. Or perhaps we both did. I wasn't sure and didn't really care. Something hard and heavy poked me in the abdomen.

Then, he broke away and stepped back. We stared at each other, breathing hard. I placed my fingers lightly over my mouth.

"Oh my, what did we just do?" I asked in a throaty whisper.

"I don't know, but now is not the time to explore the possibilities."

"What?"

"I mean we cool it, Hilary." He turned and strode to my door. "I'll see you in the morning. We'll work in Ross's study from now on. No more bedrooms."

He left, closing the door behind him and leaving me with a profound sense of loss.

It had been the most explosive kiss of my life and I wanted more—a lot more.

Chapter Nine

Descending the staircase the next morning at the ridiculous hour of seven o'clock, I wondered how to handle Colin. That kiss had seriously changed things between us. He was no longer the enemy.

My sleep had been interspersed with disturbing dreams of Don's body and not-so-disturbing ones of Colin. At three in the morning, I stared into the darkness, my mind a jumble of who killed Don and Ross—and whether Colin would break his promise to cool it.

I pushed open the door to the kitchen and inhaled the wonderful aromas of coffee and frying bacon. Colin looked up from the newspaper he was reading at the table.

"Well, you're up early."

"Couldn't sleep. Too much running through my mind." I took the chair opposite him and stared into his face. "You always up with the birds?"

"Usually."

"Good morning, miss," Effie said placing a cup of coffee in front of me. "Would you like some breakfast? The bacon's almost done and the eggs won't take but a minute."

I sipped the hot brew cautiously. "That sounds wonderful."

"Would you like toast, too?"

"With whatever jam you have."

She nodded and walked across the room toward the stove.

I took another sip of coffee before asking Colin, "So, what's on your agenda for today?"

He shot a glance at Effie. "Oh, nothing much. I think I'll spend most of it on the computer."

I got his drift—no discussing our arrangement to work together in front of third parties. Made sense. Apparently, I needed to learn a lot about investigating.

"Me, too, I guess. I was also thinking I'd go back to my place and pick up the mail."

"I'd wait another day until the police are done gathering evidence."

I shifted my gaze to Effie's back, and then to him again. "But what if something important comes?"

"It'll be just as important tomorrow." He frowned and shook his head.

I drank again, not sure what to say next. "So, have you talked to Ian lately? Any word on when Ross's funeral can be held?"

"The autopsy was performed, but as far as I know nothing has come through yet on the blood and tox screens."

"I wish it was over and done with. It'll probably be a media circus."

"No doubt, but then I'm sure Uncle Ross would be counting on that."

"One last wish granted," I muttered.

Effie set a plate of fluffy scrambled eggs, perfectly cooked bacon, and toast in front of me. A jar of strawberry preserves accompanied it. Colin got the same.

My mouth watered like Pavlov's dog. I grabbed a fork with one hand, a slice of bacon with the other, and plunged in. I was immediately transported to culinary heaven.

"Effie, how do you do it? This is fabulous."

"I don't know, miss. Just comes natural, I guess. Been cooking ever since I was six. By the time I was ten, Mama said I was better than her—and that was saying something, 'cuz she was an excellent cook."

"Well, your mother was right," Colin said through a mouthful of toast and jam.

"Thank you, Mr. Colin."

I spread jam on my toast and bit in. "I hope Ross complimented you often."

"Mr. Patterson wasn't one to compliment. If he said nothing, then I knew it was all right. Now, Mrs. Patterson says 'nice meal' every once in a while."

"Every once in a while? Should have been every night. Sorry, Effie, but Mother can be thoughtless."

She waved a hand. "No problem, miss."

"All I can say is I'm glad you found your way to Ross's doorstep. Mother said the old cook quit and you showed up the next day. What luck."

"No luck about it. I knew Rosie from church. She was getting on in years and when her daughter moved to Florida, she decided to tag along. Winter in Tampa is better than winter in Memphis. I didn't let any grass grow under my feet. The instant I heard she'd gone, I was here."

"Both Ross and Priscilla should have been thankful for that," Colin said.

Effie left and entered the laundry room. Over the gushing of water filling the machine, I leaned closer to

Colin.

"Why can't I go to the house? I want to get that jump drive to the cops. The sooner the better and the only way it can come is through the mail."

"Because you might look just a tad too eager the day after finding a body in the place," he replied. "Besides, I want a head start on those files. Maybe I can get in to interview some of those people before the cops, assuming they can legally use the information on the drive."

"Don't you mean 'we'?"

He forked the last of his eggs into his mouth and shook his head.

"Is that a no? I thought we had a deal." I crunched into a piece of bacon for emphasis.

"Most of those people are the scum of the earth. I'm not sure you should be exposed to them."

I didn't know if he was being a prude or not. In any other circumstances I might have been amused.

"I don't plan to expose myself, but I can be a distraction. I'm good at being a distraction. I can wear a short skirt, sit there, smile, cross my legs, and do any number of things. The person you're questioning might not give any thought to his answers."

"Does a low cut blouse also make an appearance?"

"If necessary."

Colin frowned, set his silverware on the empty plate with a clatter, and pushed it away.

"I'll think about it." He rose from the table. "I'll be upstairs if you need me."

"Think hard," I called after him as he left the room.

I finished my breakfast and carried the dirty dishes to the sink and opened the dishwasher. *If he thinks I'm going to just sit by and do nothing, he's in for a hell of a surprise. I have a stake in this now. Ross gave me the jump drive and I discovered Don's body in my house.*

Effie emerged from the laundry room with an armful of folded clothing. She looked at me with a horrified expression. "Oh, miss, I can get that."

"That's all right, Effie. It's only a couple of plates. Believe it or not, I like feeling useful."

"Well, miss, if you'll pardon me, you need to feel useful somewhere else. I'm paid to be the housekeeper."

The earnest look on her face made me want to laugh. I'd just been told to mind my own business in a very polite manner. I put the dishes in the washer anyway.

"Point taken. From now on I will not interfere in your domain."

"Oh, miss, I didn't mean…"

I laughed now. "It's okay, Effie. I'm going upstairs for a while, and then maybe out for lunch. I'll let you know."

At her nod, I left the kitchen and climbed the stairs. The door to Colin's room was closed indicating he wanted no interruptions. Well, two can play that game. Once inside, I closed the door to my room, too.

Even though it came under housekeeping duties, I made the bed and tidied my bathroom, then turned on the computer and slid the CD into the drive. Pulling up Don Merrick's file, I reread it again. Nothing jumped out at me.

I sat back to think. Why come back for the jump drive at all? The information about his drug deals would surface with any background check.

Yeah, but not information about Ross's blackmail. And since I'd obviously been reading the files, did he assume I'd get to his sooner or later?

Okay, so Don returned in an act of self-preservation. But who else had shown up? And why? The only reason Don knew of the device's existence was because I'd left the screen visible. It had never occurred to me he'd be interested. Someone else *must* have known.

Or maybe, Don told someone else about it. A partner in crime? Perhaps that someone else had more to lose than Don.

Which meant another third party knew I had the damned thing, too.

****

I descended the staircase a little before eleven. I'd finally finished the case files a while ago. There'd been seventy-five of them. Some I skimmed, others I read more thoroughly. Not all seventy-five people were involuntary contributors to Ross's retirement fund, but it did add a bundle of new suspects. How on earth would anybody ever get to the bottom of this mess?

Colin remained closeted in his room. Still irritated with him from this morning, I decided to ignore his advice and return to my townhouse. I'd pick up whatever mail was there, see what kind of damage forensics had done, and contact the police about the jump drive later. Whether or not the courts allowed them to see it wasn't my problem.

I informed Effie I wouldn't be in for lunch and left. Pulling into my driveway, I breathed a sigh of relief that the newshounds had departed. Don was yesterday's news. I assumed juicier, more timely murders and crimes now occupied their attention. The crime scene tape was gone, which suggested there hadn't been much to find.

I fished the mail out of the mailbox, and then hesitated before unlocking the door. A ripple of uneasiness slithered up my spine making me shiver.

Don't be an idiot. No one's going to break into a crime scene after *the police have given it the once over.*

Lifting my chin and straightening my shoulders, I opened up and entered. The sliding glass door in the dining room had been boarded over telling me maintenance had been on the job this morning. Other than black fingerprint dust on every horizontal surface, the mess wasn't as bad as I'd feared. I crossed to my desk, relieved to see the computer still there. A quick scan of the drawers showed very little disturbed. Even my old phones were intact. I couldn't tell if the cops had confiscated anything down here.

I made my way upstairs to find the same black dust. It would take a lot of cleaning to get rid of this crap. A stain on the carpet where Don had lain made me bite my lip. He'd lived long enough to bleed. I made a mental note to have the room re-carpeted soon.

The drawers to my vanity, dresser, and nightstand were ajar. In my panic of yesterday, I'd never noticed if the room had been searched. Had the police done that or Don? I fished through them, but found nothing missing.

Don's body had been over near the vanity. I closed my eyes and tried to visualize his actions.

He broke in, searched the dining room first because it was the first room he entered, and then moved on to the desk before heading upstairs. Or, he searched the desk first and not finding what he wanted moved on to the rest of the downstairs. In my room he went to the nightstand, then the dresser, and finally the vanity. My jewelry boxes are unopened, so he hadn't investigated them yet. Someone follows him in. He sees the person in the mirror and turns. Maybe he rushes at them. The killer blocks his path and stabs him.

I opened my eyes. Sounded as good as any other theory.

"What the hell do you think you're doing?"

I screamed and whirled. Colin stood in the doorway.

"Goddammit, Colin! You scared the crap out of me." I'd been so intent on my reenactment, I hadn't heard him either enter or come up the stairs.

"I thought I told you not to come here alone. You left the front door unlocked. Anybody could have waltzed in."

"Anybody did!" I snapped, my heart still pounding with fright. "How the hell did you know where I was?"

"When Effie told me you wouldn't be in for lunch, I had a hunch. I take it you picked up your mail."

"It's on the desk downstairs. I'll contact the police later and tell them I found the jump drive in the mailbox."

"They might even believe you." He glanced around the room. "What are you doing up here?"

I told him about trying to visualize Don's movements.

"Could have happened that way. I wonder if the killer also searched after killing Merrick."

I shrugged. "My jewelry boxes don't appear to have been opened."

"Maybe they were and the second man was more meticulous. Perhaps Merrick came with somebody or met them here. He searched the downstairs while Merrick searched upstairs. Could be the killer planned on eliminating Merrick all along. Maybe even had a gun, but decided to use the letter opener instead."

"Seems you're just chocked full of interesting scenarios, too."

"Come on, let's get out of here. There's nothing to find."

"The place is a mess," I grumbled.

"So, call a cleaning service. Let's go."

Back in the foyer, I headed for the front door.

"Did you open the mail?"

I paused with my hand on the dust-covered doorknob. "What?"

"I said, did you open your mail?"

"No, why should I? It's just bills and assorted junk."

"Open them anyway. Then toss the envelopes and take out the trash. When's pick up?"

"Tomorrow morning. Why?"

"If you received the jump drive in the mail, the cops will want to see the envelope it came in, too. And they'll also want to know why you didn't notify them immediately."

"I can always say…"

"Will you just open the damned mail?"

Heaving a sigh, I crossed to the desk and ripped open the envelopes, then stacked the four bills next to the computer.

"Don't forget to dump the junk mail. Now, let's empty the trash."

Shooting him an exasperated glance, I popped the remains into the wastebasket in the kitchen and pulled the drawstrings tight. "There, satisfied?"

"Yes. Come on, I'll buy you lunch."

I tossed the plastic bag into the dumpster on my way out, and then followed him to a chain restaurant. It was almost noon, but we snagged the last booth along the outside wall. The waitress came by for a drink order. I requested white wine and he chose iced tea.

"Did you find anything interesting in Ross's files?" I asked.

"He had quite an interesting sideline."

"I counted the files. There are seventy-five, which means each of them is a suspect."

"Some of them are very dead."

"Like who?"

"Don Merrick for starters."

I swallowed my irritation. "Don't be a smart ass. You know what I mean."

"I recognized some of the names. Sleaze often ends up dead." He unwrapped his napkin and placed the silverware on the table. "I never realized Uncle Ross was such a greedy son of a bitch."

"I just had him pegged as a son of a bitch." I opened the menu and scanned the lunch items.

The waitress arrived with our drinks and we ordered. When she left, I continued. "Did you find anyone to interview?"

"A couple of people. Most of the files are for small potatoes criminals—sleazy and dangerous, but small time. He wouldn't put the bite on someone like Joey Lazarus. Too powerful to be blackmailed."

"So, he went after clowns like Don Merrick

instead."

Colin nodded. "I'm thinking I'll pay Sally Ransom a call. Find out if Ross was blackmailing her, too. Her husband was pretty upset that she got off with a slap on the wrist while he did time."

"Sally Ransom, the accused madam? She's still around?" If I'd been arrested for pimping, I'd have left town as soon as possible.

"She couldn't afford to leave. The house, the cars, the furniture all had to be sold to pay Ross's fees."

"And let me guess, she also had to pay his little monthly entitlements," I said in a dry tone.

"That's why I want to talk to her. Plus her husband made threats as he left the courtroom."

"I'm surprised it took someone this long to off Ross," I muttered.

"They'd pay as long as Ross held their files."

"I can't understand why he'd go public with anything in a book deal."

Colin frowned. "I wonder if he used it as his blackmail swan song. Extort one last hefty payment, then burn the files."

"Except the book would be published. How did that help the criminals?"

"Haven't figured that one out yet." He paused and tapped a finger on his chin. "Unless he planned on changing the names of his clients, the attorney-client privilege would still be in effect."

"So he refers to Scumbag A as Sleazeball B and gets away with it?"

"More or less, but a thinly veiled switch could leave the reader with enough description to figure out the real identity yet keep him in the clear. It's the whole 'names have been changed to protect the innocent' thing."

What Colin said made sense. Tinker with the truth just a tad and publish. And Ross had been a real winner at tinkering.

"Innocent? None of these clowns were innocent. Is his tinkering ethical?"

"Nope, but it might not have crossed the line far enough to get him disbarred or sued." He frowned. "Somebody sure has something to lose by that book being published."

The waitress brought our food. My salad didn't look overly appetizing. Colin was busy slathering mayo on the bun and cramming the lettuce and tomato on top of the char-grilled burger.

Like most people, I didn't really think about how healthy I ate. It was an on again, off again thing.

"You're going to give yourself a heart attack with that mountain of cholesterol and fat."

He grinned. "Will you miss me if I die?"

"Yeah, like a rash on my ass."

He laughed as I speared a chunk of romaine and a bite of chicken. I thought about his words. Yeah, I'd miss him. The last few days had shown me he cared at least a little bit for me. He could be funny when he wanted, and I knew he was damned good at his job. He didn't have to give me a heads up on the mail thing. I'd have just left things on the desk. The envelope never even entered my mind.

But then, I'd never been a suspect in a couple of murders before either.

I'd managed to push last night's kiss into the back of my mind for most of the morning. Now with a little salad and wine in me, I let the images flow. My heart fluttered at the memory of his lips on mine not to mention the gush of desire that had swept through me. Three days ago, Colin Blackwood had been an irritating pain in the ass. His sarcastic remarks on my lifestyle often hurt as much as they'd angered. His concern for my future had come as a surprise. The kiss had come as a shock—the kind of shock I wanted again and again. Being in the same house with him would be a constant temptation. Could I resist that temptation?

Do I want to?

I pushed the salad bowl away from me. Close to a third remained. It hadn't tasted any better than it looked. Colin had left a sizable portion on his plate, too. Guess the grease had gotten to him.

"So, when do we go see this Sally Ransom?" I asked, finishing my wine.

"I see her tomorrow morning."

"*We* see her tomorrow morning," I reminded him.

"I don't think Sally Ransom will be impressed with low cut blouses or short skirts."

"Maybe she's still in the business."

He shot me an exasperated glance and signaled the waitress for the bill.

I leaned forward when he didn't answer. "Colin, I'm in a lot of trouble here. I want to be involved."

He sighed and stared. "All right, but keep your mouth shut and let me do the talking. I know what questions to ask. Okay?"

"It's a deal. And I had a thought about…" My cell rang interrupting my train of thought. "Hello."

"Oh God, Hilary, what am I going to do?" Mother practically sobbed.

"About what? What's wrong?"

"The police are here demanding I come down to the police station with them. I've already called Jim Price. Do you think they're going to arrest me? How can they? I have an alibi. Oh damn, I don't know what to do."

I looked into Colin's eyes. "The police are at the house demanding Mother come to the station."

His brows drew together in a scowl. "I was afraid of this. Tell her to call a lawyer, go with them, and not answer any questions until he shows up. We'll meet her there."

I relayed the information and hung up.

They hadn't arrested her yet, but once they had her at the station anything could happen. A more sinister thought crossed my mind.

Suppose Mother had lied to them, too?

Chapter Ten

We rushed into the police station and headed for the information desk.

"Has Priscilla Patterson been brought in yet?" Colin asked.

The cop in charge cast a bored look at us. "About ten minutes ago."

"Can we see her?" I pleaded.

"She's in an interrogation room and can't be interrupted," the officer at the desk said. His tone matched his expression—bored and disinterested.

"Does she have a lawyer present?" Colin pressed.

"I have no idea. If you want to wait, have a seat."

The Moreland police weren't being helpful, but I had no choice except to sit and wait.

"What do you think is going to happen?" I asked Colin.

"Offhand, I'd say they're going to question her again, probably about her alibi."

"Oh Lord, she didn't kill Ross, and she certainly didn't kill Don. She didn't even know who he was!"

"I doubt this is about Merrick."

"Well, she didn't kill Ross!"

"The cops brought her back for a reason." He shot me a look. "I told you, it's never a good idea to lie to the police."

I felt the rebuke. "I didn't exactly lie. I just didn't

tell them everything."

"You were at the house on Friday. Kinda forgot to tell them that at first, didn't you? And you're about to lie to them again about the jump drive."

"Yeah, well you're aiding and abetting with that!"

Before he could answer the entrance door opened and Jim Price entered with another man. I recognized him immediately—Jerricus Monroe, the premier defense attorney in the tri-state area.

I rose and called, "Jim!"

He headed for us. "Hello Hilary, Colin. This is Jerricus Monroe. I've asked him to handle the situation with Priscilla. Jerry, this is Ross's nephew, Colin Blackwood, and his stepdaughter Hilary Watson."

Jerricus Monroe needed no introduction. His face was splashed all over the Mid-South on billboards, TV, and in newspapers. He was the best of the best—better than Ross. Ross knew it and hated the guy's guts. The fact he was here probably had my stepfather attempting resurrection.

The man stepped forward and extended a hand. "Mr. Blackwood, Miss Watson, I wish we could meet under happier circumstances."

I'd never seen Monroe in the flesh before. At six-five, he bore his two-hundred fifty pound weight well. The mane of white hair was a trademark in the Memphis area. His grip was firm, but not crushing.

"I take it you'll be representing Priscilla," Colin said.

"For the moment."

Price shook his head. "I told you all the other day that criminal matters aren't my line of expertise. I've known Jerry for years. He's the expert."

Jerricus Monroe loved the dramatic and played to it often both in and out of the courtroom. He defended the rich, the socially connected, and upon occasion, took on pro bono work for a client he believed was innocent— or that he could get off with a maximum of media coverage thrown in. With the exception of the pro bono part, he wasn't all that different from Ross. Only I didn't think Monroe blackmailed his clients.

"Has Mrs. Patterson been brought in yet?" Monroe asked.

"A while ago," Colin replied.

"Well, Jim, let's go find her and hope she hasn't said anything without an attorney present."

Price nodded. "I told her to refuse to answer questions until I showed up."

"Miss Watson, Mr. Blackwood, we'll see you in a while."

The men moved off down the hall.

"Now what?" I asked.

"Now we wait."

"Any idea how long?"

"As long as it takes. Want some coffee or a soda?"

I shook my head. "No thanks. I'm just worried about Mother. She won't do well in a situation like this."

"She wouldn't do so hot in jail either."

"You don't seriously think they'll stick her behind bars, do you?"

Colin shrugged. "Anything's possible."

I sat silent for a couple of minutes. The silence got on my nerves. I fidgeted, crossing and re-crossing my legs, picking at the strap on my purse, and glancing at my watch every few minutes. Time crawled.

"Have you done any investigating into the family yet?" I asked just to hear my own voice.

"Some."

"And?"

"My Uncle Sam has major financial problems. The gins are doing well, but he mortgaged the hilt out of that five bedroom monstrosity he calls home in order to buy more farm land and commercial real estate. When the housing market took a dive, he found himself underwater on the house. He's about to lose it. He's also behind on his car payments. At least two out of the four he owns are about to be repoed."

"According to Effie, he met with Ross several times in the last couple of weeks. He probably asked his brother for money and was turned down. Ross's death would certainly help him swim to the surface."

He raised his eyebrows and shrugged. "Possibly."

"What about good old Bonnie? I don't believe she and Sam got back together out of true love."

"Haven't started with her yet."

"And Ian? Anything on him?"

"Not a whole lot. He and his investors lost a bundle on a parcel of land he planned to develop up in Tipton County. It was supposed to be a strip mall. When the economy went south, so did the mall owners. Plans fell through."

"So, he's in financial straits, too?"

"Not as badly as Sam, but bad enough. The real estate market's beginning to turn around. As far as I know, he didn't borrow too heavily against his personal assets."

"If we had any more suspects, we could hold a convention and title it 'Why I Wanted To Kill Ross

Patterson'," I muttered.

"Yeah, if the cops get their hands on that jump drive they'll be running in more directions than there are on a compass."

"How far through the files did you get?"

"Just about finished."

"Have you made a list of people to interview?"

"I have some ideas, but to be honest, pinning this on someone from that list will be damned near impossible."

I glanced toward the hallway leading to the interrogation rooms. "No, I guess it would be easier to nail someone close, like family."

"Which explains why there was no sign of forced entry."

I sneaked another peek at my watch. "What do you think is happening now? Will Mother be arrested?"

Colin sighed. "If an arrest was imminent, they'd have done so at the house. The first thing Jim and Jerricus will do is demand a meeting with their client. Jim will request what new information the police have, then undoubtedly bow out of the action, leaving Jerricus full rein. He'll demand they release your mother so he can properly talk to her. When that's done, they'll come back in to answer any questions. I'm sure this is not a new experience for Monroe."

"I'll bet Detectives Parker and Smiley-Face won't be happy to see Monroe walk in."

"I think they're going to be damned upset."

I picked at the stitching on my purse. "The irony is unbelievable. Ross hated Jerricus Monroe, and now he may be defending my mother on charges she murdered him."

He smiled. "Life does have curious twists, doesn't it?" His gaze snapped to the hallway. "Well, that didn't take too long."

Mother walked out next to Jerricus. Jim trailed behind. I leaped to my feet and met her halfway across the room.

"Mother, are you all right?" I demanded giving her a hug.

She hugged me back and patted my shoulder.

"I'm fine now that Jerricus has stepped into the picture." She glanced up at her new attorney sending him a dazzling smile. "We're on our way to his office to discuss things. Jerricus, would you like to come to dinner at the house tonight?"

Monroe smiled. "I'd like that a lot, Priscilla."

"Say seven o'clock for cocktails?"

"I'll be there. Now if y'all will excuse us, we have some work to do."

They sailed out of the police station leaving us standing there with Jim. Ross was dead less than a week and already Mother was eyeing a new conquest. I wished her luck. From what I'd heard Monroe had the same marital track record as my late stepfather.

"So, why did they bring Priscilla in?" Colin asked.

Jim heaved a sigh. "Seems her alibi wasn't as strong as she thought."

"What do you mean?" I said.

"Can't discuss it, but I'm sure your Mother will tell you." He headed for the doors. "I'll be in touch about the estate."

After he left, I stared at Colin. "Well! We've been dismissed."

"So it would seem. We've got a few hours until

dinner. How about we go see Sally Ransom, the ex-madam?"

"Sure, why not?"

Colin called Sally while I found the vending machines and got us each a soft drink. Suddenly, I was thirsty as hell.

He slipped his phone into a pocket as I returned.

"Sally's agreed to see us. Should be there in less than twenty minutes."

We departed the Moreland Police Department and headed south. I was looking forward to meeting Sally. I'd never met an ex-madam before. This private investigating thing had promise.

****

Sally Ransom lived in a seedy looking apartment complex in Horn Lake, Mississippi, where rents were cheap and discount stores plentiful. The Lake Edge Apartments were non-descript and as far as I could tell, nowhere near a lake. After several knocks, she finally answered.

"Yeah?"

"Ms. Ransom, I'm Colin Blackwood. I called earlier. May we come in?"

Her gaze swept Colin from head to foot before shifting to me. Her heavily penciled right eyebrow rose as she eyed my clothing—a short skirt and clingy jersey top.

"Yeah, sure, why not? Who's she?"

"This is my assistant, Miss Watson."

I pulled the notebook Colin had given me on the drive down from my purse.

"It's a pleasure to meet you, ma'am," I said as she stepped back and we entered the cluttered, cramped space.

I'm not sure what I expected an ex-madam to look like, but for the prices she must have charged I was disappointed. Her blonde hair had a brassy tone making her skin take on a sallow hue. And no amount of make-up could hide the lines on her forehead or running from her nose to her mouth. Bright red lipstick, bleeding slightly into her upper lip, further enhanced the fact that age had caught up with her. Thin as a rail, she wore a pair of skintight leopard print leggings. An equally tight low cut black top stretched across her ample breasts. She was barefoot and I couldn't help noticing the scarlet nail polish on her toes was almost as chipped as that on her fingers.

"Have a seat," she said, waving us toward an oversized sofa in the tiny living room. She sat in a recliner, and reached for an ice-filled glass on the table. "Now what is it you want again?"

She took a large gulp of the glass's contents. From this distance I couldn't tell if it was iced tea or something more substantial. Then I caught a whiff of a distinctive odor. Ah, rum.

"I wanted to ask you a few questions concerning your late attorney, Ross Patterson," Colin began.

"Shame he got murdered like that. He was one hell of a lawyer, I gotta tell ya. Got me off with barely a ripple."

"The same can't be said for your ex-husband," he continued.

"That bastard. Dumped me for a younger bitch just before the cops showed up. Would give a bundle to know who turned us in. I think the new squeeze did it, hoping to see me end up in jail and *him* acting all shocked about what went on." She giggled. "Didn't quite work out that way."

Younger and maybe more cultured? I had the impression this was the real Sally Ransom, not the upscale Webster housewife as described in Ross's file. Hell of an acting job. I remained silent as per Colin's instructions, but pretended to write in the notebook.

Colin cocked an eyebrow. "He was pretty upset when your verdict came down. Swore he'd get even."

She giggled again. "Even more upset when he was found guilty. At least I had the brains to hire the best. He made do with a cut-rate mouthpiece."

"He got out about a year ago. Think he could have made good on his threats?"

She gulped more of the amber liquid and curled her lip. "Him? He was full of shit. He wouldn't have the balls to do something like that. And if you find him, don't believe his crap for a minute that it was all my idea to run a dating service. He ran the business end of things. I ran the girls. We were partners all the way."

"Except Patterson got you off with declaring you'd been forced to do it."

She grinned. "Like I said, I hired the best."

Sounded like a match made somewhere considerably south of heaven. I wondered if she realized how old and used she looked. Was she still in the business with a few girls in the stable or did she freelance on her own?

"So, what are you doing now, Sally?" Colin asked with a smile.

"Not what you think. I work over at the Style Right Beauty Salon. That's what I used to do years ago, before I met Mr. Asshole. Today's one of my days off."

"Any ideas on who'd off Ross Patterson?"

"Not a clue."

"Know where I can find your ex?"

"Nope. Heard he got out and that was it."

"He never contacted you?"

She stared into her glass and rattled the ice cubes before draining the remains. "Nope. If he'd showed up here, I'd have kicked his ass across the parking lot."

Colin rose. "Thank you for your time, Ms. Ransom."

I put the notebook away and also stood. Sally walked us to the door.

Colin had exited and stood on the narrow walkway leading to the stairs. Before I crossed the threshold, Sally grabbed my arm.

"Honey, you got class. If you ever want to earn a couple of extra bucks, I can set you up with some work. You know where to find me." She stepped back and winked.

Back in the car, Colin looked at me. "What did she say to you?"

"Said she could throw some work my way if I wanted it."

"Once a madam, always a madam."

"Probably employs half the beauty salon. Did we find out anything useful?"

"Yeah, Sally didn't kill Ross and the husband likely didn't either. And since both admitted to the charges against them, Ross had no reason to blackmail either. "

"Which only scratches two suspects from the list."

"Let's head home and get ready for tonight's dinner to impress your mother's new attorney. I have to make a few calls and want to finish up reading the last of the files. When are you going to spring the jump drive on the Moreland police?"

"I don't know. If I delay a couple of days, it'll give us a chance to interview a few people."

"It could also land you in jail."

"In which case, I'm sure Mr. Monroe would be only too glad to come to the defense of his latest client's daughter."

Colin laughed. "He'd do it, too—for a price."

****

"And I can tell you right now, Chynna Delaney can go straight to hell! Claims she took a sleeping pill and didn't hear a thing until ten the next morning. Some fucking friend!"

Mother swigged the vodka in her glass like a pro. When she got angry, those redneck roots sneaked into her vocabulary and her actions. She, Colin, and I awaited Jerricus Monroe's arrival by getting a head start on cocktails in the den.

"The least she could have done was say we'd stayed up and talked for an hour or so after we got home!"

"But that wouldn't have been the truth," Colin pointed out.

"So what? She's a friend—or supposed to be." She walked over to the bar and poured more Gray Goose.

"Mother, Chynna Delaney's husband is big stuff in Jackson. Being even peripherally connected with Ross's murder is enough to make her keep her distance. All she did was confirm you were together from late afternoon until around ten. Anything more would have been a lie. And if the cops found out she lied, her husband would not be happy. Chynna's not stupid enough to risk her meal ticket, even for a friendship."

"Bitch," Mother muttered.

I sipped from my glass and contemplated what I'd just said. Did Mother and her friends consider their husbands nothing more than a bank account? Were they really that shallow? If so, how long would it take for them to turn on a college sorority sister? Especially one who'd come from a sharecropper's background, although knowing Mother she probably embellished her childhood to having lived on a large farm. *And given time, would I have followed in their footsteps?*

Effie appeared in the doorway. "Mr. Monroe is here, Mrs. Patterson."

Mother set her glass down, fixed a smile on her face, and hurried out of the room. Voices drifted down the hallway. Then Jerricus Monroe entered the room with Mother clinging to his arm.

"You remember Colin and Hilary, Jerry. Hilary is staying with me for moral support and Colin because I like a man around the house for protection. What can I get you to drink?"

Jerricus nodded and smiled. "Good to see you again. I'll take scotch on the rocks."

"I'll get it," Colin offered, rising.

Mother sent me a stern look. I moved from the sofa to a chair.

"Please, have a seat, Jerry." He sat on the sofa. Mother plunked herself down next to him in my vacated spot.

"Here you go," Colin said handing him a glass.

Jerricus drank, and then smiled. "I imagine old Ross is turning in his grave at me sitting in his house, drinking his Dewar's."

Mother waved a hand in the air. "Oh, piffle. It's my scotch now. Enjoy."

Oh, piffle? The Southern belle was back in place. I wanted to roll my eyes. Colin did. He also grinned.

"I can't tell you how glad I am that you've agreed to help my mother. I don't know what kind of evidence the police think they have, but I know she didn't kill Ross."

Mother's new attorney sipped his drink. "They're just fishing. The suspect list is so deep I don't think they'll ever solve it. Luckily, all I have to do is show reasonable doubt if they arrest her and it goes to trial. Unless they come up with something that sticks, this will never go any further."

"They'll go over every alibi and phone call they can. Something might pop," Colin said.

"So you're a private investigator. I understand Ross was your uncle and that Ian Rogers has hired you to help with the case," Jerricus said.

"That's right. Naturally, I'll share anything I find with both sides of the fence."

Monroe sipped again and nodded. "Naturally."

Jerricus and Colin spent the next several minutes discussing private investigation while I listened. Mother hung on every word, her eyes wide with feigned interest.

"Mrs. Patterson, dinner is served," Effie said from the doorway.

Finally.

Jerricus rose and offered his arm to Mother who took it with a sweet smile. Colin also stood and with a devilish grin offered his arm to me. I drained my vodka before accepting.

Once again, Effie had done wonders on such short notice of a guest for dinner. Throughout the meal, Jerricus kept us entertained with stories of his past courtroom experiences. No doubt about it, he was full of himself, but that simply added to his charm. Mother, of course, paid rapt attention, laughing and making the correct comments at the appropriate times.

By the time he left at ten o'clock, I'd had enough. Mother waved from the entryway and closed the door behind him.

"That went very well, don't you think?"

"Mother, you might at least bury Ross before pursuing husband number four—or is it five? I lost count."

"Don't be common, dear. I just find him very interesting."

"I might remind you, that he isn't all that different from my uncle," Colin added.

Mother bridled. "Sure he is. Jerricus Monroe is likeable."

"Well, just remember, he's your attorney first. Get around to the other stuff after he gets you off, assuming you're arrested, of course," he said with a sigh.

Mother shot Colin an exasperated glance and headed for the stairs. "I think I'll go up, check my e-mail, and read for a while. See you tomorrow."

Colin and I wandered back into the den for a nightcap—brandy for him, Drambuie for me.

"I guess tomorrow we'd better start calling people on your list," I said. "By the way, who's up first?"

"Even though he isn't on the jump drive, I'd like to have a chat with Joey Lazarus. Effie IDed him from a photo I showed her yesterday as the man who came here last week all hot and bothered. I researched him and he does have a sister named Carlotta."

"And he was probably the guy I saw leaving the study with Ross the night of the murder. When do we tackle him?"

"I'm not so sure I want you along on this one. Lazarus is scum, and dangerous in the bargain. He's not likely to meet me alone."

"I'm your trusty assistant, remember? He won't pay any attention to me."

"He probably knows who you are."

"I'll dress down."

He shot me a sardonic look. "You? Dress down? Yeah, right."

"Don't be nasty. Besides, I doubt he'd admit to being here. I'd rather talk to the sister, Carlotta. She was the one having the affair with Ross."

"I'll think about it."

Colin finished his brandy and rose. I did the same. He wasn't about to brush me off.

"Hold it, buster. Don't humor me."

He turned and placing his hands on my shoulders, gave a little shake. "This is not some game or TV show where the hero and the heroine solve the crime before the cops. Joey Lazarus is a hood—a damned dangerous hood. He won't let us anywhere near his sister."

His close proximity did strange things to my breathing and heart rate. Last night's kiss floated in my mind. I swayed toward him. His fingers tightened and his eyes went storm cloud dark. He lowered his head, then stopped just inches from my mouth.

"No, baby, not tonight."

Did I detect a trace of regret in his voice?

He dropped his hands and stepped back. "I'll see you in the morning."

I stared, feeling bereft as he walked out of the room. His touch and the almost-kiss had my insides churning. My nerves hummed to the tune my imagination sang of what could be. With a deflated ego, I refilled my glass.

"Well, shit."

Chapter Eleven

"I'm a wreck, I tell you, an absolute wreck!" Mother exclaimed from her bed the next morning. She wiped tears from her eyes with the corner of the sheet. "Do you think I could take a trip to the Bahamas or something? You know, just to relax for a few days. Would the police mind?"

I wanted to heave an irritated sigh, but refrained. "I think the police would mind very much. You're a suspect in Ross's death and have been seriously questioned twice. Plus your alibi is now on shaky ground. I don't think your lawyer would approve either."

Her face brightened. "Maybe he could come with me."

"I doubt it. He's a busy man. You're not his only client."

Mother's eyes widened as though the possibility of Jerricus having other clients had not occurred to her. "But this is a high profile murder case!"

"Which is why you need to stick around here."

She poured a glass of water from the pitcher on the nightstand, shook a pill from a bottle next to it, and quickly downed it.

"I seem to be living on Xanax and liquor the last couple of days," she complained.

"Just be careful not to mix the two."

She shot me an irritated glance. "I'm not stupid."

"But you are upset. Mistakes happen."

I didn't like her popping pills like candy. And last night she'd had at least three vodkas on the rocks, plus several glasses of wine with dinner. Stress related, I guessed.

"Mother, why don't you call a couple of your friends and go to lunch? Shopping, a movie, anything to get out of the house for a while. You can't hide in your bedroom forever."

She fingered the lacey ruffle of the sheet. "Maybe Jerricus is free for lunch at the Peabody."

Yesterday had been a series of highs and lows for her. Terrified at the police station, she turned into a flirting dynamo with her new attorney. So far this morning, she'd been teary-eyed, and then mentally chasing after Jerricus Monroe. The sudden mood swings disturbed me and I wondered if she had any other medication hidden away. Mother was thoughtless and vain, but not scatterbrained. Unless, of course, chemicals no one knew about were involved.

I dismissed that notion. Mother had never shown signs of drug abuse. And besides, where would she have gotten them? Don Merrick's face flashed through my mind. I blotted it out.

"If I were you, I'd let your attorney do his job for a couple of days. Don't chase."

She frowned. "Hilary, I do *not* chase. Men gravitate in my direction. I can't help it. I know Jerricus finds me attractive or he wouldn't have come to dinner last night."

I shrugged. Nothing I could say would change her mind.

"You *are* right about one thing—I need to get out of the house. Maybe I can arrange lunch or dinner with Dorothy, Victoria, and Janine," she mused naming some of her longtime cronies.

I turned to leave. "You do that, Mother. I'll see you later."

In the kitchen, Colin was finishing breakfast.

"Good morning, miss. Would you like something to eat?" Effie asked.

"I'm not very hungry this morning. Just coffee and toast will be fine."

I poured my own coffee while she stuck two slices of bread in the toaster. I sat across the table from Colin.

"So, what's on our agenda today?"

"Joey Lazarus is proving elusive, so I was going to check out a couple of the writers of the hate mail letters."

I'd forgotten about those. "Only a couple?"

"Most of them wrote once just after the trial. People vent their anger and frustration, then move on. Others can't let go and write more than once. There are some who threatened Ross off and on for two or three years. Those are the ones I want to talk to."

"That's a long time to carry a grudge." I sipped my coffee as Effie placed buttered toast in front of me along with a jar of cherry preserves. "Thank you, Effie."

"My pleasure, miss, and if you don't mind my saying so, I didn't know Mr. Patterson received hate mail. Were there many letters?"

"Quite a few. Some of them date back as long as ten or twelve years. Uncle Ross saved them all."

"Well now, it's been my experience that some

people are more silent about holding grudges than others. They keep quiet, letting it smolder and grow until it has to come out or kill them. Why my dear, sainted mother and her sister went for ten years without saying a word. At family gatherings, they'd sit on opposite sides of the room. Wouldn't even spare the other a glance."

"Did they ever get together?" I asked taking a bite of the toast.

"Eventually."

"What made them change their minds?" Colin said.

"It was a big barbeque one summer down in Coldwater, Mississippi. Most of my family is from that area. Well, my Aunt Bessie got tired of the whole thing and made them sit next to each other at the picnic table. The next thing we knew, they was good friends again."

Colin chuckled. "Probably forgot what they were fighting about."

Effie beamed. "Exactly! Can I get you anything else, Mr. Colin?"

"No thanks." His attention turned to me. "I have to make a couple of calls. Can you be ready to go in say an hour?"

"Sure, no problem."

He nodded, finished his coffee, and left.

"Miss, may I be so bold as to ask you a question?"

"Yes, of course."

"Are you helping Mr. Colin investigate your stepfather's murder?"

I nodded. "If the case isn't solved, the entire family will have a sword of suspicion hanging over their heads forever."

"Well, you be careful. People who write hateful

things can be dangerous even years after the fact."

"I will. I promise. We're also looking into some of his cases. That book deal could have scared someone badly enough to commit murder."

"Could be. If I was you, I'd tread real light."

"I'm just along for the ride. Colin does most of the work. And he's good at his job."

She picked up the dishes and turned toward the sink with a worried look on her face. "That he is, miss. You be careful, hear? Don't want anything bad to happen to you."

I finished my toast and returned to tidy up my bedroom. With that chore done, I explored my choice of clothing for the morning. I wanted something nicer than the jeans and top I wore now. Yesterday, Colin had given me the once over in the short skirt and clingy blouse. He didn't say anything, but I knew appreciation when I saw it.

And he hadn't been immune to my charms in the den after dinner either.

A devilish imp inside me made me select another short skirt—black with a hint of spandex—and a long-sleeved turquoise blouse. The ruffle running down the front of the deep v-neckline stopped just short of my lacey bra. My breasts showed enough to be considered mild advertising. I added a pair of high-heeled sandals.

I inspected my reflection in the mirror. Not bad at all. A trifle questionable for daytime attire, but not too trashy. I had the feeling Sally Ransom would approve.

Someone knocked on my door. I opened it and stared at Colin.

He stared back, his gaze sweeping me from head to foot, lingering for a fraction of a second on my chest, then he raised an eyebrow and smiled. "Very nice. Shall we go?"

"Just let me get my purse." I sashayed across the room to the dresser and slung the item over my shoulder. I was certain his eyes followed my swaying backside.

"So who do we talk to first?" I asked as he drove down the driveway.

"Roger Bunting. His son was shot in the head during a drug deal gone bad. Unfortunately, he lived in a vegetative state for the next four years until the family finally pulled the plug. He wrote seven or eight times saying how he'd get even with Uncle Ross for getting the defendant off."

"Was the kid an innocent bystander?"

"According to the father he was. According to Ross's notes and the defendant, he wasn't. Naturally, the defendant swore he'd never been near the scene of the shooting."

"Naturally. And since the only witness was incommunicado the piece of scum walked."

"There was another witness who swore the kid went into the alley to buy some crack. Next thing he knew shots were fired and someone ran out. *Naturally*, he swore the defendant wasn't the shooter."

"Was it true?"

"I found Ross's file on this one. His client did it."

Roger Bunting lived in a seedy looking trailer on a weed choked lot in Walls, Mississippi. He answered the door wearing a pair of ratty cutoffs and a wife-beater tank top with a lewd message scrawled on it. I smelled beer and body odor even at this distance. He was so stereotypical redneck trailer trash he could have come from Hollywood's central casting. His gaze swept over me much like Colin's. Colin's admiration had made me feel good. Roger Bunting's made my skin crawl. I immediately regretted my wardrobe choice.

"Yeah, waddaya want?"

"Mr. Bunting, my name is Colin Blackwood. I'm a private investigator working on the murder of Ross Patterson. This is my assistant, Miss Watson."

At the mention of Ross's name, his eyes narrowed and his lip curled. He hacked up a huge loogie and spat it on the ground not far from my foot. I moved back a few inches.

"That fuckin' sumbitch! He got what he deserved! My boy was a good kid. He was walkin' along, mindin' his own business when this punk come out an alley and shot him." He spat again. "Kept him alive until his mother died, then I told the docs to forget it. Didn't have no money left anyhow. If that miserable piece of shit killer hadn't gotten off, I coulda sued for some of the hospital bills, but no, his lawyer made it sound like my boy was the guilty one. Fuckin' asshole."

I wasn't sure who the last comment was aimed at—Ross or the defendant.

"Can you tell me where you were last Friday night between say ten in the evening and approximately two in the morning?"

Bunting glared, his yellowed teeth, what few there were, bared. "Why should I?"

"An alibi. You wrote several nasty letters to Mr. Patterson. I believe one of them stated you'd get even if it were the last thing you'd do. A cliché, but a threat all the same."

I doubted Bunting knew what a cliché was, but he

got the words alibi and threat.

"I didn't kill 'im, but hope whoever did gets away with it."

"So, where were you?"

Bunting scratched his ample belly with dirty fingers. "I was drinking at The Bird of Paradise. It's a bar and strip club off Brooks in Memphis. Got home, it was after three."

"Can anybody confirm that?"

"Hell yes. The bartender and the bimbo who gave me the lap dance of a lifetime."

The imagery made me want to puke.

"Thank you for your time, Mr. Bunting."

Colin took my arm and led me back to the car where I slammed the door and rolled up the window.

"Oh my God," I said as we drove away. "He sure hated Ross's guts."

"Yeah, but I don't think he did it. If he tried to get into the house during the party, he'd stick out like a sore thumb. And I can't see Ross opening the door to him afterward. Plus, if he wanted to kill Ross, he'd have used a twelve gauge up close and personal. A frying pan would never occur to him."

"Do you realize you've been talking in clichés ever since we got here?"

Colin grinned. "Must be the redneck atmosphere."

"Who's next on the list?"

"Virginia Connelly. Her sister was brutally murdered by an ex-boyfriend with money. Ross got him off. She sent a letter a month for six months. While she didn't threaten him, she did call my uncle a lot of names and claimed she knew people."

"Knew people?"

"As in hit men, I assume. That's why I want to talk to her."

Virginia Connelly was a quiet, dignified woman in her mid-thirties. Her sister's death four years ago had hit her hard. She admitted to hating the ex-boyfriend and Ross, but also admitted not really knowing any assassins. She'd been visiting family in St. Louis on Friday.

The next two people on Colin's list were also washouts. Three more had solid alibis. Yet another insisted he'd been at home the entire weekend with the flu.

"So, that's it?" I asked as we headed home.

"Looks like it."

"I'd love to read some of those letters. I'll bet they're priceless."

"Some are. I'll give them to you when we get home."

We walked into the house a little after noon and hurried into the dining room. To my surprise, Mother was seated with a glass of wine and a salad in front of her.

"You're late. Where have you been?"

"Checking out some of Ross's less happy acquaintances," Colin said as we seated ourselves.

Effie must have had the hearing of a lynx. She appeared immediately with salad plates, and then poured wine for us.

"I'm sure the list must be endless," Mother commented.

"I thought you were going out to lunch with friends," I said.

"Effie asked for the night off. Some kind of family

thing. She won't be here to make dinner. I've arranged to have dinner with Madeleine and Robert, and then take in a play. You're on your own. As soon as I'm done here, I'm heading for Orion's Day Spa. I've booked the works—facial, massage, body wrap, manicure, pedicure, and a few things I've forgotten. I need pampering."

Orion's was the most expensive spa in Moreland, but customers got their money's worth. I'd been once and dropped a quick four hundred bucks in less than two hours. God only knew what Mother would shell out today. Sounded like she'd be there all afternoon.

We finished our meal. Mother disappeared upstairs only to reappear ten minutes later. She waved goodbye and left. Colin brought his laptop down to the study along with an accordion folder of hate mail. He sat at the desk. I chose the nearby loveseat.

This was the first time I'd been in the study since Ross's death. I couldn't keep my gaze from settling on the desk where Effie had found his body. The blotter had been changed. *Probably soaked with blood.* Either the cops confiscated it or it had been thrown away.

Oddly enough, I didn't feel uncomfortable. My stepfather's ghost didn't drift in front of my eyes. I'd always liked this room. It was large, but I'd managed to make it feel cozy. At least, that's what Mother had said. Ross had merely said something like "not bad" and gone on with his day.

Colin worked on the Internet while I read through the letters. Most were mildly threatening, but not specific. Others were very specific about how Ross was going to get it. Colin had penciled notes on the senders in the margins. Some were dead, and some were no longer in the area. I had neared the end of the file when I picked up a real beaut.

"Colin, listen to this one," I said chuckling.

"You rat-bastard, scumbag! You must drink pond scum for breakfast…"

"Boy, did somebody nail his personality or what?" I chuckled before continuing.

"You call yourself the best, but if people ain't got a lot of money you ignore them. My son was accused of armed robbery. He didn't do it. The husband and I wanted a good lawyer. Figured to pay you off a little at a time, but you laughed and said no. My boy had to make do with a public defender. He got found guilty and sent to prison at Parchman. He was a good boy who skeered easy." I paused to decipher the awful spelling and grammar. *"He lasted two months afore some low-life kilt him in the shower. I blame you. You cudda been nice and taken what little we had. Instead, my Eddie is dead. I hope you are soon, too. God will get you in the end. I hope you fry in hell. My whole family does, too. You ain't fit to live on this earth. Every night I pray you meet a horble death. I hope no one finds the body for days and that the worms eat you.*

Sinserly…"

I had to squint at the barely legible name. "Sincerely, Pascagoula Haskins? Sincerely? After all of that, she signed the letter 'sincerely?' And what the hell kind of a name is Pascagoula?"

"Other than a town on the Mississippi Gulf Coast, I have no idea," Colin replied. "I remember that letter."

"You've got 'deceased' written in the margin."

"Yeah, if I'm not mistaken, the woman died about six years ago. Her husband passed away a couple months before that. They lived a scratch existence on a small farm near Senatobia."

"Was the son innocent?"

"I don't know. Since Ross obviously didn't take the case, there are no notes or files. My guess is he probably did it."

In spite of the glaring spelling and grammar errors, this letter made me shiver. It was spot on delineating my late stepfather's character and he *had* died a horrible death. Divine retribution?

Effie appeared in the doorway. "I'm fixin' to leave now. If there's anything you need, better ask now or forever hold your peace."

Colin laughed. "We're fine. We'll go out to eat. Priscilla said you had a family matter. Hope nothing's wrong at home."

She waved a hand. "Oh no. My brother's third daughter is getting married soon. She wants me to do the cookin'. I gotta go down and see what they want."

"Well, enjoy an evening with your family," I said.

"Yes, miss, I will. See you in the morning."

Colin powered down his computer. "Don't know about you, but I'm about ready to call it a day. It's after four. Where would you like to go for dinner?"

"Rather early for dinner, isn't it?"

"I have a few calls to make. Shouldn't take too long. I was thinking cocktails at the Peabody, dinner at that Brazilian steakhouse across the courtyard, and then a little fun on Beale Street."

"You and Beale Street? That sounds like the kind of evening I used to indulge in. If I'm not mistaken, you sneered at it."

"You went every other night. I only sin once in a

while. How about it?"

A night on the town with Colin? The possibilities were endless.

"You're on." I rose and handed the file back to him. "I'm going to take a long, hot soak in the tub, and then dress to impress."

He smiled and shook his head. "I expect nothing else."

****

I leaned my head back on the headrest and closed my eyes. What the hell was wrong with me? It was a little after midnight and Colin and I were on the way home from Beale Street. Beale Street! Where the real action doesn't pick up until midnight! Yet I had wanted to leave.

"Are you sure you feel all right?" Colin asked.

I opened my eyes and stared through the windshield. "I don't know. A week ago, I'd have closed the bars. A week ago, I *did* close the bars. I wonder if my life from now on will be BRD and ARD."

"BRD? ARD?"

"Before Ross's Death and After Ross's Death. I find myself getting up by eight o'clock and actually eating a real breakfast. No sleeping in until noon and no highly Tabascoed tomato juice with a splash of vodka for hair of the dog."

"Maybe you've matured in the past week. Murder has a way of sobering people up real fast."

He had a point. Tonight I'd enjoyed conversation over cocktails in the lobby of the Peabody Hotel. Dinner at the Brazilian steakhouse was superb. We'd taken our time eating and to my amazement, discussed both politics and religion without getting into an argument—mainly because we both had the same basic views.

But oddly enough, when we finished, I wanted to head home for a nightcap in the den. It made no sense.

"Finding Merrick on my bedroom floor scared the bejesus out of me." I sighed heavily. "Maybe I should take a page out of Mother's book and call a few friends. Go to lunch or shopping. At least try to get back to my old life."

"Why would you want to? I thought you were all enthused about design school." His voice held a hint of censure.

His words struck a chord. I took on a defensive tone. "I checked out a couple, but the past week has been rather tumultuous. Oh, what the hell do you know, anyway?"

"A lot more than you realize."

I turned my head to stare at him. "What do you mean?"

"Fifteen years ago, I was on the same path as you. Out every night and carousing. How I made it as far as I did in law school is a mystery. Funny how a chance encounter with a private investigator changed my life. I was tired of waking up hung over, tired of the same people night after night, tired of drifting into a profession I didn't like with a man I didn't like."

"You...you went through the Beale Street routine, too?" My mind had a problem processing the information. I tried, but couldn't picture Colin Blackwood staggering out of a club at three in the morning.

"Sometimes. Most of my so-called friends went on to do what they'd planned on doing. Most make three times what I do. Several have had nasty divorces. And a few are downright unhappy with their lives. I don't see any of them much anymore. I like what I do and can honestly say I'm pretty content with life at the moment."

"Is that why you didn't like me? Because I reminded you of you?"

"I never disliked you, Hilary. When we first met, I saw a beautiful, intelligent woman who was wasting her life. Don't let the old ways creep back. Move on. If you really want to be an interior designer, then contact one of the schools and go."

He never disliked me? Beautiful? Intelligent?

Oh my God, how many years have I wasted? Not only with my life, but possibly with Colin, too?

I wanted to please him, but more importantly, I wanted to please myself. Did I really have the chops to attend school again? Did I have what it takes to open my own business? The fear factor had kept me down for so long.

He pulled into the subdivision and inserted a card into the machine that opened the gate. Mother had arranged for him to have one. The night guard waved as we entered.

"Look, Hilary, in the end you are the only person who can make the decision. Which is worse—taking a chance and perhaps failing, or never taking the chance and wondering if you could have succeeded?"

He had a point. For years I'd avoided making any kind of decision other than what to wear and where to go for the night. Old doubts and insecurities lingered. Would I have the courage to give it a try?

We rolled into Ross's driveway and parked off to

the side.

"I see Priscilla isn't home yet," he commented.

"It's only a little after midnight. She's probably having an after theatre snack and nightcap with her friends."

He took my hand and raised it to his lips. "I didn't mean to preach, honey."

My heart rate accelerated and my breath caught in my throat. "You didn't. And what you say makes sense. It's time I put my fears behind me and moved on with a meaningful life."

Did I really just say that? I sounded like the heroine in some really bad novel.

He chuckled, kissing my hand again. "Good girl."

Much to my disappointment, Colin dropped my hand and moved to open the door, then froze with his gaze along the side of the house.

"Stay in the car. Lock the door and duck out of sight. Call 9-1-1."

"Why?"

"Someone's in Ross's study. I saw a flashlight beam."

I followed his gaze. Sure enough, a flash of light crossed the window.

"What do we do?"

He reached into the console between us and pulled out a nasty looking gun. "You are going to do exactly what I told you to do. Got that?"

I stared at the gun like it was a living entity. I didn't like guns, even though, like many Southerners, I had one stuffed in my glove compartment. It was a .22 and I'd never touched it since the day I'd put it there.

"What are you going to do?"

"Find out who's here, of course." He opened the door, exited, and then leaned against it hard to close it quietly.

The click of the latch sounded like a gunshot. My heart raced and tremors radiated from the pit of my stomach. I fumbled in my purse and dialed 9-1-1 giving the operator the necessary information, then scrunched down across the console, keeping my head out of sight.

A minute passed. Two. Where was Colin? Had he gone in the front or around the back? Was he all right? Had the prowler bopped him over the head and made his escape? Were they, at his moment, scuffling like a couple of combative schoolboys? *Is Colin all right?*

I sat up. My questions drove me nuts. I couldn't just sit here and wait. Not with Colin possibly in danger. What kind of loyal sidekick was I?

Following Colin's example I exited the car in the same manner and tiptoed up the porch steps to the front door. I had no clue what I was going to do, but if nothing else, I could be a distraction. Like I'd told Colin earlier, distracting was easy for me.

I reached for the doorknob when suddenly the door was flung open. A man ran out and crashed directly into me. I landed flat on my back crushed by the weight of his body pinning me to the floor. A few seconds later, another man rushed out and lifted the bozo off of me.

"Okay, you, inside," Colin said in a hard voice. "Hilary, are you all right?"

I picked myself up and tried to catch my breath. "Yeah, I'm fine."

I followed Colin as he dragged the man into the foyer and switched on the light.

The intruder was Ross's brother, Sam Patterson.

Chapter Twelve

"Sam!" I said with a gasp. "What the hell are you doing here?"

"Let's go see what was so important in Ross's study that you felt you had to come in the dead of night with a flashlight," Colin added.

I noticed a lump forming near Colin's hairline.

"What happened to you? Are you hurt?"

"I'm fine. He must have heard me come in through the kitchen and hid behind the door. When I walked in, he nailed me with his flashlight."

"Didn't know it was you in the dark," Sam muttered.

"I'm surprised you didn't see our headlights or hear the car when we parked," I said still trying to catch my breath.

"I was busy and didn't think anyone would come home so early."

Colin jerked his uncle down the hallway to the study. In the room, he turned on the lights. A large painting used to conceal Ross's wall safe leaned against the wall. The safe gaped wide open. Papers littered the floor.

"Sit down, Uncle Sam. What were you looking for?"

Sam sat, but said nothing.

"Did you call 9-1-1?" Colin asked me.

"Yes, they should be here any second."

"Better open up fast or you're going to be arrested," he warned.

Sam wiped a line of sweat from his hairline with the sleeve of his jacket. His gaze shifted from Colin to me, and back to Colin.

"There was something of Ross's I needed," he mumbled.

"What?" Colin demanded.

Sam shifted in the chair, and then heaved a sigh. "Ross recorded every conversation he had with family members who came begging for money. I was afraid if the cops got a hold of it, they'd look at me in a different light. I figured me, Bonnie, Ian, and Elaine were on it." He shot a glance at me. "You and your mother were probably on it, too."

Uh-oh. If the cops had the recording then they already knew about the jump drive he'd given me that afternoon. But since they hadn't demanded I turn anything over, I came to the conclusion someone else had it. The killer? If so, then Ross *had* been dispatched by family.

"What kind of a recording?" Colin demanded.

"I don't know. I was looking for a tape recorder."

"Like a cassette? I don't think they even make those anymore."

"Maybe my brother went digital. How the hell should I know?" Sam rose. "I don't have to answer your questions. I'm outta here."

Colin pushed him back into the chair. "Not yet, you aren't. How did you know we would all be out tonight?" In the distance, sirens sounded. "Better hurry."

"I didn't. I got here and took advantage of the situation."

"How'd you get in?" I asked.

"Had a key. Have for years."

I didn't believe him for a second. Besides where was his car?

"And the safe combination?"

"Ross liked to keep things like that simple. He had a problem remembering long number sequences, so I guessed. Got it with his landline telephone number."

Which just goes to show even smart attorneys can get stupid.

The cops rolled into the driveway.

"All right, let me do the talking," Colin said.

We all walked back down the hall to the foyer. I opened the door and four policemen walked in, guns in hand. For the first time, I noticed Colin no longer held his gun. Where was it?

"Officers, I want to apologize. This was all a misunderstanding. Miss Watson and I came home from dinner, saw a light where none had been left on, and the front door was open. Seems my uncle came over to tell us about the arrangements for his brother's funeral. I'm sorry for the inconvenience."

"You all right? Looks like you got hit in the head," one of the officers stated with a frown.

Colin touched his head. "Oh? This? I stumbled over a rug and hit my head on the doorframe. No big deal."

Mother chose this time to roll up. She dashed out of the car and into the foyer with the rest of us.

"What the hell is going on here?" she exclaimed.

"It's all a misunderstanding, Mother. Come with

me into the living room and I'll explain."

I grabbed her arm and shoved her along in front of me.

"Hilary, stop that! Why is Sam here? Any why are the *cops* here?"

As soon as we were out of earshot of the police, I gave her a condensed version of the last twenty minutes.

"That's bullshit and you know it. Have him arrested," she insisted.

"Mother, that might not be in your, or my, best interest," I hissed. "Let Colin handle it."

She hesitated, nodded, and swept into the foyer.

"Officers, I'm sure my brother-in-law meant no harm. He simply wanted to let us know the update on my late husband's arrangements. His murder has been very upsetting for me, and I'm grateful he's taken charge. Let's just forget about this misunderstanding."

The cops looked at all of us. They knew we lied, but could do nothing about it. In the end, they left—alone.

Mother immediately whirled on Sam. "I want the truth. What the hell are you doing here? And don't give me any crap about funeral arrangements. Kinda late to be dropping by, isn't it? A phone call would do."

His nostrils flared and he sucked in a ragged breath. "Ross had something here I needed. It's personal."

Mother's eyes narrowed. "Uh-huh. What did Ross have that's got you so scared?"

Sam glared at her, but said nothing.

"Go home, Sam," Colin said. "And you better hope that recording isn't already in the hands of the police."

"What recording?" Mother said, her eyes wide and harboring a hint of fear mixed with wariness. She stared harder at Sam.

"By the way, where's your car?" I asked.

"Down the street. I parked in the driveway of an empty house that's for sale."

"What recording and how'd you get past the gatekeeper?" Mother demanded.

Sam shrugged. "Told him I needed to talk to you. He knows me by sight and didn't call through. I'm family—a blood relation, not a stranger." Sam left without a backward glance after that snarky remark.

"I'll have that guard's ass for this," Mother muttered.

"I need a drink," I said heading for the den. Everyone followed me. I glanced again at Colin's head. "Are you sure you're not hurt?"

He waved a hand. "I'm fine. Nothing a good stiff scotch won't cure."

"What happened to your gun?"

"Gun!" Mother said with a startled expression.

"Dropped it in the study when Sam whacked me with the flashlight—which reminds me." He detoured into the study, retrieved his gun, and dropped it in his pocket.

In the den, Colin poured three glasses of Dewar's. He bolted his in a single gulp and poured another. Mother and I sipped.

"Not too smart to walk into a dark room knowing an intruder is there," I commented.

He frowned as if knowing I was right, but not liking to admit it. "I didn't walk in all the way. I was feeling for the light switch when he rushed out and nailed me."

It was still stupid, but I kept my mouth shut.

"And I thought I told you to stay put in the car. What the hell were you doing on the porch?"

"I got scared not knowing what was happening. If it hadn't been for me, Sam would have gotten away."

"I'd have caught him. He's older and out of shape."

Mother's gaze traveled to each of us during the conversation as though she watched a tennis match.

"You attempted to enter a house knowing an intruder was here? That's not too smart either," she commented to me.

"Mother!"

"Okay, maybe we were both a little on the stupid side tonight," Colin interjected.

"We have other things to worry about," I said.

Mother sipped again. "Like what?"

"Like where is the recording Sam was looking for?"

"Which goddamned recording?" she snapped.

I explained what Sam had told us earlier.

She shrugged one shoulder and brought the glass to her lips one more time avoiding eye contact. "I'm sure it's around somewhere."

"So it exists?" Colin asked eyeing her with a narrowed gaze. "And what do you mean by 'which'?"

"Ross always recorded his private conversations with family members if they involved money."

Colin's forehead wrinkled. "That means you and Hilary are on it. Sam was telling the truth."

"Well, someone has the damned thing," I concluded. "And I don't think it's the cops."

Colin looked at me and nodded. "I think you're

right." He turned back to Mother. "How did you know he recorded things? Was it an old-fashioned tape recorder or something more up to date?"

"He used the old cassette recorder for ages, but switched to a digital toy about a year ago. He showed it to me and got a laugh out of how no one would ever suspect it was anything other than a lighter."

"A lighter?" I asked.

Mother nodded. "He kept it in the top right hand drawer of the desk. Whenever he wanted to use it he simply put it in the ashtray next to his humidor. It looked just like a slim lighter. Son of a bitch even had it faux gold-plated."

Colin scratched his head. "Well, this is a new wrinkle. If it's not here, then I suspect the killer not only knew about it, but took the damned thing, too. It is definitely not in his desk. I looked in the drawers the other day."

"Which means, a family member killed Ross," I said.

I'm not sure if Mother got the implications, but a wary look crossed her face. She drained the rest of the scotch.

"Whatever. This has been an interesting day. I'm going to bed."

She whirled and strode from the room, her high heels clacking on the hardwood between the rugs in the hall and foyer. Her total lack of curiosity concerning the whereabouts of the recording device and who had taken it disturbed me. *Unless she knows.* The possibility scared the crap out of me, but I knew better than to try and tackle her about things now. I turned back to Colin.

"The police can't have the recording," I said. "If

they did, they'd have asked about the jump drive."

"I know. Did you know Uncle Ross recorded conversations?"

I shook my head. "Never had a clue."

I finished my drink and walked over to him, my hand lightly brushing against the rising lump on the side of his head.

"Must have hurt like hell," I whispered.

"Only for a moment." His hands lightly caressed my shoulders.

"Want me to kiss it and make it better?" I moved closer. His fingers tightened.

"I think I'd like that a lot."

My arms slid around his neck. Our lips met.

A sweet, glowing warmth spread from the pit of my stomach to the tips of my fingers and toes. Our tongues tangled in delightful exploration. Colin's hands roamed up and down my back, slipping lower each time until he cupped my derriere and pulled me hard against him. His erection stabbed me in the abdomen. I groaned deep in my throat.

Desire made my legs go weak. The sofa was only steps away, and while I'd prefer a bed, it would do.

Then, like the other night, he stepped away. This time, he maintained the embrace and rested his forehead on mine.

"Hilary, I want you, but this isn't the time or the place. Your mother is upstairs and I'll be damned if I make love to you with her in the house." He pulled back, breaking the contact. "Besides, we need to keep our heads on straight."

"My head will never be on straight again. Mother's room is on the other side of the house. She won't hear a thing."

"No, but she'll be there just the same. And what's worse, I'll see her in my mind."

I had to laugh. "You've got a house, haven't you?"

He didn't answer, merely took my hand, turned off the light, and walked with me down the hall.

I paused by the study door, the mess clearly visible. Colin turned off that light, too.

"Shouldn't we clean up?"

"I'll do it tomorrow. I'll also look for that recorder again."

"We," I corrected.

"We."

Upstairs, he walked me to my room and lightly kissed me again.

"Goodnight, Hilary. Sleep well."

Sleep well? Not possible with my hormones so stirred up.

I opened my bedroom door as he continued on to his room.

"Hope your head feels better."

He chuckled as he entered his room and shut the door. It wasn't until a moment later I caught the double entendre and laughed, too.

****

I overslept badly the next morning, not making an appearance until after ten. In the hallway, I paused by the open study door. All was neat. Colin had been busy. Was he still here? I hurried on to the kitchen. Effie stood at the island chopping veggies.

"Good morning, Effie. Is Colin around?"

"Oh no, miss. He was up when I got here this morning. Said he'd already had his breakfast. Told me to tell you he'd be in for lunch. Then he left. Can I get you a cup of coffee?"

I waved my hand. "I'll get it. Go on with what you're doing."

I poured a mug and took it to the table. So, Colin was out and about. Doing what? Had he found the tape while cleaning up the room? And if so, had he listened to it? Was he now out asking questions of family members? Without me? Obviously, he hadn't mentioned Sam's intrusion to Effie. I followed his lead. I'm sure it never occurred to Mother to comment on the fact to a servant.

"Would you like some breakfast, miss?"

"No thanks. I had a rather late night and slept in. I'll just wait until lunch. How's everything with your family? Did you get the wedding menu planned?"

"Oh yes, miss, my niece and I got it all planned out. Won't take a great deal of work, thank goodness. Should be a right nice ceremony. Just family and close friends at the groom's home. Has her heart set on an outdoor event. Sure hope it doesn't rain." Effie sighed. "Only seventeen. So young to take such a big step."

I didn't like attending weddings. My last experience with one had been two years ago as a bridesmaid. A sorority sister had tied the knot down in Oxford. I hadn't heard from her since, and still had the strapless, floor length, grass green dress hiding in the back of my closet. The color had been atrocious on me.

After finishing my coffee, I wandered back upstairs. Mother's door was still closed telling me she either still slept or just didn't want to talk. Worked for me.

In my room, I sat on the chaise lounge and let my

mind drift over last night. Dinner, Sam, Colin. Our conversation in the car replayed through my head—at least the part about wasting my life.

In the past week not one of my friends had called to offer condolences or suggest I join them for an evening out. Not even a lunch invitation had appeared.

I picked up my phone and scrolled through the contact list. Maybe it was time to make a few calls.

An hour later, I tossed the phone onto the foot of the chaise. Not one of my friends was available for anything.

"Oh, Hil, honey, I'm going out of town," "Darling, I've got a spa appointment," "So sorry, but I've got relatives in town. Maybe next week," were just a few of the excuses.

"Next week, my ass," I muttered out loud. "Face it. You've been dropped like last year's fashion."

For some reason, I wasn't as upset as I should have been. They weren't true friends. A true friend would be at my side with words of encouragement. It dawned on me that I had no real friends, merely shallow acquaintances.

Except for Colin. He'd stand by me through whatever trouble I was in. He has already.

"Hilary Watson, you are a dope. The best thing in your life was in front of you for years and you never noticed."

Someone tapped on my door.

"Come in."

Colin poked his head around the corner. "Hi. Just thought I'd let you know Effie has lunch ready."

I rose and joined him in the hallway. Mother met us at the foot of the stairs.

"Ah, there you are. Where have you been hiding?" she asked leading the way into the dining room.

"Just catching up with a few friends."

She shot me a keen glance, but said nothing. I wondered if she'd been given the brush off by some of her friends yesterday.

"So, did you find any sign of a recording device or a lighter when you cleaned up Ross's study?" I asked as Effie set a small salad plate in front of me.

"No, not a thing. I even looked in the humidor. All I found were some contraband Cuban cigars. Wherever that recorder is, it isn't here."

We all concentrated on the salad for a few minutes.

"What else were you busy doing this morning?" I finally asked him.

"Checking out where I can find Joey Lazarus."

"Who's that?" Mother asked.

"A friend of Ross's," I said.

"A former client of Ross's," Colin corrected.

"Oh. Why do you need to find him?"

"Because his sister is named Carlotta," I stated.

Mother sat back with her nostrils flaring. "Carlotta? As in the Carlotta my husband was boinking? Can I come and snatch her hair out by the roots?"

"No, you can't tag along and, yes, Colin and I need to talk to her."

"Why?"

"Because I'm helping Colin."

"Do you think she could have killed Ross?"

"Right now, the door is wide open as to who bumped off my uncle."

"Maybe we'll never find out who did it," she said,

finishing her salad.

As if on cue, Effie entered with a tray and placed it on the sideboard. She cleared away the smaller plates and set our lunch in front of us.

I inhaled the delicious aroma of basil and garlic before answering Mother. "Well, you'd better hope we do. Otherwise, the entire city of Memphis will wonder if it was one of us."

Effie served Mother next. She acknowledged the food with a nod and picked up her knife and fork.

"Nonsense, there has to be dozens, if not hundreds of people who hated Ross and wanted him dead."

"Yeah, but the circumstances indicate it wasn't a stranger or even an old client. No forced entry," I said.

Colin received his plate last. He looked up at the housekeeper and smiled. "Effie, this looks and smells wonderful."

"Thank you, sir," she replied in a quiet tone.

"Maybe it was an old client he didn't know was out to get him," Mother said. "My money's on this Carlotta. Or her brother."

"That's why we have to find them," I told her.

Effie had opened and now poured us each a glass of white wine.

"I already did," Colin answered.

"Where?" Mother and I said at the same time.

"Hot Springs."

"Why Hot Springs?" I asked over the sound of dishes clanking as Effie put them on the tray.

"Because Joey likes the ponies and they're running at Oak Lawn."

"And when do we leave to interview them?"

"Tomorrow morning. We'll go, talk to them, and

head back here. Should take the whole day."

"Is the wine all right, Mrs. Patterson?" Effie asked.

"What? Oh, the wine." Mother sipped. "Yes, it's fine."

Effie nodded and left.

"I think they're in Hot Springs to avoid answering questions from the cops," I said, sampling the perfectly cooked chicken. "How does Effie do it?"

By the time we finished I was stuffed. Almost like I'd had dinner.

"Why the big lunch?" I asked.

"Why not?" Mother countered. "I've heard it said that a large meal in the evening is bad for the digestion."

I stared. Since when did Mother become so concerned about digestion or nutrition? My glance shifted to Colin who shrugged.

"Let me guess, you won't be in for dinner again tonight," I ventured.

"Jerricus and I are having dinner at the Peabody."

"Discussing your possible case, no doubt," Colin said.

"Amongst other things. We won't be eating until late. He's escorting me to some kind of reception or cocktail party he has to attend first."

"Hence a large lunch to tide you over," I commented.

Mother pushed back her chair and rose. "Exactly."

With that said, she exited the room.

"I wonder if she's bothered to plan a meal for us," I said to Colin.

"Why don't we give poor Effie a break and the night off again? Think Priscilla will mind?"

"Don't see why she should care. She won't be here."

"Been to that new Italian place on Moreland Way yet?"

"No, but I heard it's wonderful."

"Then why don't we do that?" He stood and placed his napkin beside his plate. "I'll go inform her now. Then I have to go out for a while."

"Out? Where?"

"I do have other clients, you know. Plus, I have to be in court on Thursday. I need to review my notes on that case, too. I'll be back by six. I'll make reservations for seven. Is that too early for you?"

"No, that's fine."

He left me alone in the dining room with a half-eaten slab of apple pie and melting ice cream. Disgruntled at not having been asked to join him, I finished the dessert and headed upstairs.

I paced in my room. What the hell was I going to do all afternoon? Once again, our conversation in the car last night came to mind. I walked over to the desk, turned on my computer, and pulled up the website of the Lighthouse School of Interior Design.

Located near the University of Memphis, it had much of what I sought. I clicked on the online application, and then spent the next ten minutes staring at it.

Can I do this? What if I bomb out? Will anybody be even interested in paying me to redecorate their homes? And if so, would they like what I'd done?

Taking a deep breath, I filled out the form then stared for another couple of minutes before hitting the send icon.

There! I'd done it. Whether or not they accepted me was another story, but at least I'd taken the first step.

I liked the feeling of accomplishment suddenly filling me.

Maybe it isn't too late, after all.

Chapter Thirteen

Hot Springs, Arkansas, was approximately three hours west of Memphis, and the natural thermal springs had made it a monster tourist attraction over a hundred years ago.

That's all I knew about the city. I knew even less about Oak Lawn and horse racing. If I gambled, it was at a casino. The facility was located in the center of town with ample parking. We pulled in a little after one. Fifteen minutes later we were seated in a box seat.

"What is it you expect to learn from Lazarus?" I asked watching a machine smooth the track from the last race.

"Why he showed up at the house twice in one week, and why at the party."

"Think he'll tell you?"

Colin raised a pair of binoculars to his eyes and scanned the crowd.

"He'll probably tell me to go to hell."

"To which you will reply...?"

"That he can talk to me or the cops since he was identified by two people as seeing Ross that week." He handed the binoculars to me. "Four boxes down and to the left."

I peered through them. The backs of two dark heads—one male, the other female—suddenly enlarged. I lowered the glasses.

"All I see is a lot of dark hair."

"He'll get up to place a bet sooner or later. When he does, take a good look. I need your ID that he was the man you saw talking to Ross the night of the party."

"I thought hoods traveled with an entourage."

"Not always."

Colin had bought a program and the board in the infield said the next race would start in fifteen minutes. Current odds on each horse updated every thirty seconds or so. I picked up the program and scanned the entrants for the second race.

"How do you know which horse to bet on?" I asked.

"Race history, odds, tipsters, track conditions, and gut instinct. I can't explain the fine art of horse betting in a couple of minutes. You gonna play?"

"I don't know. Never done it before." I gazed at the program. "What the hell kind of a name is Whatchamacallit?"

"I once bet on a nag called Down And Out. It was appropriate. He finished dead last."

"How do I do this?"

"Make your selection, go to the betting window, give the man two bucks, the horse's starting position and race number, plus where he'll finish—number two in the sixth to win. He'll give you a ticket."

A trumpet sound came over the loudspeakers.

"What's that?"

"The call to the post."

A few minutes later the horses appeared on the track parading in front of the grandstand in single file. Number four, Whatchamacallit was a beautiful rusty brown with a black mane and tail. I also like the color of the jockey's shirt—turquoise and black, two of my favorite colors. The geometric diamond pattern appealed to my sense of order.

"Okay, I've made up my mind. Now where do I go again?"

Colin shook his head, an amused expression on his face. "Just give me the information. I'll place the bet for you."

"How much does it cost?" I asked fishing in my purse for my wallet.

"At least two dollars."

I handed him a five. "Here. I want to bet on Whatchamacallit, number four."

"You realize the odds on this horse are fifteen-to-one. He's not likely to be anywhere near the front of the field. Why not go with the minimum?"

"I don't have any ones."

"Why this horse?"

"Because he's pretty and I love the colors the rider is wearing."

Colin rolled his eyes. "Oh God. All right. Win, place, or show?"

"What?"

"Do you want to bet on him coming in first, second, or third?"

I didn't know it was possible to look amused, yet sound irritated at the same time. Colin managed to pull it off.

"Well, I want him to win, of course!"

He looked up and nodded to the left.

The dark haired man stood, spoke with his companion, and left his seat, climbing the steps toward us. He passed by, his eyes glued on the program in his hand. My breath caught in my throat.

"Well?" Colin asked.

"It's him. That's the guy I saw coming out of the study with Ross that night."

"Okay. I thought so. I'll be right back."

He rose and left me alone. I used the binoculars again to look at the woman. She sat staring straight ahead as if bored or pissed off. Not seeing her face, I couldn't tell which.

On the track, some contraption had been wheeled across the backstretch. I knew enough to assume this was the starting gate. The horses were loping along the turn to my right. I trained the glasses on them. Lord, they were beautiful creatures. Muscles rippled and flexed with the movement. So elegant, so powerful.

Colin returned and handed me a ticket. "Here you go. Good luck."

"Did you bet?"

"Two dollars on number seven, BeerHere. His odds are three-to-one."

Lazarus walked past our seat to his box.

"Did you talk to him?"

"Lost him in the crowd. I'd rather talk to the sister."

"She won't talk to you, especially about Ross. Next time he goes to bet, you follow and I'll tackle the sister—assuming that's who's with him."

"It is. Joey's latest squeeze is some blonde stripper from one of his clubs."

"Ladies and gentlemen," a voice boomed from the loudspeaker. "It is now post time."

While we'd been talking, the horses had been loaded into the gate. A bell sounded, the doors flew open, and ten horses shot out of the stalls like rockets.

"And they're off!"

I listened as the announcer called who was in front down the backstretch and around the third turn. Whatchamacallit was fourth. BeerHere was first. They rounded the fourth turn with my horse now in third. The people in the stands stood and cheered. So did I.

"Come on, Whatchamacallit! Go, baby, go!" I fist pumped to cheer him on.

He edged up to second. BeerHere dropped back to third. Slowly, my guy inched up on the leader and drew ahead at the finish line. He'd won!

"Wow, that was exciting!"

"I don't believe it," Colin muttered.

"So, how much did I win?"

"The jockeys have to weigh in to make sure everything's the same as when they started, then the payoffs will show up on the board."

"How did your horse do?"

He ripped his ticket in half and dropped it on the concrete.

"Seventh. The nag took his starting position to heart."

When the payoffs were listed, Colin took my ticket and returned a few minutes later with a wad of cash.

"Holy cow, this is more fun than blackjack."

He groaned. "Do you know there are people who make their living from handicapping, and your system is a pretty horse and colors?"

"Worked, didn't it?"

I studied the program for the next race, finally deciding on a horse named Tomato Soup. His jockey wore bright orange with a white diagonal stripe. The odds were five-to-one. This time I gave Colin ten bucks.

Joey Lazarus passed us on his way to the windows. I glanced at his seat. The sister was once again alone.

Colin nodded and rose. I headed down four rows.

The woman sat staring at nothing.

"Carlotta?"

Her head swiveled toward me. She was lovely. Even seated, I could see she was of medium height and possessed a terrific figure. Her long dark hair cascaded over her shoulders. Her oval face and big, brown eyes fringed with the longest lashes I'd ever seen stared at me. No wonder Ross strayed. Mother never had a chance.

"Yeah, who are you?"

"My name is Hilary Watson. Ross Patterson was my stepfather. Can we talk for a moment?"

She cast a glance over her shoulder as if to seek help from her brother.

"No. I don't wanna talk."

I sat in the vacant chair next to her anyway. "Look, this isn't about recrimination or anything. I just wanted to know about your relationship, that's all."

"It's none of your business. Go away. I'm in mourning."

"How did you meet?" I persisted.

She sat silent for a moment before finally answering. "Ross was my brother's lawyer. He came to the house for a couple of meetings." Her eyes clouded with tears. "I'd never met anybody like him. He was so charming I never noticed the age difference. We started going out, and then he bought me a condo on the riverfront. Before I knew it, we were having an affair."

I felt sorry for her. She was young enough to have actually fallen in love.

"I take it your brother objected."

"Long and loud. Said Ross was old enough to be my grandfather. He told me to break it off immediately. I told him to drop dead. He went to see Ross one day. Ross told him the same thing. He and his wife had just separated. I guess Ross told him he planned on marrying me as soon as his divorce was final. Then, last Friday night Joey came to the condo. He was not happy. He'd crashed some kind of party Ross was having and talked to him again. I suppose it was about me." A tear trickled down her cheek. She brushed it away. "Ross was serious. He loved me and I loved him. The next day, his murder was all over the news. A couple of days later, we came here to get away from any reporters or cops. I can't stop crying."

"And they're off!" the PA system blared. We both ignored the calling of the race.

I didn't have the heart to tell her Ross likely wouldn't have gone through with the vows. He wanted a nice young thing to squire around for a while. Her brother's reputation would never have fit into the Patterson family—or business plans.

"I'm so sorry. Really, I am. Carlotta, do you think your brother may have killed Ross?"

"I don't know. He was certainly mad enough. If he did, I'll hate him forever." She looked me in the eye. "When's the funeral? Do you think I can come?"

I could just see Mother's reaction to Carlotta's appearance. On the other hand, if she stayed out of Mother's sight, it might not degenerate into a catfight. I was certain the church would be packed, and Mother, intent on playing her role as the grieving but stylish widow, might not notice.

"I'm sure that won't be a problem. The funeral's on Monday," I replied patting her hand and giving her the time and place. "Thanks for talking to me."

I rose and made my way back to our seats as the horses flashed by the finish line.

"And the winner is Tomato Soup by three lengths!"

Joey Lazarus passed and glanced at me with a glare. I plunked myself next to Colin.

"I don't believe it. You won again." He shook his head. "I'm going to start betting on whatever you do. What did Carlotta have to say?"

I gave him the gist of our conversation. "Poor girl. She really was in love with Ross."

"She's twenty and has lived a sheltered life. Her parents died in a car crash when she was twelve. Joey more or less raised her. Sent her to a good private school in Memphis, and an even better finishing school in Switzerland. She'll find true love eventually."

"She's not sure if Joey killed Ross or not."

Colin shook his head. "Not likely, but his story backs up hers. He argued with Ross a couple of weeks ago, and again on the night of the murder. He was about to ship his sister to relatives in Los Angeles to get her away from Ross's influence."

Joey and Carlotta climbed the steps past us. Joey sent us another glare. Carlotta kept her eyes downcast.

Colin watched their progress until losing them in the crowd.

"Guess they're calling it a day. How about you? You ready to go?"

"Are you kidding? I just won again. This is fun.

Let's stay for a while. Who do you like in the next race?" I asked picking up my program.

"I have created a monster," he proclaimed. "And I should be asking you that question."

We stayed for the rest of the races. I won four more times and pocketed a little over a thousand bucks. It was dusk as we headed for the car.

"Since I'm a big winner, I'll treat you to dinner for a change."

"Damned straight you will. And I just happen to know a great restaurant not far from here."

"Now aren't you glad I'm your devoted assistant?"

He didn't answer, but just shot me an exasperated glance as we pulled out of the parking lot.

I chuckled. All in all, this had been a great day.

****

It was after nine when we left the restaurant. A popular place, we'd had to wait for a table, and then took our time ordering and eating. The good food and even better wine made me drowsy. I dozed while Colin drove only to start awake at an unfamiliar noise.

"What…what was that?" I muttered, rubbing my eyes.

Colin chuckled. "You woke yourself up snoring."

Oh, crap. He had to be kidding.

"I did not."

"Yes, you did."

"I do not snore."

"Then you must have a chain saw hidden in your purse."

I ran a hand through my hair. "I do not snore! I might breathe heavily upon occasion, but I do not snore."

He laughed outright.

"Where are we?"

"About half an hour outside Memphis."

Wow, I'd done more than doze. Before I could say anything else, his cell rang.

"Blackwood here." He listened for several long seconds. "Tonight? I'm not even in town… If you have such hot information, call the police… Yeah, I'm familiar with the area. I suppose I can find it… Give me an hour and fifteen, maybe twenty minutes."

"Who was that?" I asked as he hung up.

"An anonymous caller who claims to have information about Ross and one of his less than pure clients. He wants to meet at a bar off Ridge Road just west of Hernando."

"Are we going to do it?"

He sighed. "I don't like anonymous calls or anonymous anythings for that matter. They're usually bogus and all you do is go on a hunt for nothing. That's the good part. The bad part is it could be dangerous, especially if this guy happens to be the killer. I think I'll drop you off at a respectable diner in Horn Lake and go alone."

I sat up straight and shot him a glance. "Oh no, you don't! If something happens to you, I'll be stuck in some greasy spoon."

"Your confidence in my abilities is overwhelming."

I ignored his sarcasm. "Besides, I'm your assistant. Now where is this place?"

He gave me the name of the bar. I punched in information on his GPS system. Within seconds a map appeared. He glanced at the display as he drove.

"It's out in the boonies. We'll have to hustle to make it in time."

"So what are we waiting for?"

Colin pushed the speedometer up to eighty. Forty minutes later, we swung off the beltway around Memphis and south onto I-55. Shortly after that, we exited at Hernando and headed west. A series of turns led us to Ridge Road.

I leaned forward to peer out the windshield. "Sure is dark."

"Yeah, too dark. I don't like this."

Ahead I spotted the glow of neon beyond a curve in the road. Colin slowed as we came up on the place called, The Last Stand. A preponderance of motorcycles told me this was a biker bar. He sped up again and passed it by.

"No way. Not with you."

"Hey, I can hold my own. Besides, this guy might have valuable information."

"I don't think so."

"I think we should go back and see. You forget— I'm a suspect. So's my mother. I'd like to hear what he has to say."

"I don't like the set up. A biker bar in an isolated area of Desoto County just sends up red flags."

"Maybe he wants to meet here because he's familiar with the place. Maybe a biker buddy is the killer," I argued.

"Then he wouldn't be meeting us here. We'd stick out like priests in a synagogue."

I sat back and crossed my arms over my chest. "I can't believe you'd pass up a lead. What kind of private investigator are you?"

"The careful kind, Hilary. If it's a set up, I'd be dead as soon as I walked in the door and the cops would find your raped and strangled body next week sometime."

Knowing he wouldn't change his mind, I stared out into the inky darkness. Trees flashed by on either side of the road.

"Where are we?"

"I'm not sure, but as soon as I find a place to turn around or a side road that looks like it leads to civilization, we're outta here." He paused to glance into the rearview mirror. "Shit."

"What?"

"There's someone behind us. Coming up fast."

I twisted around to look out the back window. A car was gaining ground on us fast. The high beam headlights made me squint. The driver would be on our bumper in seconds. Before I could ask a question, he was there. He never slowed and rammed us with a teeth-rattling jolt.

The car swerved as Colin fought for control. My heart pounded. I looked back again as we increased our speed. The vehicle looked to be a pick-up or SUV. It fell back a few yards, then came at us again. This time the hit was harder.

"Goddammit," Colin swore, once again fighting to keep the car on the road as we fishtailed.

"Colin! Go faster!"

We had to be doing close to sixty miles an hour. Ahead, our headlights picked up a curve. The attacker kept pace. The car screeched around the curve, drifting across the double yellow line into the other lane. The impact from another hit sent the car broadside down the road.

"Hang on!" Colin yelled.

I looked out the passenger side window. Headlights filled my view. He was coming right at me. I screamed and covered my eyes with my hands. He nailed us again in the right rear door. My world turned upside down as the car barrel rolled down the roadway.

Chapter Fourteen

The other vehicle roared off into the night. Our car had finally come to rest roof side down on the weed-choked berm near the tree line. I hung by my seat belt. Escaping steam hissed into the silence. My heart lurched at a crackling noise.

"Hilary, are you all right?"

I batted the deflating air bag out of my face. "Yeah...yeah, I think so. You?"

"More or less."

"What's that sound? Are we on fire?"

"Maybe. Probably an oil line. Stay put. I'll get you out."

He released his restraints and twisting, crawled out of the shattered driver's side window before running to my side. He reached in and fumbled with my seat belt mechanism. It refused to work.

"Jammed. Just a second."

The crackling sounded louder. My heart pounded in my throat and my panicked breath came in panting bursts.

"Colin, hurry!"

Lying prone on the ground, he reached in and sawed the belt off with his pocketknife. Once free, he helped me from the mangled car and to the other side of the road. I clung to him while sobbing into his shoulder.

"Are you sure you're all right?" he asked.

I nodded and gulped. "Just scared. Is the car going to blow up?"

"I don't know." He whipped out his cell and dialed. "Yeah, I've had an accident on Ridge Road just west of The Last Stand bar... Not really. Just shaken up... Hit and run... Car's in bad shape, some fire... Thanks." He hung up. "Cops are coming."

I finally caught my breath and my wits. "I guess you were right. This was a set up."

"All the way. I should never have agreed to meet the guy, especially with you along." He pulled me into his arms and rubbed his hands up and down my back, then cupped my face and kissed me. "I'm sorry. A total lack of judgment on my part."

I shook my head, wishing he'd kiss me again. "I was gung-ho to talk to the guy, too."

The flames from the underside of the car licked brighter illuminating our position.

"Let's move further away. The gas tank may explode."

"Who do you think did it?" I asked as we stumbled another thirty yards from the scene.

"We only talked to one person today—Joey Lazarus."

"Did he want us dead or just scared?"

"It was a warning. If he wanted us dead, we'd have been shot in the head and left by the side of the road."

I shivered and nestled closer to his shoulder again. Something wet dribbled onto my forehead. I leaned back and brushed away a slick film, then put my hand along side his head.

"Colin, you're bleeding!"

"Probably cut by glass on the first roll. It was

toward my side. It's just a scratch."

"But you're hurt!"

I heard sirens in the distance, indicating help was on the way. The sound grew louder until a car rounded the curve followed by a large fire truck.

The fire department quickly put out the fire. For once I kept my mouth shut and let Colin do the talking. By now, an ambulance had also arrived. The paramedics patched up the cut on Colin's head and gave me a quick exam.

"No cuts, thank goodness. I'm just shaken up," I told them.

"You'll probably have some dandy bruises and hurt like hell tomorrow morning," one of the medicos said shining a small penlight into my eyes. "You weren't unconscious, were you?"

"No. I think I put my arms around my head so it wouldn't hit anything."

"Airbag helped."

Funny, while I remembered knocking it out of the way, I didn't remember it deploying.

"Here, let me help you to the ambulance," he said taking my arm as if to guide me.

"Oh, I don't think that's necess—"

"Yes it is," Colin said. "We need to get a thorough check-up."

"But I feel fine," I protested.

"I took a pretty good wallop on the head, and the guy nailed us right behind where you were sitting. You could have hit your head and not remember it. Don't take chances with possible concussions."

Like not remembering the airbag popping out?

Giving up and getting into the ambulance, I still

felt shaky. A trip to the hospital wasn't a bad idea. I stretched out on the gurney and closed my eyes, then reopened them again when all I envisioned was the SUV coming at me. Nausea gripped my stomach as the interior of the vehicle spun. I swallowed hard.

Maybe I did hit my head after all.

I had no idea how long I laid there. Finally, Colin entered and sat on the foot of the cot. He handed me my purse.

"Thanks. How much did you tell the cops, and what did they have to say?"

"I told them the truth. This is a felony hit and run. You…we…could have been killed. No time for lies or bending the facts."

"I guess not."

The paramedics entered the ambulance, one behind the wheel and one back with us. The drive to the hospital didn't take long. On the other hand, once there, the exam did. In the end, we were both admitted overnight for observation. My night was complete when as I settled into bed, Mother rushed into the room.

"Darling, are you all right?"

"Mother, what are you doing here?"

"Colin called me, of course. Is there anything I can do? Do you need anything?"

"I'm fine. This is just a precaution."

"What on earth were you doing out in the middle of nowhere in the dead of night?"

"It's a long story, and I'm tired. It's after two. Can we discuss this later?"

"You were investigating something, weren't you? Where's Colin?"

"Across the hall, and yes, we were supposed to

meet someone."

Mother straightened her spine. "Well, I'll have to have a chat with him. He had no business involving you."

"I wanted to go. And when we saw how isolated the place was, we didn't stop. I'm sure we got hit by some drunk." I said that to ease her mind. A dart of pain slashed through my head, but whether from the accident or Mother's presence, I wasn't sure. I was touched she was here, but doubted she could do anything constructive. "Go on home. We'll be released in the morning."

"Nonsense. I'm staying here. And who's to say someone won't take a shot at ramming me? That chair in the corner will do fine."

"Oh, God," I muttered as she marched from the room, no doubt to bully the hospital staff into scaring up a pillow and a blanket.

I slept fitfully what with nurses coming in to check on me every couple of hours, but by nine the following morning could honestly say that other than being sore, I felt fine. The rumpled pillow and a blanket thrown across the chair told me Mother had made good on her promise. I had no clue as to where she was now.

Other than a large bandage on his head, Colin didn't look any the worse for wear either. He smiled at me as we were wheeled to the hospital entrance.

"How did you sleep?" he asked.

"So-so. And you?"

"The same. May I suggest that when we get home, you go to bed and catch up on your sleep?"

"Will you?"

"Sure."

He lied. I could tell from the look on his face. He would investigate this down to the last dent in the foam-covered bumper.

Mother met us out front and drove us home. For once, we were all quiet. Effie rushed in from the kitchen when we entered the foyer.

"Mr. Colin, Miss Hilary, are you all right?"

"We're fine, Effie," he answered. "Just a little bruised and sore."

"I swear I don't know what this world is coming to. Drunk drivers hitting respectable people, and then running off like cowards when it comes time to face the music. I'm sure the police will find who did it. Would you like some breakfast?"

"I had a lousy night's sleep," Mother said. "I'm going straight to bed. I'll be down for lunch."

"Well, I'm starving," I told her, having refused the hospital food earlier. "I'd love something to eat."

"Same here," Colin added. "Priscilla, before you go, I need to ask a question."

"What?"

"Did you tell anyone where we were going yesterday?"

Mother hesitated. "I think I may have mentioned it to Ian."

"Ian!" I exclaimed.

She nodded. "Yes, he called around noon with a couple of questions about the funeral and asked to talk to you, Colin. I told him you were over in Hot Springs checking out a lead or something. He said, 'Good, at least someone was working on the case.' I don't think he has a whole lot of confidence in the Moreland police."

"Okay, Priscilla, thanks."

She swept up the staircase as Colin and I headed for the kitchen.

"So, Ian knew where we were," I said. "I wonder if he shared the information with Sam."

"If he did, I'm sure he'd tell me."

"Not if he and Sam are in cahoots regarding Ross's murder and the break-in the other night."

"I'll deal with it. Let's eat."

Link sausages, scrambled eggs, and banana nut muffins satisfied my empty stomach along with the coffee.

Back in my bedroom, I gazed at the bed and stifled a yawn. Maybe a little nap wasn't out of the question. Lunch was only a couple of hours away, but I had the feeling I'd skip it today.

I stripped off my clothes from the day before, tossed them into the hamper, and slid naked beneath the sheets. I yawned again and nestled my head deeper into the pillow, but sleep refused to come. Instead, my mind replayed those headlights bearing down on me like a video caught in a never ending loop. Neither could I get the sound of the collision out of my head. The screech of protesting tires, fiberglass ripping, and metal shredding had me opening my eyes to make sure I was in my own bedroom.

After an hour, I finally gave up, showered, dressed, and went in search of Colin. He was in the study seated at Ross's desk and on the phone.

"Four o'clock is fine. I'll leave your name with the guard at the gate." He hung up as I entered. "Thought you were going to bed."

"Couldn't sleep. What are you doing?"

"Getting a rental car and doing some research."

"What kind of research?" I asked, settling on the leather sofa.

"The police have been busy. They traced the call that sent us out to the Last Stand. It came from a cell tower near Hernando. Turns out the phone was stolen in Senatobia earlier in the day."

I rubbed my forehead. "Maybe I'm still groggy from the accident, but I don't get it. Why way out in the boonies when they could have run us off the interstate and gotten better results?"

He tapped a pencil on the desktop. "Joey Lazarus is the only one who knew we'd be leaving Hot Springs for Memphis, yet this doesn't sound like his type of thing. And he'd be after me, not you, too."

"Not if he was pissed because I talked to his sister. But then Joey doesn't strike me as the kind to care who else was in the car." I paused. "He was out of his comfort zone in Hot Springs and didn't have his usual contacts. He could have followed us from the track to the restaurant, and then called a confederate in Hernando to lure us to a dark, deserted road. And don't forget, Ian knew, too."

"I'm wrong," he said slowly. "Lazarus wasn't the only one who knew we'd be heading home. Carlotta knew."

"You think Carlotta set us up?" I thought for a moment, and then shook my head. "No, I don't see it. She was genuinely grief-stricken by Ross's death and wants the killer found."

"Unless she's the killer and one hell of a good actress. We only have her word for it that Ross told her brother to kiss off. Maybe he bowed to pressure and broke it off with *her*. Isn't there some saying about a woman scorned?"

I tried to imagine Carlotta in the role of villain. It just didn't fit. "My money's on her brother. He's protecting his sister. Ross is dead and no longer a threat to him. I wonder if she'll come to the funeral."

He rolled his eyes. "That ought to make for an interesting day."

"The church will be packed. Mother will be too busy portraying the grieving widow to pay much attention to who attends—other than the media."

His cell rang. "This is Colin… Oh, really. That's interesting… Any idea how it got there…" He listened for a long time. "So this wasn't a spur of the moment thing. It was premeditated… Yeah, thanks for the call." He hung up and stared at me.

"Who was that?"

"That was Detective Parker. You're not going to believe this one. He got the tox report back on Ross. Seems he had enough Xanax in his system to down an elephant."

"Xanax? Ross didn't take Xanax. To the best of my knowledge, he didn't take any kind of medication. Why would he take a bunch of pills? Was he trying to kill himself and met another killer along the way?"

"He would never check out with a bunch of happy pills. Ross had a nightcap every night before he went to bed. The coroner also found a lot of alcohol in his blood—at least point oh-six."

"Well, of course, he'd just hosted a cocktail party."

"Ross was a creature of habit. Right?"

"Right," I replied in a low tone. "So, the last guest leaves, he goes into the study and pours himself a drink.

Just routine."

"That's right. Which means the Xanax was likely in the Dewar's bottle, *which* means someone wanted him at least semi-incapacitated, *which means* his death was planned."

"Which explains how the killer got near him as he sat at his desk."

"Exactly. Ross is comatose or close to it. The assailant has a nice docile target that can't fight back. He nails him with a cast iron frying pan before switching out the tainted bottle for a new one."

I thought about Colin's comment regarding Carlotta possibly being dumped. Ross may have called her with the bad news after the party.

"Or she," I repeated. "Carlotta comes to the house. Ross would let her in. She slips the drug into the Scotch, waits until he's woozy, gets the frying pan from the kitchen and wham—nails him." I still had a problem reconciling Carlotta's behavior at the racetrack with my words. And why go to the kitchen for a weapon when all those golf trophies graced Ross's bookshelves? And would she even know where the kitchen was located? "But why would she want to kill him."

"We know Lazarus came to see Ross on Tuesday. It was a heated discussion. Effie attests to that. We also know he returned on Friday night, probably unaware of the party. You saw him leave."

"He wasn't happy then, either." I sighed. "And the gate guard likely assumed Joey was a guest, didn't consult the guest list, and waved him through. Where are we going with this?"

"I'm not sure." He paused for a moment. "We're assuming both visits revolved around Carlotta. What if they didn't?"

"I'm lost. What are you talking about?"

"Suppose on Tuesday, Lazarus demands Ross break it off with Carlotta. At this point, my uncle figures she might not be worth the trouble of having Joey on his back, so he agrees."

"He gives Carlotta the bad news, and she decides to extract revenge. But why would Lazarus come back on Friday?"

"For some other reason—something not connected to his sister."

"Or to warn Ross that Carlotta is furious and maybe he'd better get out of town for a while," I suggested.

"I don't think so. You said Lazarus was angry when he left."

"Not angry, exactly, more like perturbed. He was scowling and walked quickly, but that's all."

"How did Ross act after he left?"

I shrugged. "Like normal. He drank, he talked, and that's about it."

"So Joey was upset, but Ross wasn't." Colin frowned and drummed his fingers on the blotter. "I'm thinking I need to talk to Joey Lazarus again."

"You think he'd agree to that? He wasn't pleased with us at the track."

"I'll play nice. Tell him I don't think he's involved, but could help us with just a little information. And I won't mention the accident at all."

"And guarantee no cops."

"Without a doubt."

"Do you know how to get a hold of him?"

"He owns a gentleman's club on Winchester. Does

most of his business out of it. If I show up about ten tonight, he'll be there."

"We."

"Hilary…"

"We. You may be used to getting chased by thugs, but I'm not. Besides, I've never been to a titty bar."

He sighed. "All right. We."

Effie appeared in the doorway. "Lunch is ready."

We trooped into the dining room. Mother was a no-show. I assumed she was eating in her room. The meal was a mostly silent affair, but it gave me time to think.

Carlotta as a killer? The old adage about a woman scorned might prove true. I wondered if she'd taken any acting classes at that fancy Swiss finishing school. It was certainly something to consider.

Inevitably, my thoughts turned to tonight and a possible confrontation with Joey Lazarus again.

And what the hell do I wear to a titty bar?

****

I crammed my body into the rental car and fastened the seat belt.

"Couldn't you have gotten something smaller?"

"Hey, its got an engine and four wheels. This was all they had. I'll upgrade tomorrow."

The Golden Harem was located on the seedier side of South Memphis. But then, I'd never heard of a strip club in a nice section of town. It was Saturday night and the parking lot was jammed. Big surprise.

I'm not sure what I expected to find inside, but the place lived up—or down—to what I imagined. Music boomed from loudspeakers. Small tables jammed close together dotted the floor as scantily clad waitresses sidled past customers. Girls danced on platforms set among the tables. Men sat with drinks in their hands, their eyes glued to the gyrating, half-naked dancers. Other muscle-bound men walked around constantly scanning the crowd.

A rectangular bar took up the rest of the space. Mostly nude women shimmied on the top and curled themselves around poles. Colin managed to find two seats in front of one. I slid onto the stool, unable to take my eyes off the girl. She twisted and wrapped her legs around the three inch pipe only to bend backwards, suspend her body over the bar, and shake her boobs at the same time.

"Beer in a bottle for both of us," Colin said to the bikini clad bartender.

"I don't like beer," I said in a low tone.

"The booze will cost a fortune and is watered down. Beer will last longer."

The girl now hung upside down from the pole, her undulating body drawing whistles of appreciation from several patrons.

"I had no idea how much athleticism this required," I said in awe.

"Yeah, well they get a lot of practice. And whatever you do don't make eye contact with any of the guys. Just look at the bar or pretend to talk to me."

Naturally, I didn't do it. I let my gaze swing toward a man sitting around the corner from me. He leered and winked. My skin crawled. I was glad I'd followed my intuition and worn a simple skirt and modest top. I turned my attention back to Colin.

"So, come here often?"

"I told you not to look. Any woman in here who isn't a performer, waitress, or bartender, is a potential performer, waitress, or bartender."

Our beers arrived. I pretended to take a sip.

"That'll be fifteen bucks and I don't run a tab," the bikini mama said.

Colin paid. "Hey, sweetie, is Joey around?"

She swiped a damp rag at one of the many sticky spots on the counter. "Joey who?"

"Come on, Joey Lazarus."

"Never heard of him."

Colin peeled a twenty from a wad of bills and stuffed it down her cleavage.

"That help your memory?"

"Still never heard of him."

Another twenty followed. "How about now?"

Her gaze flickered from him to me and back again. "Who wants to know?"

He handed her his business card. "Just tell him the fellow from Oak Lawn yesterday wants to apologize and would like a word with him."

She tapped the card on the bar top, eyed us again, and then left.

"That was disgusting," I said. "How could you stuff money down her bra?"

"It wasn't her bra, but a bikini top, and she's used to it. She probably makes more selling information than she does from tips. They all do."

"Think Joey will talk to us?"

"I have no idea, but if nothing else, he'll be curious."

We waited a good fifteen minutes. In the meantime, the bartender returned and went about her duties. She didn't inform us of anything. I took another sip from the beer bottle.

A scream echoed from behind me. I twisted on the stool. One of the patrons had grabbed the leg of a dancer and was kissing his way up her thigh. A huge man approached, clasped the offender around the neck, lifted him out of his chair, and dragged him toward the entrance.

"Holy crap!" I muttered.

"Joey takes care of his girls. Most of them work for him off hours, too."

"You mean they're prostitutes?"

"Joey lets them keep their tips here, but takes a hefty ninety-five percent on all other activities."

I shook my head. How could a woman do this? They were all pretty, and looked like they had a modicum of intelligence.

Colin shrugged when I asked. "Low self-esteem? Adventure? Some just might like it. Remember Sally Ransom? My guess is she knows Lazarus."

Another large man walked up to Colin.

"You, follow me."

I slid off the stool.

"You, not her."

Colin eyed the man. "Come on, do you really think I'm going to leave her sitting out here all alone? Besides, she's my assistant."

He shrugged, led us through the club to a back hallway until pausing to knock discreetly on a door, and opened it. He gestured with his chin indicating we should enter.

Joey Lazarus sat behind an ornate desk, his beady eyes boring a hole through Colin. He ignored me.

"Okay, Blackwood, whaddaya want?"

"To apologize. I didn't mean to upset either you or

your sister."

His gaze shifted to me and then back to Colin. "Yeah, well you did upset her."

"Mr. Lazarus, I know you didn't kill my uncle, but eyewitnesses can place you at his home on Tuesday and again the night of the party. So far, I don't think your name has come up to the cops. What I'd like to know is why you saw Ross."

"Why should I tell you anything?" he countered.

"Because some people might think your sister had something to do with it."

Lazarus's eyes turned almost black with anger. He half-rose and leaned forward. "Why you..."

Colin held up his hand. "I don't think that, but if your name surfaces, so will hers. Too many people have seen them together. His wife hired a PI. He took pictures. Maybe what you tell me can help keep you both in the clear."

I held my breath. If Lazarus didn't buy Colin's explanation, neither of us would make it out of this office in one piece. To my relief, his expression changed from furious to thoughtful. He resumed his seat.

"I don't like the idea of my sister screwing anybody, especially my attorney, a man old enough to be her grandfather. When I found out, I warned Carlotta to drop him. She refused. Knew I shouldn't have sent her to that Swiss school. They taught her how to stand up for herself." He muttered the last two sentences in a low tone. "At any rate, I warned her again, and then I warned him. That was a couple of months ago. I thought I'd gotten through to both of them. Seems I didn't. Found out that instead of a motel, he'd bought a condo for their get-togethers. This time I didn't phone, I went to the house. Told him Carlotta expected a wedding band. He back pedaled fast. Said he was going through what would be a nasty divorce and had no intentions of tying the knot again. He agreed to tell Carlotta it was over."

"Did he?"

"So she said. Told me he met her the next day and gave her the news. I arranged for a trip to Los Angeles to get her mind off him. Besides, I wasn't sure if she lied or not. I canceled the trip when he got killed."

That wasn't quite how Caroltta had described things at the racetrack. Could Ross have told her they'd have to cool it for a while, and Carlotta had simply lied to her brother?

Lazarus glared at me. "And thanks to Miss Watson, she's now going to go to the funeral on Monday."

"You needn't worry about her reputation, Mr. Lazaurus," I said. "The crowd will be huge. With any luck no one will notice her."

"They better not. One whiff of who she is will make me very unhappy."

"Why did you show up again on Friday night?" Colin asked.

He shifted his eyes down to the desk. "Other business."

"What other business?" The silence stretched. "Look, that other business could lead me to another suspect."

Lazarus laughed. "Oh, brother."

"What's so funny?"

"I have a lot of businesses."

"Such as?"

"I loan money from time to time."

"Yeah, okay, so? Are you telling me Ross went to a loan shark?"

"Naw, not him. He didn't need to do that."

"Then who?"

Lazarus remained silent and smiled.

Colin's chin rose as understanding swept over his face. "A family member?"

"Into me for close to twenty-five grand. Loves those casinos."

"Who?"

"Mrs. Sam Patterson."

Chapter Fifteen

"Bonnie?" I said with a gasp. "Bonnie borrowed money from you?"

"Yeah," Lazarus answered. "And she's not real good about paying on time. Had to remind her last week."

"How long has she been a client?" Colin asked.

"A little over a year."

"I see. So why bring that up with Ross?"

"I talked to Mrs. Patterson on Wednesday. Told her to make a payment. If she didn't, she might not like the consequences. She told me the next day her brother-in-law would make good on the loan. I didn't believe her, so I went to see him. He had a bunch of people there. The front door was wide open. I walked in and saw him first thing. We spent five minutes, maybe less in his study."

Colin frowned. "Let me guess. He refused."

"Said his brother's wife was on her own. I left the party, called Mrs. Patterson with the bad news, and told her she had twenty-four hours to pay up. End of discussion. And speaking of ending discussions, this one is over." He waved his hand in dismissal.

My mind reeled with this information. I could just see Bonnie, on the edge of desperation, coming to the house. Ross would let her in. Did she beg? Threaten? Cry? And when Ross said no, did she go to the kitchen, grab the first thing she saw—the frying pan—and whack him over the head with it?

And was that the reason Sam had broken into the house the other night? Had Ross recorded the conversation? *My God, was the murder recorded?*

"Thank you for your time, Mr. Lazarus."

Colin and I walked from the room, through the club, and out to the parking lot.

"Holy cow, I didn't expect this," I said as we drove away.

"The time frame fits on when she and Sam were separated. She runs up debt at a casino, can't pay, and goes to Lazarus for a loan. She and Sam get back together, and he either won't or can't pay it off. Remember, I said his finances are shaky at best."

"So, Lazarus warns Bonnie on Wednesday. She goes to Ross on Thursday and he tells her to take a hike. To buy time, she tells her friendly neighborhood loan shark Ross has agreed to pay."

"What she doesn't count on is Lazarus talking to Ross and learning the truth."

I gave him my theory. "Could she have done it?"

"Maybe, if she was scared enough. And once Ross was dead, she knew she'd get something out of the estate."

"Awfully convenient, him getting killed like that. Just in time to save her sorry ass. No wonder she was so concerned about her cut of the pie last Sunday. Think Sam knew about her owing money to a loan shark?"

"Maybe. My guess is that if he didn't know, he sure as hell suspected. On the other hand, like I said, Sam's got money problems of his own."

"Wouldn't it be ironic if he'd gone to a loan shark,

too?"

"What? Dueling loan sharks? In this town, I can see that happening. My question is; when did she spike his Scotch?"

"I forgot about that. Could she have slipped in earlier in the day or maybe during the party? With so many people and the staff busy, it's a possibility."

"She'd be taking a chance, but who knows?"

I directed my gaze out the windshield. We were nowhere near Moreland or even on a street leading to it.

"Where are we?"

"Going to my place. I need some clothes and a private conversation with Sam. Or Bonnie. Or both. I'll set it up for tomorrow."

"Can I listen in?"

"I'd rather you didn't. Neither is likely to talk with you in the room."

"I can stay out of sight. Hang in the kitchen or bedroom while you talk to them. They'll never know," I said in a wheedling tone.

"I'll think about it."

We were silent for the rest of the drive until Colin pulled into a driveway.

"Nice house," I commented.

"It's home."

Colin's house was located in East Memphis just off Walnut Grove Road. The single story white clapboard with black shutters and a cranberry colored door looked inviting. The landscaping consisted of evergreens and was what I'd call minimalist. But then, who was I to talk? I lived in a townhouse with a homeowner's association that took care of all things nature related.

The open foyer led into a great room on the left.

Through an archway, I caught a glimpse of a dining room. I assumed the kitchen was beyond another door at the far end of the room. The furniture had a comfortable look to it yet with simple lines. My mind immediately wanted to redecorate, not because I found fault with his choices, but because that was my nature.

On the right a hallway led to the bedrooms. I speculated about those, too.

"Can I get you something to drink?" he asked walking toward a wet bar in the corner of the room.

"Sure. You choose."

"Drambuie all right with you?"

"Fine. Is there somewhere I can freshen up? I need to get the cooties from The Golden Harem off me."

"Down the hall, first door on your left."

I hadn't lied about feeling slimy from Lazarus's club. Thank God, I'd had the sense to wear non-revealing clothes. Leaving the bathroom, I resisted the urge to tiptoe down the hall and check out the master bedroom.

Back in the living room, I found my glass on the bar, sipped, and walked toward the kitchen where I heard Colin on the phone. I leaned against the doorjamb and listened.

"That's right, tomorrow morning, ten o'clock. I need to talk to both of you... It concerns Ross and money... No I'm not going to talk about it over the phone or at this hour... Let me talk to Sam... Where is he...? Well, get a hold of him if you can. I'll talk to you tomorrow." He hung up and frowned.

"She giving you grief?" I asked.

"Sam isn't there. He moved out again. She's not sure where he's staying. No matter. I want to talk to

Bonnie first anyway. I'll tackle Sam at the funeral."

"It's occurred to me that we may never wade through the suspect list. Heard anything else from the cops?"

He shook his head and plugged his phone into a charger on the counter.

"Not since this morning. They're busy checking phone records and credit card receipts."

"Credit card receipts?"

"It's routine. Probably seeing if Ross had any big expenditures lately. I'm sure bank statements are also getting overhauled."

I sipped my drink, and then made the mistake of looking into his eyes. Our gazes locked. Heat that had nothing to do with Drambuie slowly worked its way from my stomach to my chest and beyond. I read the desire in his face and sensed his struggle to contain it. I made no attempt to contain *my* desire. I set my glass on the counter.

"Need any help selecting those clothes?"

"No, I'm a big boy. I can do it on my own."

"Even big boys need help now and then."

Our gazes never wavered. His hands reached out to clasp my shoulders. Slowly, he drew me toward him. My arms slid around his neck. His arms cradled me, and then tightened. This was where I belonged.

"It's just you and me," I whispered.

"And your mother is nowhere in sight."

His lips claimed mine and I surrendered to the bliss of it. As the kiss deepened, his hand roamed up and down my back before clutching my derriere and jamming my hips against his. His erection nestled just where I wanted it. I moved my hips and moaned. His answering groan told me tonight would show no holding back.

With our lips still locked, I pulled his polo shirt from his slacks. My hands slid up his smooth chest. Muscles rippled under my fingertips. His nipples were hard as stone. I fumbled with his belt buckle.

Not to be outdone, Colin's hands moved under my top. His nimble fingers found and released the clasp on my bra. Within seconds, he covered my breast, kneading and pinching until my nipples resembled diamonds. I groaned.

We broke apart and stood staring. My breaths came in rapid bursts. The blood pounded in my ears. Then he reached for me again and yanked my top over my head. It drifted to the kitchen floor. It was joined a moment later by his shirt and my bra.

"The bedroom. Now!" He gasped in a hoarse voice as he pulled me toward the hallway.

We staggered and groped our way through the living room and down the hall. My skirt and sandals disappeared along the way. In the bedroom, I unzipped his slacks and plunged my hand inside past his boxers. It was like touching a shaft of hot steel. He groaned again, leaned over, and threw back the covers on the king sized bed, then pushed me down. His body covered mine.

I was beyond reason or coherent thought. All I wanted was him. His lips trailed down my cheek to suck on that delicate pulse point in my neck. I gasped and moaned. His hands caressed my breasts only to be replaced by those lips a few seconds later. My body squirmed and moved with a neverending need.

He worked his way down my body, fingertips light

and arousing, teeth nipping and sending signals to my nerves I'd never felt before. I was damned near out of control by the time he reached my inner thighs.

"Colin! Now!"

"Not yet, honey."

His tongue found and tickled the one spot that counted. I cried out as pleasure rolled over me in waves. Then, just seconds from fulfillment, he pulled away, leaned over, and fumbled in his slacks.

"Don't stop now, for God's sake!"

"This'll just take a second," he replied in a raspy tone.

He returned, his shaft now shielded. Without another word, he kneed my thighs apart and lunged. In one swift move he filled me, paused, and then moved to the ancient movement of love and pleasure. I wrapped my legs around his waist and rode the wave with him. My gut tightened. I burned like a fuse racing to the explosive. Leaving rational thought behind, I lived in the moment.

Detonation! I came hard. Spasm after spasm ripped through me. I cried out, tightened my legs, lifted my hips off the bed, and let the motion carry me to whatever Nirvana awaited. Then with an unintelligible shout, Colin lunged deep. His release pulsated. My dying orgasm rejuvenated before finally dissipating.

Groaning, I let my legs relax. My arms flopped to the mattress. He rolled off to the side. Neither of us said a word. I couldn't if I'd wanted to. I was nearly breathless and sucked in huge gulps of air.

Several minutes passed while my vital signs returned to normal. His hand found mine and squeezed.

"Holy crap," I said between breaths.

"Yeah," he replied. His words also had a breathy quality.

"And here I thought you didn't like me."

He gasped a partial chuckle and raised my hand to his lips. "I always liked you. I just hated watching you waste your life. This past week has shown a whole different woman. You've been helping me investigate and you've taken some action on your future, perhaps a real career."

"I feel like a different person, too. Suddenly, my old friends seem—I don't know—useless."

Colin got up and disappeared into the bathroom. I lay satiated and thinking about what I'd said. I hadn't seen any of my so-called friends since Ross's death. And the strange thing was how I didn't miss them. Not one bit. In fact, if one of them were to call with an invite, I'd decline. I'd make up some excuse and do... *Do what?* I didn't know, but it had to be better than bumming around on Beale Street or drinking myself senseless.

Colin returned to the bedroom. I'd been too excited earlier to appreciate his well-toned body. Not quite six-pack abs and no bulging biceps, but just a nice body— the kind a girl could get used to in a flash. His erection had not completely withered.

He crawled into bed, and then leaned over to kiss me.

"Miss me?"

In a swift move, I pushed him onto his back and straddled his hips.

"Yeah, what took so long?" I let my lips play with his chin and neck.

He grinned and caressed my shoulders. "Oh, this

and that."

"Well, I want more of this." I kissed him, then gently squeezed his rapidly hardening penis. "And a lot more of that."

His hands moved down to the small of my back. I squirmed. His erection hardened more. He laughed outright.

"I think I can oblige."

I kissed him hard on the mouth again. The night was just beginning.

****

I awoke the next morning to an empty bed. The sheets still held warmth telling me Colin hadn't been up for long. Stretching, I groaned a happy groan. We'd made love several times throughout the night before finally sleeping. I hadn't had this much sex in a long while. Never, in fact. I may have led a dissipated lifestyle, but chose my bed partners with discrimination. One-night stands weren't my thing. I didn't see them being Colin's either.

I wonder where this takes us. I had no answer.

Tossing back the covers, I sat on the edge of the bed. My clothing from the night before lay folded on the dresser. After a quick shower, I dressed and ambled down the hallway. The sounds of pots and pans, along with the smells of coffee and bacon frying, led me into the kitchen.

"Good morning," Colin said with a smile. "Pour yourself a cup of coffee and have a seat. Sleep well?"

"When I finally got around to sleeping." I picked up a mug next to the coffee pot and poured, then doctored it with sweetener and cream. A clock on the wall read eight forty-five.

"How do you like your eggs?"

"Any way you want to make them." I took a seat at the kitchen table and sipped. It figured he'd make perfect coffee. I had high hopes for the breakfast.

The silence stretched as that awkward time after spending the night with a man lengthened. Don't we have anything to say to one another? I finally spoke.

"So, think Mother missed us last night?"

"No. She was probably vamping Jerricus."

"Wouldn't doubt it."

He turned the bacon and cracked the eggs into a bowl. Once again quiet descended.

"Uh, Colin…"

"Hilary…"

We'd spoken at the same time. Colin laughed.

"It's kind of awkward, isn't it?" he said.

"Yeah. You having regrets?"

He looked over, his gaze soft. "No, no regrets. How about you?"

I shook my head. "None whatsoever. So, where do we go from here?"

"I don't know, but one fabulous night in bed does not make a relationship. Those take time."

"Do we have time?"

"Maybe. Let's take it slow for now."

"All right. I guess it's hard to build on anything with me being a suspect in Ross's death. When this is over, we can talk."

"I agree." He laid the bacon on a paper towel to drain, and slid the eggs into another slick coated pan. "Sunny side up or over easy?"

"Up and staring at me. If you're going to fry them, why put them in a bowl first?"

"Do you know how many times I've burned my fingers trying to get bits of egg shells out of a hot frying pan? Much easier to remove them from a bowl."

I sipped my coffee as he arranged the food on the plates. What he said made sense—about both the eggs and us. Ross Patterson, even in death, hung in the air like an old shirt on a clothesline. Until the killer was found, any type of relationship had to hit the back burner.

He set my plate in front of me and took a seat. I nibbled on the bacon. Not too soft, not too crisp. The eggs ran just the way I liked them and the butter melted into the toast. I didn't even bother with the jam.

"You know, you could give Effie a run for her money."

"I can make breakfast. I'm not so hot with dinners that require any more than four ingredients."

"That puts you way ahead of me. I can barely boil water."

"Guess that's how you stay so thin."

"Too thin?"

He grinned. "No, sexy thin."

Warmth spread throughout my body. His grin faded. He lowered his gaze to his plate. I resumed eating, too.

He said to take it slow. He's right. Focus on something else.

"So, did I hear you right last night? Bonnie and Sam are coming over this morning?"

"At ten—at least Bonnie is. I want to tackle her about Joey Lazarus."

"I think Sam knew his wife owed big time."

"It might explain why he was in the house the other

night."

"If Ross recorded everyone, then Bonnie must be on it. Maybe Lazarus, too."

"Could be. At least his name might be mentioned."

"I know I said I'd stay out of the way, but I think I'd like to sit in on this."

He sighed. "I guess it can't hurt, but she won't like it."

I helped with the clean up, poured another cup of coffee, and settled on the sofa to wait. The doorbell rang a few minutes early. Colin opened the door. Bonnie walked in alone.

"Where's Sam?" he asked.

"I...I'm not sure. I couldn't get a hold of him. He packed up and left night before last." She turned and saw me. "What the hell are you doing here?"

I said nothing, but lifted the cup to my lips.

"She's here, because I want her here," Colin said. "Would you like a cup of coffee?"

"Yeah, that sounds good." Her posture was ramrod straight and her nervous glances around the room suggested she was anything but comfortable. Her fingers plucked at a button on her jacket.

"I'll get it," I said, rising. "Cream? Sugar?"

"Black."

"Have a seat, Bonnie," he said.

I poured a mug and returned, setting it on the coffee table in front of her chair. She picked it up with shaking hands and sipped.

"What's this all about, Colin? Why do you want to see me?"

"Had a long chat last night with an old friend of yours—Joey Lazarus."

215

She jerked. Coffee slopped over the rim and splashed onto her slacks. She wiped it away with an unsteady hand and set the mug on the table with a sharp clink.

"Who?"

"Joey Lazarus. He's a loan shark, amongst other things. He was also one of Ross's clients."

"I…I have no idea who that is."

"Of course you do, Bonnie. You borrowed a whole buttload of money from him," I said.

She shot me a hate filled glance. "I'm not saying a goddamned thing with you here."

"Let me handle this, Hilary." His gaze never wavered from his aunt's face. "She's right. You borrowed a lot of money. He wants it back—with interest."

"Why should I tell you anything?"

"You can either tell me or the cops. Your choice."

Colin spent the next few minutes telling Bonnie about our talk with Lazarus and our speculations about her asking Ross to pay him off. For once, I kept silent.

When he finished, a sick look came over her face, but she said nothing.

"The other night Sam told me he broke in hoping to find a recorder. Did you know Ross recorded his visits from family members?"

"Not until the other day. We were at Ian's planning the memorial service when Ian mentioned it. We all thought it was a sleazy thing to do."

"So, you suspected your conversation with him about your gambling was on it."

She nodded and bit her lip. "Look, Colin, I was at loose ends when Sam and I split. One night I went down to Tunica. Sam and I know the casino manager at Good Times. We'd been there often over the years. At any rate, I signed a couple of markers. When it came time to cover them, I wrote a check. No big deal— then."

She picked up her cup and stared into the dark liquid before gulping.

He paused before speaking. "Only it turned into a big deal."

She nodded. "Every few months turned into every few weeks. By the time Sam and I reconciled, I was having problems paying. Sam was furious and told me my gambling days were over. He just about stripped our savings to pay Lazarus, but couldn't cover everything I owed."

"But you continued gambling, I take it," Colin said with a frown.

"I signed more markers, lost big, and knew I was in trouble. Sam would leave me again and regardless of what you think," she glared at me, "I do love him."

"How did you know to contact Joey Lazarus?" I asked.

"I... I asked a friend—a gambling buddy—if he knew of someone who could loan me money without asking a lot of questions. He gave me Joey's name."

"And Joey was only too happy to oblige," Colin said. "I'm surprised he gave you that much money."

"He didn't. The original loan was for about five thousand. Sam's reputation as a local wheeler and dealer helped. Plus, I threw Ross's name out. Didn't know until later, he had been a client. When I had problems paying the full amount, he added enormous interest. The price tag skyrocketed. Then, he called to say he wanted the money by Monday morning or else. I was scared to death of the 'or else', so I went to Ross."

"Who turned you down," he said.

Bonnie nodded. "Called me a fool and said he wouldn't pay for fools. I begged, but he just laughed." She broke down in tears. "The son of a bitch just laughed!"

She rooted in her purse for a tissue and took a moment to pull herself together.

"Aunt Bonnie, I have to ask, did you kill him?"

"No! I swear it! I didn't kill him! I told Sam the truth. He was livid. The next day he went around to every banker and friend he could to try and swing a loan. He made up a story about a new business venture or something, but money's tight. No one was interested. Friday night we had one hell of a fight. Said he'd had it. He was leaving and I was on my own. He wouldn't even talk to Ross for me. Then on Saturday morning, we got the call from Ian about Ross's death."

"And your troubles were over," I murmured.

She looked at me with a curled lip. "So were yours, and your mother's."

"Meanwhile, Lazarus still wants his money," Colin said.

"I called him as soon as Jim Price read the will. Told him I could get him what I owed, as soon as the will went through probate."

"And he agreed?"

"Only with interest, of course. So, on Monday, I called our stockbroker and cleaned out what Sam hadn't already. I took it in cash and paid off most of what I owe Lazarus. There's only about five grand left to cover the original loan."

"Plus interest," Colin stated. "Wait here. I'll be right back."

He disappeared down the hall leaving a weepy Bonnie and me alone.

"You must be getting a kick out of this," she said. "I suppose you can't wait to tell Priscilla."

"I'm not getting a kick out of anything and why should I tell Mother? Funny, but for years I've loathed you. Your snide remarks and obvious disdain had no basis in anything except that it put two more people ahead of you in line for Ross's money. Oddly enough, I don't feel loathing right now, but pity. And to be honest, you're not really worth that."

I rose and walked over to the fireplace, my back to her. She said nothing, but sniffed repeatedly. She may have denied killing Ross, but I placed her at the top of the suspect list anyway.

Colin returned. I faced him. He handed her a slip of paper.

"Here's a check to cover the remainder of the debt. Take it to Lazarus immediately. Tell him I said the debt is paid in full—no more interest."

She accepted the check with shaking fingers. "What if he says no?"

"He won't. He's a businessman."

"Th...thank you, Colin. I promise to pay you back as soon as I can." She put the check in her purse and rose. "Are...are you going to tell the police?"

"If they have the recorder, they already know and are investigating."

"And the rest of the family?" She shot a look at me.

"They won't hear about this from me or from

Hilary."

She nodded and left the house.

"That was generous of you," I commented.

He rubbed his forehead. "Sam's my uncle. She's family. I can't let her stay in the clutches of a piece of shit like Joey Lazarus."

"More coffee?"

"No thanks."

I gathered up the cups and took them into the kitchen when another thought popped into my head. I returned to the living room. Colin stood in front of the large picture window overlooking the pool.

"Do you think she could have killed Ross?"

"She's got one hell of a motive. So does Sam."

"They may have a motive for killing Ross, but where's the motive for killing Don Merrick? Colin, we may have two murderers."

Chapter Sixteen

I followed Mother and Colin down the center aisle of the church as they made their way to the front pew for Ross's memorial service. The place was about three-quarters full. Ian and Sam had decided to scrap any type of viewing at the funeral home. Too many people, not to mention media, would fill the place to overflowing, so this was it. They made a wise decision. News vans, reporters, and photographers had jammed the sidewalk outside. The click, click, click of cameras had almost deafened me. Nothing like the murder of a wealthy, socially connected, controversial attorney to bring out the best of the worst.

I had to hand it to Mother; she looked great and acted the part of a grieving widow. She clung to Colin's arm like a lifeline. Her hesitant walk suggested uncertainty on how she'd survive without Ross. The occasional tear, wiped away with a delicate hankie, was a nice touch. She'd taken my advice about attire. The navy blue suit with a cream-colored silk blouse spelled taste, and while she eschewed any kind of veil, she did manage a large navy blue, wide brimmed hat.

I wore a fitted, sapphire blue dress—very demure for me.

Mother slid into the pew first, followed by Colin, and then me. Ian and Elaine with their two children plus Sam, Bonnie, and their brood occupied the pew on the opposite side of the aisle.

Neither Bonnie nor Sam had said anything to us. I hadn't expected them to be chatty. Colin reported that his check had been deposited this morning. I assumed Joey Lazarus already had the money in his hot little hand.

Ross's casket, solid mahogany with brass trim, sat in front of the altar, a huge arrangement of red roses blanketing the closed lid. At precisely one o'clock, the minister walked to the podium.

He gave the usual spiel about what a great man Ross Patterson was and how he had lived to serve his fellow man.

I wanted to throw up at the hypocrisy.

Next came a succession of eulogies. Ian spoke for the family. Jim Price made a speech covering the law profession. Even a few of Ross's more respectable clients got into the act with words of gratitude and praise.

I let my attention wander. Colin and I had spent most of yesterday going over Ross's files again, searching for someone who wanted Don Merrick dead. I let part of the conversation replay in my head.

"My uncle dealt with several drug distributors. Merrick was small potatoes selling to friends. He sees your computer screen and the jump drive plugged into it."

"Only I come back into the room before he can do anything."

"Maybe he recognizes a name or the significance of what he's seeing and makes a call to a third party."

"Like Joey Lazarus?"

"Last week, I'd have said no. Now, I'm not so

sure."

"Then he returns to my place to get the jump drive. Except I've taken it and my laptop with me to Ross's. The third party decides Don is a liability and nails him with my letter opener."

He'd nodded with a worried look on his face.

Organ music welled, bringing me out of my thoughts. As we walked back down the aisle, I nodded to people I knew, but didn't speak. I spotted Jerricus Monroe a couple of pews behind us. Keisha, the former maid, was near the middle of the church. I spied Carlotta, accompanied by the large man I'd seen in the club the other night. They sat not far from a side entrance. My final nod was reserved for Detectives Parker and Hamilton. Their presence reminded me that I still hadn't informed them about the jump drive.

We filed into the limo waiting at the curb for the trip to the cemetery. Not everyone would follow, just like not all were invited to the house afterward for refreshments.

The graveside service was mercifully short. A few words about ashes and dust, a few prayers, and the whole affair ended. Would anybody bother to come visit the grave? Mother? No. Me? No. Any of the family? I doubted it. In a few years, the name Ross Patterson would bring blank looks to the faces of those who heard it.

As I headed back to the car, Jim Price walked across the grass and stopped at a tombstone not far away. He bowed his head as if in prayer, and then bent to place something on the ground before leaving. I didn't see his face, but was curious, so broke from the procession. Picking my way around tombstones, I finally stopped at a gravesite. Two single red roses lay at the base of a couple of markers.

Caroline Rose Price was the name on one, and the dates indicated she had died a year ago at the age of nineteen. Jim's daughter?

How sad to lose a child. It goes against the natural order of things. Parents aren't supposed to outlive their children.

The second marker was for Martha Grimes Price. The dates indicated she was close to Jim's age and had passed away five months ago. His wife?

He'd lost both his wife and a child? And I think I have problems.

"Hilary, come on. We need to get back to the house," Mother called out in an impatient tone.

I turned and walked quickly back. Within a few seconds, we were once again on our way home.

In the limo, Mother jerked off her hat. "Thank God, that's over!"

"We still have to get through the crowd at the reception," Colin said.

"I'm sure Mother will retire to be alone with her grief," I replied.

Mother sent me a stern look. "Don't be nasty, Hilary. I will mingle and thank people for attending. *Then* I'll retire to my room."

At the house, the guests arrived to drink, eat, and discuss anything except the recently departed. Mother immediately latched on to Jerricus. Effie and a crew of servers circulated with trays of noshes. A bar had been set up in the dining room. The list had been kept short, so I was surprised to see Parker and Hamilton walk in the front door.

"Why are they here?" I asked Colin.

"Because they're the police. They will mingle, talk to people, and see if they can learn any new information."

"It's been over a week. I'd have to say they don't have much to go on."

"My uncle was a very high profile person. They don't want to make a mistake that can be challenged in court."

"I wonder if now is a good time to mention the jump drive or just to ignore its existence."

"Ignoring it might not be the way to go. They'll be annoyed, but unlikely to cause a fuss—at least for the moment."

"Are you going to tell them about Bonnie's Lazarus connection?"

"Yes. It's damning evidence. I'll go talk to them. Meet me in the study."

I set my drink on an end table and took a moment to rehearse what I'd say to them. I hoped they bought my explanation. After giving Colin a chance to tell them about Bonnie, I knocked on the study door and entered. Colin sat behind the desk. The detectives occupied two chairs in front of it.

"So you gave her the money?" Detective Parker said as he wrote in a notebook.

"Yes, I wanted her out from under her debts, especially to someone like Joey Lazarus. She's family."

"Thank you, Mr. Blackwood," Detective Hamilton said. "We'll ask that she come in to tell us the facts in her own words. We also saw a report of an intruder here a few nights ago. Turns out to have been Mr. Sam Patterson. We may want to talk to him, too." She looked at me with that damned smile on her face. "Nice to see you again, Miss Watson."

Yeah, right.

"Thank you for coming. I know this is in the line of duty, but we do appreciate it. By the way, there's something you should know." I explained about the jump drive.

"When did you receive this?" Detective Hamilton demanded.

"I went back to my house a couple of times to retrieve mail and such. I think I found it last Wednesday or Thursday. I'm not sure."

"Did you read what's on it?" Parker asked.

"No."

Hamilton's eyebrows rose. "You received a jump drive from a dead man—your stepfather—and didn't plug it in?"

I got her point. It wasn't logical *not* to have read it.

"Okay, yes, I did. They're just old case files. I only read one or two, and then stopped. It was too boring."

"And you didn't turn it over to us immediately?" she asked in a hard tone, the smile gone.

"Well, they are case files, and I'm not sure if the attorney-client privilege covers it. I meant to call you, but things have been hectic around here the last few days."

"Yes, we saw another report regarding your accident down near Hernando the other night," Parker said. "Do you still have the envelope the jump drive came in?"

"No, I'm sorry. I tossed it. I didn't think it was important."

Hamilton's gaze bored into me, but I didn't look

away. I stared straight back at her. Innocent people and those telling the truth do that, don't they?

"Why would he send a jump drive full of case notes to you?" she asked.

I shrugged. "I have no idea. Maybe he didn't want to keep sensitive material in the house. He *had* signed a book deal, you know. Perhaps he was afraid someone would come looking for it, and he wanted it somewhere safe—like with me."

Hamilton's smile was making me sweat. I was giving too much information.

Apparently, Colin agreed. He spoke up.

"And my uncle isn't here to tell us the reasoning behind his actions."

"No, he isn't," Parker replied. He shoved his notebook into his pocket and rose. "We need to see that jump drive."

"Not without a court order," Colin replied.

Hamilton, her smile back in place, also rose. "We'll do that and be in touch."

Call it the smart ass in me, but I couldn't resist asking, "How is the investigation going?"

Her smile widened. "Coming along nicely. Don't worry, we'll find the killer."

When they left, I collapsed in a chair. "Not as bad as I thought it would be. What happens now?"

"They may pull you in for more questions, but my guess is they'll have their hands full trying to get that court order. Might be a good idea to hand it over to Jerricus or Jim. Let them deal with the legal angle."

Someone knocked discreetly on the door.

"Come in," Colin called out.

Effie poked her head in. "Some of the guests are

leaving. Your Mother requested an early dinner tonight. Is six satisfactory?"

"That's fine, Effie."

"You had to deal with this reception and make dinner?" I asked. "That's a lot of work."

"Not too bad, miss. I had the reception catered, and dinner will be a simple chicken dish. It'll mostly just be cleaning up."

"Effie, before you go, I'd like to ask a question," Colin said.

"Yes, sir?"

"The week before my uncle died, you said family members had been to see him, some more than once over the last couple of weeks."

"Yes, sir, that's right. Mr. Sam and Mr. Rogers were in about a week before the party. Mrs. Elaine came on Monday morning, I believe, and Mrs. Bonnie on Thursday."

"I don't suppose you heard what they talked about, did you?"

She hesitated, and then sighed. "I wasn't eavesdropping, mind you. I was cleaning the living room. Mrs. Elaine didn't bother to close the door and I heard her say Mr. Patterson was mean not to give her husband the money. Something about how he'd miss out on a good development deal if he couldn't raise it. I was in the library when Mrs. Bonnie came. I didn't hear what went on, but she left crying."

"Did you hear what Ian and Sam wanted, too?" he asked.

She shook her head. "No sir, but Keisha may have. She's the one who let them in. I was busy with lunch both days."

"Thank you, Effie, you've been a great help."

She nodded and left the room.

Colin tapped a pencil on the desk. "I'll bet both Ian and Sam came asking for money and were turned down. Elaine showed up to ask for a change of heart. We know why Bonnie was here, but my guess is Sam needed money to get out from under some of his business debt."

"He didn't know Bonnie's little problem was still a problem until later. Have you talked to him yet?"

"No. I'll pull him aside in a while. I'll also talk to Keisha tomorrow and see if she overheard any conversations."

He rose and came around the desk to pull me out of the chair and into his arms. He kissed me hard.

"Been wanting to do that all day."

I snaked my arms around his neck. "So why didn't you?"

"Too many damned people, including your mother."

I laughed and kissed him back.

A moment later, he stepped away. "And speaking of people, we'd better get back out there and mingle."

"Mother's probably already gone upstairs."

"Only if Jerricus Monroe has left."

I laughed again and followed him out to the living room and the reception. I couldn't find either Jerricus or Mother. *Please tell me she didn't have the bad taste to leave with him—or to take him upstairs.*

For the next two hours we chatted and mingled with the mourners, if you could call them that. The whole affair resembled a cocktail party, not an after-funeral get together. Most of the people were business acquaintances with a few judges and political figures added in. Gradually, the crowd thinned. I saw Colin tap Sam on the shoulder and speak to him. Sam nodded and they walked toward the study.

I played hostess as the last of the mourners left, shaking hands and thanking them for coming.

Colin and Sam exited the study as the rest of us all beat a fast retreat into the den. Neither Sam and Bonnie's nor Ian and Elaine's children were present, thank God. I wasn't sure I could deal with Bonnie's offspring.

"Thank goodness this day is over," Elaine murmured, sipping a glass of scotch.

"Amen," Sam echoed. "I noticed those detectives were here. Who invited them?"

"I imagine they invited themselves," Colin replied, pouring the two of us a drink. He gave them the same reason he'd told me.

I was dying to ask him what Sam had to say, but kept my mouth shut.

"They don't honestly think one of us did it, do they?" Elaine asked in a huffy tone.

Bonnie didn't make eye contact with anyone, but stared into her Bloody Mary.

"From what I understand, in situations like this, the family is always at the top of the suspect list," Ian added. "Right, Colin?"

"They'll check us all out first."

"I'll bet they never find out who did it," Elaine offered.

"You'd better hope they do," I told her. "Otherwise, we'll all have a cloud hanging over us. Our friends will always wonder if one of us got away with murder."

"When's dinner?" Sam asked abruptly.

"Six," I said.

"It's almost that now. Where's Priscilla?"

"I'm here," Mother said from the doorway.

Her suit had been replaced with a pair of designer jeans, an expensive red silk top, and red, medium heeled, peep-toed Jimmy Choos. The mourning period was decidedly over.

Bonnie, looking slightly dumpy in an ill-fitting black dress, glared, but said nothing.

Mother accepted a drink from Colin and stood next to him. "I thought the service was excellent. Very tasteful. Thank you for making the arrangements, Ian."

The next few minutes found the conversation somewhat stilted until finally Effie announced dinner. Dinner wasn't any better, and even though the food was up to its usual standards, I couldn't wait for it to be over and for all of them to leave. I was exhausted.

Finally, by eight o'clock, the house was empty. Mother had gone up to do whatever it was she did by herself, while Colin and I had a nightcap in the den. He poured us each a small brandy, then held the bottle in his hand.

"You know who deserves a little bit of this? Effie. Come on."

I followed him to the kitchen. Effie stood at the sink washing dishes too delicate for the dishwasher.

"Effie, it's been a long day."

She turned, wiped her hands on a towel, and nodded. "Yes, Mr. Colin, it surely has."

"Did anyone even bother to say thank you?" I asked.

"I don't need thanks, miss. It's my job."

"Have a seat Effie. You've done more than your fair share of work." He lifted the bottle. "How about a spot of brandy?"

"Oh, I don't know sir. I'm not real good with liquor."

I got a glass out of the cupboard. "Oh, one won't hurt. And Colin's right. You've earned a moment to relax."

She hesitated. "Well, maybe just a tiny bit."

Colin poured. He and I sipped, but Effie downed a good portion, and then coughed.

"Oh my goodness. That burned all the way down!"

"Sip it," he cautioned.

She obeyed, and then smiled.

"So, how are the plans for your niece's wedding coming along?" I asked.

"Oh, just fine, miss." She sighed and took a larger sip. "I do worry about Passy though. She's so young, but her fiancé, Bobby Lee, is a nice man. He'll take good care of her. He's got a fine job at one of those home improvement stores over in Senatobia and is renting a nice house nearby close to her family. I just wish she'd waited a bit longer afore tying the knot."

"I'm sure they'll do fine," Colin said.

Effie drank again, blinked, and held out the glass. "Mind refreshing that? This isn't so bad once you get used to it."

I refrained from chuckling as Colin added more brandy to the tiny bit remaining in the glass.

"I hope you're right, Mr. Colin." She heaved a sigh. "Young folk today always seem in a hurry."

"That's the way it goes sometimes," I told her.

"There's no accounting for love."

"Now, miss, you're exactly right. That's the way it was with my dearly departed first husband, the late Mr. Smith. Ah, what a man. Now, don't get me wrong. Mr. Tolliver was a good man, but not quite up there with my Rafe." She drank again with a far away look in her eyes. "Oh yes, he was something else. Not real good looking, mind you, but Lordy could he ever charm the birds outta the trees. It ran in the family. Why his brother, Jackson did the same thing to my oldest sister at the same time Rafe was courting me. Had us a double wedding, we did. I do miss those boys. Been gone close to thirty years now. Drowned, both of 'em."

"Good heavens, Effie. How did that happen?" I'd never really thought of Effie as having a life outside of this house.

"Fishing on Lake Sardis. They went out in a rowboat along with a whole lot of bait and a case of beer. Don't really know what happened. Police came knocking on the door and said the boat musta overturned and they drowned. Neither one of 'em knew how to swim."

"No life jackets?" Colin asked.

"Nary a one."

Drinking, boating, no lifejackets, and not knowing how to swim was a recipe for disaster.

"That wasn't very wise," I commented trying to be diplomatic.

"I said they was charming, not smart." She downed the last of her brandy, and then hiccupped. "Oh, dear, I think maybe I've had enough."

Colin smiled and removed the glass from her hand. She rose and walked back to the sink.

"Thank you kindly for the little pick me up. Sorry if I bored you with my life story."

"You didn't bore us at all," he reassured her.

"Now, why don't you two go on and do whatever you need to do. I'll be done here real soon."

"I'll call you a cab when you're ready to leave," Colin said.

"No need, Mr. Colin. I'm fine."

We left Effie to finish cleaning up and returned to the den.

"So what did Sam have to say?"

"He'd known about Bonnie's gambling and her paying off the casinos the first time. But he claims to have had no knowledge about Joey Lazarus or the large sum she owed this time around until Thursday. That's why he left. Matches what she told us. And we already know that's why he was here the other night."

My mind was unsettled and I had the feeling something was about to pop. Detective Hamilton's coy remark about the investigation "coming along" sounded slightly ominous. Either the detectives had nothing, or something explosive.

Either way, it wasn't going to be good news for me. Nothing meant the family might never get out from under the shadow of being suspects. Something explosive suggested an arrest—but of whom?

Chapter Seventeen

Colin called me into the study shortly after breakfast the next morning.

"Let me have the CD you burned of Ross's files."

"Why?"

"If the police do get that court order, they'll suspect we may have copied it. I'll take the CD to my place, transfer it back to an old jump and toss it into a desk drawer."

"I think I'll hand the original jump drive over to Jerricus."

"Sound idea. Now, let me have the CD."

I ran upstairs, ejected it from my computer, and handed it over. "Why do you want to transfer it?"

"I've been thinking. Parker and Hamilton were on a mission here yesterday. They were talking, listening, and watching. They may be back, and this time with a search warrant."

My stomach clenched. "A search warrant? Why?"

"They've pulled both you and your mother in twice. And your mother's alibi is shaky. Plus, they aren't sharing information like they did earlier. It's just a feeling I have."

Funny he should have the same reaction I'd had last night.

"What's on our agenda for today?" I asked.

"I have a court appearance at nine-thirty. I'll stop

by the house first, make the transfer, and get rid of the CDs. This afternoon, I'll talk to Keisha."

"Anything I can do to help? I'd like to hear what she has to say."

He shook his head. "Not today."

"I suppose I can find something to do. Maybe go over those hate letters again." A sudden thought hit me. "Whoa, if the cops do show up with a search warrant, will they confiscate those?"

"It's possible. I'll take them home with me, too."

"If I want to read them, I'll need a key to get in, won't I?" I kept my voice neutral, but gave him a look I hoped was full of promise for better things to come.

He grinned, pulled out his key ring, and unhitched a key, tossing it to me.

"My spare."

I caught it in mid-air, happy he'd handed it over so freely. "I might wander over after lunch. I think we should both go over them again. That could lead to a long evening. Perhaps we should order in if it's going to go on into the night."

He rose to kiss me long and hard. "I'm partial to pepperoni pizza and beer."

"Regular or thin crust?" I asked, nibbling on his ear.

"Regular." His hands moved to squeeze my rear end.

"Hmmm. A man after my heart." My voice took on a breathy quality.

Colin chuckled, swatted my ass, and backed off, reaching for his briefcase.

"I'll see you this afternoon."

He set his case on top of the box of letters, hefted

it, and left.

I informed Effie neither Colin nor I would be in for dinner, then headed upstairs. I had no idea how I'd pass the time this morning. I attached the key to my key ring and tossed it into my purse. *I wonder if this is the start of something important in my life. Might not be a bad idea.*

The first order of business was to contact Jerricus Monroe. He wasn't available, but I discussed the matter with his secretary who advised me to get the jump drive to the office ASAP. I promised to do so.

Yesterday had been hectic. I hadn't checked my e-mail, Facebook, and Twitter pages in over twenty-four hours. *Might as well catch up.*

I tweeted about the funeral and added several more about my day so far. Bored, I sat back and stared at the computer screen. I just wasn't into Twitter all that much. *Who the hell cares what I had for breakfast?* And I certainly didn't care that one of my vapid followers broke a nail just before a big event. Nor did I give a shit about another friend's golf score.

I moved on to Facebook. I posted about the funeral, scrolled down previous postings from friends, made a few comments, reposted some funny cartoons and sayings, then logged off. I was bored with this also. That left e-mail.

Between social media and texting, my e-mails had diminished in the last couple of years, so I didn't expect much. The third e-mail from the bottom, however, caught my eye. It was from the Lighthouse School of Design and had come through at eleven-thirty yesterday morning. They asked if I could come in at my earliest convenience for a short interview and to bring any portfolio I might have.

They'd actually answered! My heart beat faster. Did this mean I'd been accepted? *No, silly, it means they want to talk to you and see what kind of work you've done.*

I replied immediately that I could be there by noon today. The portfolio part presented a problem. I didn't have one, so took photos of my room and Ross's study with my cell phone. I also included the den. I hadn't actually decorated that room, but if I had, I'd have done it in the same style. It was just a tad dishonest, but my credentials were slim and I needed as many as I could get.

I printed out the pictures and put them in a manila folder. It might not be professional, but would have to do. I next grabbed a couple of pieces of copy paper and did a few sketches—one a redo of my room, another of the master suite, and one each of the living and dining rooms. I hoped they didn't look amateurish or rushed. By the time I'd finished, it was after ten. Placing them in the folder, I hurried to take a shower and dress.

I scanned my closet. Most of what I had here was casual. Would the powers that be expect to see an applicant in typical artists attire—whatever that was— or something more refined—whatever *that* was? Refined seemed to be the best choice, so I chose to wear the dress I'd had on yesterday. I'd only worn it a few hours. Some wrinkles here and there, but maybe Effie could iron them out for me. I took the dress down, told her I wouldn't be in for lunch either, and then paced in my room.

What kind of questions will they ask? Will they like my work? Am I too old to fit in with other students?

Can I do this? Do I have the desire and determination to see this venture through to the end?

The last two thoughts were the most important. I just didn't know.

Effie brought my dress back. I donned it, fixed my hair, and did my make-up. As an afterthought, I packed up my laptop. If I was going to Colin's, I might need it. Then taking a deep breath, I walked out of the house, my meager portfolio held in a tight fist.

****

I opened the front door to Colin's house with shaking fingers. It was almost four o'clock. Lacking an appointment, I'd had to wait at the school. Each passing minute had increased my anxiety making me cross and uncross my legs, fidgeting, and trying to remain patient. Patience is not one of my virtues.

Finally, I was shown to the office of some administrative person and asked to fill out yet another form. The interview itself was ordinary—at least I assumed it was ordinary since I'd never had an interview about anything before—dealing with any past experience in the field, my college degree, and why I wanted to be an interior designer. My interrogator, a short, thin man named MacCumber with a really bad comb over and rimless glasses, had looked at the photos and sketches, but said nothing substantial other than, "Yes, yes, very nice."

The whole thing had lasted a lousy thirty-five minutes. I had no idea if I'd impressed the man or not. I left the portfolio, then drove to a small bistro where I ate a seafood salad and downed a couple of glasses of wine. The salad was tasty, but the wine helped put my nerves to rest. Lastly, I made the trip downtown to drop off the jump drive at Jerricus's office. At least that was now out of my possession. Hamilton and Parker could battle *him* for it.

At Colin's, I decided the best thing to do was keep busy. The box of letters and another of old case files was sitting on the kitchen table. I'd read most of the letters, but not these particular files. I poured a glass of iced tea, sat, and picked a file out of the box.

"*The State vs. Madison*," I read out loud. "That sounds like a hot one."

It wasn't. The file dealt with a woman accused of public intoxication. Public intoxication? Ross? This wasn't a big bucks type of case. I reread the defendant's name.

"Jacqueline Jefferies Madison," I muttered. "Who the hell is she and why would Ross defend her?"

I picked another file out of the box—*The State vs. Boswell*. Richard David Boswell had been arrested for DUI, reckless driving, and resisting an officer.

This name rang a bell, but damned if I could come up with why. It finally occurred to me to check the dates on the files. I flipped through the folders. All were at least fifteen years old.

The front door slamming told me Colin had arrived.

"Hilary? You here?"

"In the kitchen." I rose, retrieved a glass from the cupboard, and poured him some iced tea.

"Ah, thanks, just what I needed," he said gulping half of it before leaning over to kiss me. "You're all dressed up."

I gave him the news about the school and my interview. "I have no clue what's next. They said they'd be in touch."

"Don't sweat it. You'll get in."

I appreciated his encouragement. Maybe I did impress Mr. MacCumber. *Keep thinking that way. Positive thoughts never hurt.*

"How was your day in court?"

He kissed me again. "Let me get out of this suit and I'll tell you."

I followed him back to the bedroom, admiring his body as he shed his clothes. He caught me staring and grinned. In a quick move, he grasped my hand and pulled me down onto the bed. My arms slid around his neck as he kissed me breathless.

"I think you're overdressed," he murmured.

His fingers found the zipper on the back and pulled. Within seconds I was naked. I pushed him onto his back, straddled his hips, and proceeded to nibble my way down his body. He returned the compliment. Heat surged throughout my body and that spring of desire coiled tighter. We didn't speak, but let our actions do the talking.

An hour later, we were back at the kitchen table. Colin had dressed in jeans and a t-shirt. I'd picked his shirt up of the floor and now sat sniffing the sleeves as I turned back the cuffs. It smelled of fabric softener—a fresh outdoors scent—and Colin.

He ordered a pizza, and then poured us each a glass of Chianti.

"So, Mr. Blackwood," I purred, still in satiated mode. "What did you testify about this morning?"

"A very nasty divorce case. The wife had the good sense to hire me. I got her husband on camera doing the deed at his girlfriend's house. You'd think they'd have had the sense to close the blinds."

I chuckled. "Did we think to do that an hour ago?"

"Nope, but then neither one of us has a reason to hide."

"Did you talk to Keisha?" I asked, taking a sip.

"She remembers Ian coming and asking for a loan. She was walking past the study and overheard Ross saying no. She doesn't recall him leaving or if he was upset.

"Sam, however, is another matter. She said he charged in demanding to see Ross, but before she could announce him, Sam stalked to the study and didn't bother to close the door as he yelled about what a cheapskate his older brother was and if he, meaning Ross, didn't give him the money, he stood to lose the house and other property in Mississippi. Keisha admits to listening from the hallway. They shouted so loud, it was hard not to hear."

"When did this happen?"

"About a week to a week and a half before his death."

"Wow, looks like a family member could have done it."

He nodded. "Means, motive, and opportunity. Ross would have let any of them in that night. The murder weapon though is still odd man out. I can't see the killer arguing with Ross, and then calmly walking into the kitchen for a frying pan to clobber him with."

"The killer could have slipped Xanax into Ross's drink, waited until he was groggy, and then grabbed the skillet."

"True, but why a frying pan? There were plenty of blunt objects in the study—the fireplace poker, several golf trophies, a couple of awards from the Bar Association and Memphis charitable organizations. Why go to the kitchen?"

He had me there. I couldn't think of one logical explanation, other than a cast iron skillet was the kind of thing a woman would use—a very strong woman. Those things were heavy. Maybe a man did kill Ross.

Colin glanced at the files on the table. "What are you reading?"

"Some of the files in the box. Did you read any of them?"

"A few. Most were old and didn't deal with anything relevant to the last decade or so. I put them aside to concentrate on more recent files. You're frowning. Why?"

"They don't make sense. Ross was a high-profile defense attorney. Why would he bother with a DUI or public intoxication?"

"My uncle was not always so high-profile. He began his career at a law firm in Nashville. That's where he and Jim met. When neither of them made partner, they split, came to Memphis and opened their own firm close to eighteen years ago. They did wills, trusts, and things like that for a while. About fifteen years ago, Ross branched out into criminal defense." He picked up one of the files, glanced at the name, and whistled softly. "Richard David Boswell."

"The name sounded kind of familiar to me, too. Do you know him?"

"Not him specifically, but Boswell is the name of a family that dominated Memphis politics over a decade or so ago. Most of them eventually ended up in jail on corruption charges." He rose and went into the living room, returning a few minutes later with his laptop, setting it on the table. "Let's see what we can find."

The minutes ticked by as he surfed the net. "As far as I can tell, no Boswell is left in jail. They served their time and are pursuing legitimate business, although most of it seems to be located off South Third Street on Brooks."

"As in titty bars?"

"And bars in general." He typed in more information and waited. The doorbell rang. "That's the pizza. It's already paid for. Just leave a tip and sign the tab."

What the delivery dude thought of a woman wearing a man's dress shirt that reached mid-thigh didn't concern me. I left a generous tip and carted the aromatic box back to the kitchen, setting it on the table. I grabbed a couple of paper plates and forks.

Colin was still at the computer. "Richard David Boswell was the oldest son of Reginald Boswell, former member of the Tennessee House of Representatives who was eventually nailed for taking bribes. Boswell has numerous arrests for DUI and such. He's now a partner in his uncle's establishment, The Hot Tamale Club." He slid a piece of pepperoni and mushroom pizza onto his plate and bit off a chunk. "Let's see what comes up on Jacqueline Madison.

I ate and sipped my wine as he once again searched.

"Here it is, Jacqueline Madison. She's the daughter of Henry Madison who just happens to own the Zanzibar and the Rumpus Room restaurants in East Memphis, plus a couple of other high end eateries in Moreland and Webster."

"I've eaten at Zanzibar."

"Miss Madison was sixteen at the time of this arrest. She'd partied a bit too hardy on Beale."

"But these people must have had their own lawyers. In the Boswell's case, they probably had him on call twenty-four seven. Why contact Ross?"

Colin finished his pizza and reached for another slice. "Ross and Jim had been partners for a few years. Ross wants to get into the criminal field. It's damned lucrative. So, he attends every Bar Association lunch and event he can, schmoozing his way around with the comment, 'If you're ever too busy to deal with the small stuff, remember me. I'll do it.' He gets his name out there and makes friends."

"And eventually, it pays off. But why keep the files so long?"

"You never know when a new blackmail opportunity will arise."

Colin's bitter words made me stare. Sometimes I forgot Ross had been a family member. I laid my hand on his arm.

"I'm sorry. Really, I am. You and Ross may not have had much in common, but he was your uncle."

He sighed. "When I first started in this business, a wise man told me to never investigate family—that sooner or later I'd find out things I'd rather not know."

I gathered up the folders and replaced them in the box. "Let's forget about these for a while. I'd like another crack at those 'I'm-gonna-get-you' letters. Maybe there's something we overlooked."

We spent the next hour reading letters and polishing off the pizza and wine. This time I took a more analytical perspective. I dismissed those who'd only written one letter as angry friends or relatives blowing off steam. The repeat offenders garnered most of my attention—with one exception—the badly spelled, lousy grammar-laden letter from the woman with the odd name.

"You know, this one really bothers me," I said.

"Which one?"

I tossed the sheet of cheap notebook paper over to him. "This one."

He picked it up and read. "Why does it bother you so much? According to this, Ross didn't even take the case."

"Maybe that's the motive. High-powered attorney refuses case because people can't pay. Defendant stuck with public defender. Defendant found guilty and is murdered in prison."

"I researched this. The people are dead, and it happened six or seven years ago. However, if it makes you happy, I'll dig deeper." He set the letter back on the table. "Ross's killer was someone he knew well enough to let in or a party crasher who hid until after everyone left. The crasher could have slipped into the study, doped the scotch, and waited. Which means somebody knew Ross's evening routine."

"Which leads us right back to family."

Colin closed a folder. "I'm tired of analyzing this stuff. Wanna watch a movie?"

I slipped out of my chair and stood behind him, my arms encircling his neck. I nibbled on his ear.

"Wanna fool around?"

He pushed the table back and pulled me into his lap where he proceeded to kiss the life out of me. Heat radiated from the pit of my stomach to the tips of my toes. Something hard, and growing harder, poked my rear end. Prospective pleasure made me throb in all the right places.

Then my phone rang.

"Shit," I muttered.

"Ignore it."

I took his advice and continued the kiss. The ringing finally stopped. A few seconds later, the "you've got mail" tone sang out. I ignored that, too.

Colin's hands worked the buttons open on the shirt, and then found my breasts. The heat and pleasure intensified. His fingers skimming over my skin sent shivers up and down my spine—the good kind of shivers that left me panting and wanting more.

His lips moved to my throat where he sucked at the delicate pulse point near my collarbone. I groaned and threaded my fingers through his hair.

"I think we need a bed," he murmured.

"Then let's go find one."

We stood and kissed some more. Then my damned phone rang again.

"Goddammit!" I picked the offending thing up from the counter. "Shit, it's Mother."

"Ignore her."

"If I do, she'll just keep calling. And why would she be calling me at almost eight o'clock at night?"

Exasperated at the interruption, I answered.

"Yes, Mother what is it?"

"Hilary, where are you? They're searching the house, poking into everything. I need you!"

Her wailing voice pushed all thoughts of sex out of my mind.

"Who's searching the house? What's going on?"

"The police! What do I do?"

I turned to Colin and relayed the information. He snatched the phone from my hand.

"Priscilla, call Jerricus immediately... Good. He'll be there as soon as he can. In the meantime, do not talk to the police. Offer no explanations about anything. We'll be there in ten minutes."

He hung up. "They finally issued a search warrant. Let's get over there."

I ran back to the bedroom and dressed in my own clothes. "Don't they have to have a reason to issue one of those?"

"It's called probable cause, and I'm afraid they may have it."

We arrived at Ross's to find several police cars in the driveway along with a couple of vans. The front door stood wide open. I rushed in to find Mother in the living room seated on the edge of the sofa. She leaped to her feet when I entered.

"Hilary! Thank God you're here. I don't know what to do."

"Is Jerricus here yet?" Colin asked.

"No. He said he'd be about twenty minutes."

He looked at one of the policemen standing in the doorway. "Who's in charge here?"

The officer jerked his chin to a man coming down the staircase. It was Detective Parker.

"Why the search warrant, Parker?"

"Hello, Blackwood. We need to take a closer look at things. New evidence has emerged."

"What new evidence?" I demanded.

Jerricus Monroe took that moment to stride into the foyer. He ignored the police and came straight to

Mother.

"Let me see the warrant." She handed it over to him. He read for a moment, then looked at her. "You haven't said anything, have you?"

"No. You told me not to and I haven't. Jerry, what's this all about? What do they expect to find? I resent strangers rooting through my lingerie."

She blinked tears from her eyes. For once they were real. Fear made my heart pound. I felt every slice of pizza and glass of wine I'd consumed churning in my stomach.

He turned to Detective Parker. "What's this all about?"

"We have new evidence that suggests your client might not be as truthful as it first seemed."

A uniformed officer came down the stairs with an object in a plastic baggie.

"Found this in the master bedroom. Xanax."

"I take it this is yours, Mrs. Patterson," Parker said holding the bag up for inspection.

"Of course, it is. Says so right on the bottle."

"Priscilla," Jerricus said in a stern tone.

Shut up, Mother.

"You take Xanax?"

Mother glared at the detective. "Why else would I have a prescription? Most of Moreland and half of Memphis is on Xanax."

"Mother!"

"Say no more," her attorney warned.

"I'd listen to my lawyer if I were you," Parker said, nodding to the cop standing near us.

He came over, turned Mother around and clasped her hands behind her back.

"Priscilla Patterson, you are under arrest for the murder of Ross Patterson. You have the right to remain silent."

Chapter Eighteen

I shifted on the hard wooden seat in the gallery of the courtroom. Colin sat next to me, his arms crossed over his chest. Mother's arraignment had been set for noon, but the court schedule ran late. The judge, the Honorable Winston Perry, took his own sweet time with procedures. It was almost three-thirty and so far, we'd had to endure a parade of criminals charged with everything from breaking-and-entering to assault with a deadly weapon.

I moved again, trying to find a comfortable position, crossed, then recrossed my legs, and played with the strap on my purse.

"Relax. Quit fidgeting," Colin said in a low voice.

"I can't help it," I whispered back. "I'm nervous and uncomfortable, not to mention worried. I haven't talked to Mother since they arrested her."

Last night had been one of the worst I'd ever spent. Colin and I had followed the cops, Mother, and Jerricus to the police station, but were denied access to her. Finally, her attorney had come out to tell us she was being taken to the Shelby County Women's Facility for the night. Arraignment was scheduled for the next day where bail, if any, would be set.

"Don't worry," Jerricus had assured me. "She'll spend an awkward night, but I'm sure that's all."

"But what made them arrest her?" I asked.

"I can't discuss that right now. Just know that this so-called new evidence is flimsy."

Colin leaned over to whisper, "My guess is this new evidence isn't so new to Jerricus. Your mother probably told him about it when she hired him."

We returned to Ross's where I had several good shots of vodka, and then did something I hadn't done since I was eight years old—I cried myself to sleep.

Colin had crawled into bed with me offering warm arms and words of comfort. They helped, but not as much as I wanted. Even Effie's comments at breakfast this morning didn't relieve my stress.

"Now, miss, don't you worry," she'd said in a soothing tone. "Your mother and Mr. Patterson may have had their difficulties of late, but Mrs. Patterson certainly wouldn't hit him over the head with my frying pan."

I shifted yet again on the bench and cast my gaze around the room. About half the seats were full. I had no idea if this was average for a Wednesday or not. Most of those seated looked slightly seedy and dressed like refugees. A woman weighing close to three hundred pounds slid onto the bench next to me. She smelled. I inched closer to Colin.

"For the love of God, how much longer," I muttered to him. "I wish they'd bring her out. She must be terrified."

"The wheels of justice grind slowly," he replied.

"I can't wait to get her out of here. I wonder what bail will be."

"Assuming the judge allows it," Colin commented.

"Why wouldn't he?" I asked.

"She's accused of murder. Bail is not necessarily a

given." He glanced at his watch.

The judge rapped the gavel. "If anyone in the gallery feels the urge to talk, please take it into the hallway. Next case."

I gulped and stared at the back of the bench in front of me.

A side door opened. Jerricus entered. I sat up straight and leaned forward, holding my breath. Mother was brought in by a female officer. I'd expected a trembling, frightened woman. Instead, she walked with a steady gait, her head held high, and a calm demeanor. She glanced into the gallery, and then took her place at a podium alongside her attorney. Dressed in a light blue jumpsuit, her hands were cuffed behind her, but no shackles were evident.

"Why is she handcuffed?" I whispered to Colin.

"The cops may have done a perp walk."

"A what?"

"They make the arrested person walk from the jail to the courthouse through a line of media hounds. The handcuffs show they mean business."

"That's barbaric!" My voice rose in indignation. I glanced toward the judge, but he paid no attention to me.

"Maybe, but it also shows the world an arrest has been made. Makes the cops look good. Remember, Ross was a brutally murdered, high profile corpse."

I turned my attention back to Mother and Jerricus as a woman also entered to take her place at another podium to the left of them.

"The state versus Priscilla Renee Patterson. Charge is murder in the second degree," the bailiff announced.

"Good afternoon, Mr. Monroe," the judge greeted,

and then read from a sheet of paper.

"Good afternoon, Your Honor."

"How does your client plead?"

Jerricus leaned over and whispered in Mother's ear.

"Not guilty," she replied in a firm voice.

The female prosecutor spoke. "Assistant DA, Janice Grant for the prosecution. Your Honor, the state requests remand for this prisoner."

Jerricus leaped in immediately. "Your honor, we ask for ROR."

"The defendant is accused of a particularly violent crime. Her estranged husband, a well-known attorney is dead. Mr. Monroe's client is a threat to the community," the prosecutor replied.

"My client has no record of any type other than a couple of traffic tickets, the last being almost three years ago. She has strong ties to the community along with family and friends in Memphis. She also owns property in the area. She is not a flight risk. She has also agreed to surrender her passport. Having her sit in jail is ridiculous."

"Let me decide what's ridiculous, Mr. Monroe," the judge said in a mild tone.

The prosecutor glanced at Mother. "We have both credit card and cell phone evidence that the accused has lied to the police about her whereabouts the night of the murder."

This did not sound good. What the hell had surfaced?

"Your honor, my client can explain. Given the times on those credit card transactions, it would be nearly impossible for her to have committed the crime."

"Nearly impossible is the key phrase here, your Honor. The prosecution believes she *achieved* the nearly impossible. Swipe card evidence from the gate at the back of the community shows she was at the house the night of the murder. We have means, motive, and now opportunity."

I almost gasped aloud in shock. Mother was at the house? I glanced at Colin. His eyebrows had risen and his expression was one of stunned disbelief.

"Your honor, the time frame…"

The judge held up his and said, "Save it for your opening argument, Mr. Monroe. Bail is set at five hundred thousand dollars, cash or bond."

The assistant district attorney quickly jumped in. "In that case, the state would like an ankle monitor to track the defendant's movements."

"Granted. Mr. Monroe, when your client makes bail she will be fitted with a monitoring device before her release." He rapped the gavel again. "Next case."

Mother was led out the door followed by Jerricus and the assistant DA.

"Come on, let's get out of here," Colin said rising.

We slipped from the bench and quietly walked through the doors to the corridor.

"A half a million dollars," I said with a sniff. "How's poor Mother going to come up with that kind of money?"

"She only has to come up with fifty grand in cash or put something of that value up for bond."

"Good afternoon, Miss Watson, Mr. Blackwood."

I turned to find Detective Parker standing a few feet away. His partner, the ever-smiling Claudia Hamilton, was next to him.

"I take it the arraignment's over. What did the judge decide?" he asked.

I resented that he sounded so calm and disinterested. "Bail was set at five hundred thousand dollars and she has to wear a monitoring device."

"That's a lot more lenient than it should be," he said. "At least she's under what amounts to house arrest."

"House arrest?"

Hamilton nodded. "The ankle monitor is in place to prevent her from taking off for parts unknown."

"Mother wouldn't do that any more than she'd clobber Ross over the head with a frying pan. You should be looking at a lot of other people—like Bonnie and Sam Patterson. Did you search their house, too?"

"Absolutely," she replied. Her smile widened. She handed me a document. "Here's a warrant to search your place." She turned back to her partner. "Shall we go?"

I took the folded paper with a shaking hand. "You've got to be kidding. What do you expect to find at my place?"

"Well, you did find a dead man in your bedroom, and were in possession of a piece of evidence for several days before informing us," she said.

"I didn't kill my stepfather. I was on Beale Street until almost four in the morning, and I paid for the cab home with a credit card!"

Her smile disappeared and her eyes turned hard. "But you don't have the same alibi for Mr. Merrick's death."

"Quit talking, Hilary, and give Jerricus a call," Colin said. "We'll all meet you at the house."

"This is ridiculous. Go find the real killer—of both men."

Parker sighed and shook his head. "As far as I'm concerned, the Ross Patterson case is closed."

He nodded to us and walked down the hallway with his partner.

"How much trouble am I in?" I asked.

"I'm thinking Jerricus may be right and what they have is flimsier than they made it sound." He looked down the corridor. "Jerricus!"

Mother's attorney turned as we rushed over. Colin quickly explained the situation.

He read the warrant. "This is pretty straight forward. Is there anything relating to Ross Patterson at your house?" he asked.

"No. You have the jump drive now. Will they get a court order to view it?"

"Possibly, but it may take a while and I'll invoke attorney/client privilege. Anything at your place regarding Don Merrick?"

"Other than what's on the jump drive, no."

"Then you should be all right."

"And if I'm not? If they arrest me, too? Do I call you?"

"Are you asking me to represent you?"

"Only if she needs an attorney," Colin reminded him.

"In that case, call me."

"How will Mother come up with the bail money?"

"We discussed the possibility of bail earlier. She's already been in contact with her stockbroker and should have the necessary funds by late this afternoon."

"And then what?"

"Once she makes bail, she'll have to be fitted with the monitoring device, and then we'll have to discuss matters again. She'll be in her own bed tonight. Have no fear."

"Why murder two? Why not murder one? Ross was drugged with Xanax," Colin asked.

"Because murder one has too many holes in it, especially when dealing with time. It's easier to get a conviction on the lesser charge." He glanced at his watch. "Now, if you'll excuse me, I have to make sure Priscilla makes it home by tonight."

"Oh my God, this is like some kind of hideous nightmare," I said with a groan as Jerricus walked away.

Colin cupped my elbow in his hand and guided me toward the elevators.

"Come on, we have a date with the cops and a search warrant at your place."

I swallowed hard, trying to remember if I had anything incriminating at home. I sure as hell hoped not or Mother and I would be sharing a cell.

****

The search took hours. The police, under the direction of Detective Parker, picked over every piece of paper and through the pages of every book I owned. They rooted through drawers and felt under them for any hidden goodies. Given Don's past, I supposed they had drugs on their minds. Naturally, they confiscated my desktop. I breathed a sigh of relief my laptop was at Colin's. Would his place be next on their list?

"You've been living at your stepfather's since the murder?" Detective Parker asked. "Yet this is all you have in the line of mail?"

"I get a lot of crap delivered, so I chuck it. And as you'll see when you jerk out the hard drive, I do most of my banking and bill paying online."

"And you say you received this jump drive in the mail when?" he questioned.

"I told you, I'm not sure. A lot has happened since then."

He sent me a hard glance at the snotty tone of my reply. I didn't care. I was ninety-nine percent sure he couldn't prove otherwise.

They finally left with my computer and my collection of six old cell phones along with a few papers, but as far as I could tell, nothing of real consequence.

After a stop to retrieve our laptops, Colin and I arrived back at Ross's around eight. A nervous, tearful Effie greeted us.

"Effie, what's wrong?" I asked. Since we'd had no idea when or if we'd be home, she'd been given the night off. "I thought you'd be home by now."

"Oh miss, while you were gone that nasty woman detective came here to ask me questions again," she replied wringing her hands.

"Questions? What kind of questions?" Colin said with a frown.

"She wanted to know if Mrs. Patterson knew the layout of the kitchen and when she'd last been in there."

"Mother? In the kitchen? Well, that should have been easy to answer."

Effie shot me a worried glance. "But I had to tell her the truth. Your mother came into the kitchen one morning as I was making lunch. She asked which frying pan I liked the best. Said she was thinking of getting one for a friend as a wedding gift."

"But…but that's absurd. Mother wouldn't buy a frying pan for anybody as a wedding gift." Then the importance of my words hit me like a bomb. I stared in total consternation.

"When did this occur, Effie?" Colin asked.

"About a week before she moved out. I…I pointed out the one what killed poor Mr. Patterson. I feel just awful about telling them."

I patted her arm. "No need, Effie. You did the right thing."

Colin put his arm around her shoulders and hugged her gently. "Why don't you go home for the night? Hilary and I will order in."

When she'd left, I turned to Colin. "I don't like the sound of this."

"I don't either. It's one more thing to ask your mother when she gets here."

"And why she was up prowling around the kitchen before lunch?"

We ordered in Chinese and cracked open a bottle of sauvignon blanc. Now, ensconced in the den with the empty cartons on the coffee table, I sipped from my third glass of wine.

"Do you think the police will find anything from my place?"

"I doubt it, and while they may have said this involved Don Merrick, my guess is they'll also look for anything pertaining to my uncle."

"At least my laptop is safe at your place. They can't come in and search again, can they?"

"Only if they get a warrant, and I'm not sure a

judge will issue a second one, especially since they have a suspect in custody. Only new evidence could do that."

"And speaking of new evidence, I'd like to know what they have on Mother besides that damned frying pan. And where the hell is she? It's almost ten. Do you think she's having trouble making bail?"

"These things take time. I'm sure Jerricus will call if she isn't coming home, so relax."

"I can't relax. I'm about to explode. Talk to me. I don't care what about, just talk."

"I chatted with Ian this morning."

"Oh? And what did he have to say?"

"Admitted asking Ross for money to buy into a new development over in Fayette County. Ross said no and according to Ian, that was that."

"Yeah, right. And Elaine? Did you talk to her, too?"

"Yep. She says she came, asked Ross to change his mind, and got the same answer. Her story confirms Keisha's account."

"So what? Ross would have let either one—or both—of them in. Ian spikes Ross's drink while Elaine hunts for a weapon—like a frying pan."

"Possibly. I also got an irate call from Bonnie this morning. She was furious I'd told the police about her debt problem. She's also scared stiff. Seems when the cops searched their place one of the items confiscated was, you'll like this, a bottle of Xanax, the prescription in the name of Sam Patterson."

I stared as a ray of hope broke through my gloom. "So either one of them could have done it. Same scenario as with Ian and Elaine—one spikes, the other gets the weapon."

Colin shrugged. "That's why I think the police are still searching for clues. They arrested and brought charges against Priscilla. They can always be dropped later if a better suspect comes along, but it gets them off the hook as far as progress is concerned for a while. The media have been howling for some kind of action."

I rarely paid any attention to the news either electronic or print. And other than that day at my house, I'd seen neither hide nor hair of any reporter. Thank God for gated communities.

The front door opened and closed. A second later the tap-tap of high heels on wood echoed toward the den along with another, more masculine set. I jumped to my feet as Mother and Jerricus walked in. I stared in astonishment.

My mother looked disheveled and unkempt. For the first time in my life, I saw her hair in disarray. Her clothes were wrinkled. Lack of make-up showed lines and grooves. She looked every inch of her fifty-two years.

Then I saw the bulky black device on her left ankle—the house arrest monitor. A cold chill marched down my spine. The reality of the situation hit me like a punch to the solar plexus. Mother might not be in jail, but she was still a prisoner.

She dumped her purse on the sofa and made a beeline for the bar cart.

"I need a drink. You, Jerry?" She held the bottle up for his inspection.

"No thanks, Priscilla. I have to get home. I just wanted to make sure you got here safely."

Mother poured a generous shot of scotch into a

tumbler. "In that case, let me see you out."

Jerricus waved a hand. "No need. I know the way. Everything go all right with you, Hilary?"

"Yes, fine. They took my computer, some old cell phones, and a few papers. That's all."

"Good. If I can help, call. Good night, Priscilla. I'll talk to you tomorrow sometime."

With that, he left. Mother didn't even ask why he'd be interested in my welfare. She drained the glass and poured another.

"This has been the most humiliating, disgusting, awful experience of my life. I'm going to drink this, take a bath, and go to bed. I may sleep for days."

"But first, you're going to tell me what the hell is going on," I demanded. "What do they have on you that's so bad you ended up in the slammer?"

She took another long drink. "Not now, Hilary."

"Yes, now, Priscilla," Colin added.

"Look, you two, I've had a perfectly miserable last thirty-six hours. I have no intention of rehashing the whole vile scene." She lifted her leg and rotated her foot. "Plus, I have to figure out how to bathe without getting this damned thing wet. I had them put it on the left side, so I could at least recline in the Jacuzzi. Now, if you don't mind, I'm going to bed."

Colin moved toward the doorway and blocked the entrance. "No, you're not."

"Goddammit, get out of my way."

I'd never seen my in-control mother so…so what? Scared? That was it. She was scared to death. I didn't blame her. Being arrested for murdering your soon-to-be ex-husband had to bring a shiver or two down her spine.

"Priscilla, we have a right to know. My family is also under suspicion. Hilary and I survived an automobile accident that was no accident. I'm doing my best to find a suspect that wasn't related to my uncle and that includes you. You owe us an explanation."

"Don't forget that I found a dead man, who may or may not have been involved with Ross, on my bedroom floor. *And* my townhouse was searched by the cops today, too. Now, if you want to get rid of that ankle monitor and never see prison garb again, you'll sit down and give us the truth—not what you've told the police, but the truth! And why the hell were you asking Effie about frying pans?"

"What?"

I told her about Effie's encounter with Detective Hamilton.

"Oh that." She waved a hand in the air. "It was nothing. Monica Childers was getting married for the fifth time. She can't boil water, so I was thinking of getting it as a gag gift."

"Did you?" Colin demanded.

"Yes! She, along with everyone else at the shower, laughed like crazy. Now, I'm going to bed."

"Not yet, Mother. The cops say you were here the night of the murder. What gives? Were you?"

Mother licked her lips, drained her glass, and turned back to the liquor cart to refill it. She sipped, walked over to a chair, and plopped down.

"Oh, all right. If you insist."

I sat on the sofa, while Colin chose the other chair. "Start at the beginning," he said. "When did you last see Ross?"

"On Monday around eleven-thirty in the morning.

We'd been arguing about the settlement and the alimony for the past two weeks. I'd finally had enough and decided to up the ante. I showed him the photos my private investigator took of him and his bitch, Carlotta. I told him that if he didn't give me what I wanted, I'd sell the pictures to the highest tabloid bidder in the Mid-South. It wouldn't look good for an attorney who could claim politicians as friends and clients having a mistress with a brother who had underworld connections." She paused to sip again.

Her words were a bit disjointed, but I got the drift. Joey Lazarus had a prime parking space in front of the Vice Squad offices. Not good for someone like Ross to be linked to him—even through marriage. Assuming marriage was what Ross had in mind.

"Go on. What was my uncle's reaction?"

"Livid, and I mean livid. Called me all kinds of names, which told me I'd get what I wanted. I left telling him to call me when the deal was set."

"How long were you there?" I asked.

"I don't know—fifteen, twenty minutes maybe. Not long."

Colin leaned forward resting his elbows on his knees. "Okay, let's fast forward to the day of the murder. You've already said Ross called you while you were on your way to Jackson."

"It was about three, three-thirty. I was almost there. I don't usually drive and talk on the phone, but since I'd been expecting his call, I answered." She paused to sip again.

This time I leaned forward. "And?"

"He told me he wasn't about to give me a damned thing. I'd get minimum at best. I told him I'd sell the stinking photos as soon as I got back. He said to go ahead. Joey Lazarus was very fond of his sister, and her face splashed all over the Memphis scandal sheets would make me a prime target for revenge. He also called my attempt to make a better deal extortion and he'd bring me up on charges."

Considering Ross's activities along those lines, his threat smacked of the ultimate irony, not to mention hypocrisy.

Mother stopped to stare into the amber liquid in her glass before taking another sip—larger this time.

"So what did you do?" I asked.

"I hung up and cursed, of course. It wasn't until dinner that I remembered."

"Remembered what, Mother?"

Colin answered for her. "The recorder. You knew about the old cassette tapes he'd made, too."

Mother nodded. She gulped the last of her scotch and sobbed.

"Oh my God, it was awful. I came back and found him, slumped over the desk with blood everywhere!"

Chapter Nineteen

For a moment, I couldn't catch my breath. I was lightheaded and slightly nauseated. Heat suffused my body followed a moment later by numbing cold. I trembled. Whatever I'd expected, it hadn't been this.

Colin, however, took it in stride. He nodded and heaved a sigh.

"I suspected that. Tell me everything."

Mother regained control and turned frightened eyes to me first, then to Colin.

"We were all at the restaurant in Jackson when it hit me. He'd probably recorded our session on Monday."

My equilibrium returned. "You knew he did this?"

"Yes. He used to get a kick out of replaying things and laughing at the supplicant. Which is why I was always careful about what I said in the study. My problem was I hadn't been in the study in a long time. When I was there that day, I'd been so focused on my mission to wring a few more bucks out of the miserable son of a bitch, I forgot all about it."

Colin rubbed a hand over his chin. "All right, so you're at dinner and remembered. Is that when you decided to return to Memphis?"

She shook her head. "No, I didn't have any plan at that time. I just remembered."

"When did you make the decision? Did Chynna

know?" I asked in a breathy tone. The shock still hadn't worn off.

"Heavens, no! Chynna had three glasses of wine with dinner and a martini before. She didn't even drive home. I did. It was barely ten o'clock when we got back. Chynna was woozy, so she went straight upstairs leaving me to my own devices, which included thinking about that damned recording. I thought if I could get it, then I'd have the upper hand."

"When did you leave?" Colin questioned.

"A little before ten-thirty. I stopped at a gas station just off I-55 in North Jackson and filled up."

"And paid with a credit card," I murmured.

Mother nodded. "It never occurred to me not to. If Ross followed his usual routine, he'd have a couple of Scotches in the study while he checked his e-mail and went over bills. Then he'd go upstairs, take a mild sedative, and go to bed."

"Uncle Ross took sedatives? What kind?"

"A very mild Valium. Sometimes he had a problem coming down from a high in the courtroom or from trying to figure out a new angle to get his client off. I assumed that just because he no longer was in the courtroom, his routine hadn't changed. He was anal that way."

"So you figured to sneak in, get the tape or whatever, and return to Jackson while he slept," I said. "I take it he slept soundly."

"Like a rock. His snoring was enough to wake the dead. That's why we had separate bedrooms."

"Go on," Colin ordered in a firm voice. "What happened next?"

"I knew I had to get back to Chynna's before her

housekeeper arrived at seven, so I jammed the accelerator down and made it here in under three hours. I used the back entry to the neighborhood—the one off Jenson Road. I didn't want anyone to see me coming and going in case Ross missed those tapes. That way, I wouldn't be seen by the guard. They're on duty twenty-four-seven, but the back entrance is swipe card only. I parked down the street in a driveway of a house for sale, walked in through the kitchen, turned off the alarm, and went to the study. The door was closed. I…I remember pausing to listen, but there was no sound at all. Not even Ross snoring upstairs. Just total silence. I opened the door. The room was dark, so I closed it behind me, flipped on the light, and saw him.

"Jeez, the blood was all over. His head looked like a smashed pumpkin on Halloween. The smell was horrible, metallic and strong. My first thought was to get the hell out and fast."

"But you gathered your wits and searched for the recorder," Colin said.

"I had to have it, especially now. If the cops got a hold of it, I'd be suspect number one. I knew which drawer he kept the recorder in, so I opened it. God, there was even blood on the drawer pull. I remember wanting to throw up. I finally found it. Then I noticed several little memory discs in a plastic baggie also in the drawer. There were also some old cassette tapes, too. I didn't have time to go through the whole bunch, so…"

"How many discs and tapes were there?" Colin interrupted.

"Three or four tapes and a couple of discs, I didn't stop to count. I just grabbed them and ran for the door. I had blood on the fingers of my right hand, so I turned the light off and closed the door behind me with my left. I stopped to wash up in the kitchen, then beat a fast retreat. I raced back to Jackson. I was so scared, I could barely function. To this day, I have almost no recollection of the drive. I pulled into Chynna's driveway around six."

"Where are the discs, tapes, and recorder now, Priscilla?"

"I…I stopped at a rest stop on the interstate just outside of Batesville, I think. I tossed them into a trash can near the parking area."

"Without listening to any of them? How could you be sure you had the right tapes and discs?" he asked.

"I don't know! I just assumed they were the ones since it had only been a few days. I'm sure they're long gone. I mean from the trashcan. They are, aren't they?"

Colin shrugged. "Hard to tell, but it's been almost two weeks. If the police pull surveillance tapes from every rest stop between here and Jackson, they could see you dumping them. Finding them is another matter."

"And they couldn't tell what it was she tossed, could they?"

"I don't know," he answered still keeping his gaze on Mother. "I take it your host for the weekend never missed you."

"No. She didn't get up until close to ten. A few minutes later I got the call I'd been expecting from Ian. I made my excuses, acted the shocked widow, stuck around to accept the condolences of my friends, and drove home. I even had the presence of mind to bundle the clothes I wore the night before into a garbage bag in case I had any blood on them. I tossed them in a dumpster at a gas station not far from Senatobia."

"And the credit card receipts show you filling up with gas twice in twelve hours when you supposedly hadn't gone anywhere," he said.

"I just didn't think about it."

"That's what all criminals say," he added.

"I am not a criminal! I didn't kill Ross!"

"Did you tell this to the police?" I demanded.

She snorted. "Hell no. I told them Ross had called during my drive down to offer a reconciliation. I filled up that night because I'd forgotten earlier and that I'd planned returning home the next day—all for the sake of love."

"Oh brother," I said with a groan. "Wait a minute. When we talked the day after Ross's death, you actually laughed about the murder weapon being a frying pan. Are you that good an actress?"

Mother glared. "I was not acting. I never saw it. I was so panicked all I did was open the drawer and take the damned stuff."

"How did you explain the second fill up?"

"Lousy gas mileage."

"In a Lexus?" My voice rose several decibels.

"It's possible if you get a bad tank of gas," she replied. "I said the car had no get up and go, and I filled up again just south of Senatobia."

"And they bought it?"

She shrugged. "Apparently not. If they get testy, I can always suggest someone must have siphoned the tank."

"And the fingerprints in the study?" I continued.

"I was often in Ross's study and could have

touched the desk at any time."

"What about the swipe card? That puts you here at the time of the murder?" Colin continued.

"I said that since Ross and I were separated, I didn't have it with me that night and only returned it to the car after I moved back in. Someone could have stolen it, and then replaced it later after the murder."

"That's so thin I could read a newspaper through it during a new moon. You'd better hope nobody saw you in the neighborhood that night," Colin reminded her.

"At that hour? Who'd be peeking out a window or walking the dog at one-thirty in the morning?"

"Someone who couldn't sleep and might remember a strange car parked in the driveway of the house that's for sale and has no one living in it," I said.

"For someone so scared, you sure thought things out in a hurry—like prior to the act?" Colin stated, his expression hard.

"I did not kill him! I swear it! I was panicked and did what I did to save myself. I also did a lot of thinking on the way back and that morning. And for the love of God, why would I use a frying pan?"

"You said you came in through the kitchen."

"Colin, don't you think Ross would have suspected something seeing Mother approach him at that hour of the morning with a cast iron skillet in her hand? And don't forget, someone spiked his scotch. Mother couldn't possibly have done that."

He ran a hand over his face. "Priscilla, you are a liar, a conniver, and almost as good an extortionist as my late uncle. In spite of that, I don't think you killed him."

Mother's shoulders slumped. "Thank God. The two

of you and Jerricus are the only ones who believe me."

"Jerricus probably doesn't believe you either, but it's his job to pretend he does so he can get you off," Colin said with a deep sigh.

Mother looked uncomfortable as though she'd already had this conversation with her attorney. She set her glass on the coffee table.

"*Now* can I go to bed? I'm exhausted and can't wait to let that Jacuzzi hammer at me."

Colin waved his hand. "Go. We'll see you in the morning."

As she left, I turned to Colin. "Do you think Jerricus can get the charges dropped with her story?"

"I have no idea, but he'll twist and turn things to make it sound like Lexus makes the world's worst fuel efficient cars or that the gas she bought came from a dealer with a history of selling bad quality gasoline. Gas stations have surveillance cameras all over, but they often run on a twenty-four or forty-eight hour loop. Your mother filling up twice might have been recorded over." He rose. "It's almost midnight. I'm tired and have work to do tomorrow. You coming?"

I nodded, thinking as we made our way upstairs. Mother's story was so outlandish it had to be true. The problem was, would the police think so and continue to look for the killer?

****

I woke frequently during the night. Visions of Mother holding a frying pan and creeping up on her husband swam through my mind. I didn't fall asleep until close to four. As a result, I'd overslept. It was after nine before I descended the stairs. All I wanted was coffee.

In the kitchen, I grabbed a mug and poured. Colin was just finishing up a plateful of pancakes.

"How'd you sleep?" he asked.

"Lousy."

"Is your mother awake?"

"I peeked in on my way down. She's out like the old proverbial light."

"She's probably good until noon." He drained his coffee and rose. "I'll be in the study."

I nodded and sipped as he walked out.

"How many pancakes would you like, miss?" Effie said.

For the first time since moving in, I couldn't eat one of Effie's breakfasts.

"Nothing, thank you. My stomach's a little upset."

"I can understand that, miss. But at least, Mrs. Patterson is home again. Glad to see the police finally came to their senses."

I didn't feel like explaining home monitoring devices this morning.

"If you'll excuse me, Effie, I think I'll join Colin in the study."

"Yes, miss. If you change your mind, I'll be glad to get you something."

I found Colin busy on his computer and took a seat in a chair in front of him.

"Colin, I'm worried. What's going to happen now?"

He stopped typing and stared over my shoulder at a painting on the wall behind the sofa.

"I'm not sure."

"The police aren't really going to look for another suspect, are they? Parker said that as far as he was concerned the case was closed. That leaves the ball in Jerricus's hands."

"Jerricus is good, but your mother's story has more holes than Swiss cheese. Luckily, all it takes is one juror to hang a jury." He fiddled with a pencil, tapping first the eraser, then the point on the desktop. "And I'm also beginning to believe you were right about having two killers. I don't think Merrick's murder is related to Ross's. *And* I'm also worried about the search of your townhouse."

"You think they're looking for enough evidence to arrest me for Don's death?"

"Could be."

Fear sent a slashing pain across my forehead. "Got any aspirin hiding in one of those drawers?"

He leaned over, fished around in his laptop case, extracted a bottle, and tossed it to me. I shook two out and swallowed them with my cooling coffee.

"We're at a dead end, aren't we?" I asked.

"Neither murder makes much sense. If Merrick's murder was drug connected, why kill him in your house?"

"Because of the jump drive? Maybe he did talk to a third person—someone whose case file was there, but we overlooked."

"Ross dealt with the upper end of the drug food chain. Merrick was a small timer and only good for a couple hundred a month. I've seen both Ross's and Merrick's financial records. The blackmail lasted for about a year, and then the checks stopped coming."

"Ross let him off the hook? That doesn't sound right."

Colin shrugged. "Maybe Merrick just stopped

paying and my uncle, who was depositing a bundle from other sources, never noticed."

"No way. Ross noticed everything concerning money. Perhaps Don's killer had been stalking him for a while. Getting to know his routine or lack thereof. He could have followed him to my place, watched him break in, and took a chance." I paused as an idea floated through my mind. "What if Don's murder was revenge? What if someone wanted him dead for other reasons?"

"You mean something outside the drug scene?"

I tugged at my earlobe. "I guess. I mean, we don't know a whole lot about his life."

"I can run a check. See if his personal life down in Holly Springs has some clutter in it."

"Speaking of checks, have you done one on that hate letter?"

"I've got requests in to several places including the prison and the public defender's office, but nothing's come back yet, other than the husband and the wife both of whom died six years ago or so." He resumed his pencil tapping. "The one thing that makes no sense is that damned frying pan."

"The frying pan is a sticking point, but try this on for size. The killer—who knows Ross's routine—comes to the party, pops the Xanax into the scotch bottle, doesn't leave, but hides somewhere until everyone is gone, then gets the skillet and whacks him. Xanax isn't hard to obtain. Mother has it. Sam has it. For all we know Ian or Elaine or Bonnie, could have swiped Sam's or Mother's at any time."

"I've seen the crime scene photos. Ross's head is on the desk facing the door, which means he must have passed out or been close to it." He rose and stood in the doorway. "If that's the case, then the killer walked in, came around the desk…" He mimicked his spoken words. "…and hammered him hard. The autopsy report says he sustained at least three, possibly as many as five, blows."

"Why bother to come around the desk? Why not just whack him?"

"My uncle may have been nodding off—or the killer was left handed and needed to come around to get a better angle. If Ross was groggy, he wouldn't put up much of a fight."

"Exactly how bashed in was his head?"

"Pretty bashed. Most of the damage was to the right side. The left side of his head was on the blotter. One blow nailed him on the back of the head."

"Which supports your nodding off theory. Know any lefties in the family?"

He nodded slowly. "Sam and Elaine."

I digested this news and thought before speaking. "The part about the killer knowing Ross's routine fits, but for Sam or Elaine to sneak in the night of the party would be taking a huge risk. Someone they know, like Effie or Keisha, could have seen them."

"A big risk could have paid off. The night we caught Sam in here, he parked in the driveway of a vacant house for sale down the street. He could have done it then, too. Hell, even your mother parked there when she came back from Jackson."

I let my imagination run. "The front door is too obvious. Ross, me, or any of the party goers could see him. So he waits outside the back door until the kitchen clears out for a few minutes. That's possible what with noshes and such going out all the time. Then he comes in, walks directly to the study—most of the people would be in the living and dining rooms, drugs the scotch, and hides out, maybe upstairs, until he's sure the place is empty."

"I suppose that's how it could have happened—until I get to the frying pan part."

"Maybe he wasn't alone. If it was Sam, perhaps Bonnie was with him. What if they worked together? What if Bonnie was the one who grabbed the frying pan? Same with Ian and Elaine."

"Those blows were hard. I'm not sure Bonnie has the strength to do it. Besides, she's right handed."

"So she hands it over to her husband. She distracts Ross by begging for money again while Sam slips to the other side of the desk and wham—nails him."

"In which case, why bother to drug the Scotch?"

I grasped my hair in both hands and pulled. "Dammit, this is driving me nuts! Maybe Joey and Carlotta did it. Or Ian and Elaine. Or the man in the moon."

"The answer is out there. We're just missing it." He glanced at his watch. "I think I'll pay Ross's secretary a visit. I didn't really talk to her much the day I got the files. Want to come along?"

I sure as hell didn't want to stay in the house all day. "Sure, why not. Will we be in for lunch?"

"No. Let's eat out. To be honest, I don't want to make conversation with your mother just yet."

"Let me go put on some nicer clothes while you tell Effie."

On the way to my room, I looked in on Mother. Still sound asleep and would remain so for at least another hour.

As I changed into a skirt and top, I wondered again about the manner of Ross's death. Three to five blows suggested a lot of hate. And strong emotions sometimes translated into strength. Why couldn't Bonnie have been the one to sneak in?

And she and Sam were about to split again because of her gambling. Admitting to the cops they were on the outs wouldn't look good.

What if Bonnie deliberately set up her husband as the murderer? Switching hands might be difficult, however. Then a random thought made me stop applying my lipstick.

Unless that person plays tennis.

Bonnie and Sam were members of the Moreland Country Club. Sam golfed, but Bonnie played tennis on a regular basis. If memory served, she was a skilled player and her backhand was—if you'll pardon the expression—killer.

****

Ross's former secretary, Janet Harrison, showed us into her living room. In her late forties, she'd been with Ross for close to ten years.

"How can I help, Mr. Blackwood?"

She indicated the sofa with a wave of her hand. We sat. I let my gaze wander around the room. The tasteful, but expensive, décor suggested my late stepfather paid well.

"I take it the police confiscated most of the files in the office," he began.

She nodded. "Yes, sir. They took just about all that was left."

"Wait a minute," I said. "I thought Ross had retired a couple of months ago, but the office was still open?"

"Yes, ma'am. Mr. Patterson was in the process of going through the files himself, shredding some and keeping others. He said he didn't want them at the house and asked if I would keep some for him until he could rent a locker or storage bin."

"You gave me a couple of boxes shortly after his death. How many more are there?"

"That was it for boxes. He destroyed more than he kept, especially old files."

"You say 'he,' but I assume you did the actual work," I said.

She smiled. "That's true."

"What kind of files did you shred?" he asked.

"A lot of old cases from when he and Mr. Price were partners."

"You said that was it for boxes. Did he give you anything else?"

She hesitated and looked around the room before focusing her attention back onto us.

"He didn't exactly give me anything, but…" She hesitated again.

"It's okay. You can trust us. Regardless of what you read in the papers or saw on TV, my mother did not kill Ross. Please, anything you can remember may help."

"A few months ago, just before he officially retired, he had me rent a safety deposit box. He then gave me a bunch of tapes to put in it."

My heart rate accelerated. I shot a quick glance at Colin who raised his eyebrows.

"Tapes? What kind of tapes?" he questioned.

"The kind that come from a tape recorder—you know, audio tapes."

"How many tapes were there?"

"About a dozen."

Mother had tossed three or four. Sounded like Ross forgot to include them in the box for his secretary.

"Did the police confiscate them, too?" Colin asked.

"No, sir. The box is under my name. He said he wanted it that way until the office was officially closed, then he'd rent a box under his own name."

"Janet, would you mind if we took possession of those tapes?"

She heaved a sigh. "To tell you the truth, Mr. Blackwood, that would be a huge burden lifted off my shoulders. I had no idea what to do with them."

"Did you listen to any of them?" I asked.

She turned a shocked gaze on me. "Certainly not! What's on those tapes is none of my business."

"Then why not turn them over to the police?"

"Miss Watson, I know there were many people who disliked Mr. Patterson intensely, but he paid me well and was always pleasant. He was also a very good attorney. I'd hate to see something come up on those tapes that would harm his reputation. Plus, the attorney/client privilege might be in effect. I was afraid to give them to the authorities. And now that..."

She halted abruptly. I knew what she thought— now that Mother had been arrested there was no need to involve the cops.

"They could be very important to the investigation," Colin said. "Would you be willing to go to the bank now?"

"Absolutely, Mr. Blackwood."

Colin rose. "Then let's go."

Half an hour later, we were on our way home, the

tapes in a plastic grocery bag next to my feet. Janet had heaved a visible sigh of relief and closed out the box rental.

I couldn't resist pulling a couple from the bag and reading the labels.

"These are all dated," I told Colin. "Wonder who's on them."

"Clients probably."

"He taped his clients?"

"Sure, that way there's no argument over what was said."

I riffled through the tapes. "The dates seem to range over the last five or six years. Why would he keep a bunch of tapes that old?"

"His little sideline of blackmail, maybe? We'll listen to them tonight after dinner. With any luck, your mother will retreat upstairs and we won't be interrupted."

Dinner was a quiet affair. Not even Mother had much to say other than to complain that the ankle monitor was ugly and made sleeping awkward.

"I'm still a prisoner only in my own home. I can't go out in public with this thing on."

"I'm sure Jerricus is working on getting it removed," I said in a soothing tone. "Did you see him today?"

"No, but he called this afternoon. He's meeting with the DA tomorrow. Something about how their evidence is flimsy and the charges should be dropped."

Colin sighed. "Unfortunately, your story also has a lot of holes in it. Don't forget, that swipe card has you here at the time of the murder. You have explanations for damned near everything including gas mileage—

like you're making it up as you go along, which you are."

That momentarily shut her up.

Then another thought occurred to me. "Mother, when you found Ross, what did the blood look like?"

She stopped with her fork halfway to her mouth and stared. "Good God, Hilary. It was blood. A lot of it, too."

"I see where this is going," Colin stated. "Should have thought of it myself. Priscilla, was the blood congealed? Did it look like jelly?"

Mother put her fork down. "Well, you've just ruined my appetite. And I didn't pay much attention, but no. I remember a pool of it near his head looked...liquid."

"Which means he hadn't been dead long."

Her face paled. "You mean if I'd arrived thirty minutes earlier, I could have been a victim, too?"

Colin nodded. "So the time of death must have been closer to one-thirty. The coroner put it at between one and five."

"Shortly after Effie left," I said. "Someone *was* hiding inside."

Mother pushed back her chair. "Excuse me, but I don't feel well. I'll be in my room if you need me."

We finished our meal and retired to the study. Effie appeared in the doorway.

"If you don't need me for anything else, Mr. Colin, I'll go home as soon as I clean up. I have to drive down to Senatobia tonight. Passy and Bobby Lee had a little tiff and only Aunt Effie can make things smooth again," she said with a shake of her head. "I may not be in tomorrow morning until late. Is that all right?"

"Of course. Take all the time you need. Hilary and I can scramble an egg for ourselves."

"And I even know how to make coffee." I waved a hand toward the kitchen door. "Go calm the troubled waters of a nervous bride and groom. We'll be fine."

When she left, we got down to the business of those tapes. Colin pulled Ross's old tape recorder from a lower drawer and set it on the desk.

"Let's start with the oldest first," he said.

I arranged them in order and handed him a tape. He inserted it in the machine and pressed a button.

I held my breath. Deep inside, I was convinced we'd hear the voice of a murderer.

Chapter Twenty

Two hours and three tapes later, not even a hint of a murderer was heard.

I banged my fist on the desk. "Dammit, why isn't there more to grab hold of?"

"Relax, Hilary. If you listen carefully, you'll hear that Ross's clients have confessed to their crimes. These tapes are his preliminary interviews. He's getting the facts, so he knows which avenue to take to get an acquittal."

"In other words, he's twisting the truth."

"That was his job."

"But I was so sure the killer would be on one of these damned tapes."

Colin sighed and inserted another tape. "He or she might be, but they had no reason to kill my uncle at this stage of the game. We have to listen for any information that could point to murder at a later date."

He pushed the button. Murder at a later date? I had no idea what to even listen for, let alone pin-point. The night wore on. We took a coffee break somewhere around ten o'clock, and then resumed the boring task of listening to Ross and his sleazeball clients. Finally, on a tape dated almost three years ago, we heard something interesting. It was Joey Lazarus.

"Good morning, Ross."

"Mornin', Joey. What can I do for you today?"

"Got a little problem. One of my employees was picked up on a DUI in Mississippi last night. Name of Don Merrick."

He stopped the recorder. "So the stiff on your bedroom floor *was* working for Lazarus."

"And the prick had the nerve to get me into the car with him?" I struggled to contain my anger. *The stinking bastard!* "I wonder if he knew Ross was my stepfather."

"Had you ever talked to him about family?"

"Not really. But that doesn't mean someone else in our group didn't."

He resumed play. Ross's voice filled the room.

"I know. He was with my stepdaughter. Got them to let her go, but those baggies in the car bought him a night in jail."

"His one and only phone call was to me. Think you can get him off?"

"What kind of work does he do for you?"

"The usual. Sells weed and coke to the college crowd. He's small time, but good. He has a lot of customers and brings in new ones every week. I'd like to have him back on the job."

This time I stopped the recorder. "And that son of a bitch told me in my own living room the day after Ross's murder that he was going to take over his father's furniture store in Holly Springs."

"He may well have been going that route. Let's listen to what else is said." He pushed the button.

"He ever been arrested before?"

"Yeah, once about five years ago here in Memphis. A couple of bribes and the charges got reduced to next to nothing. Think you can do the same?"

"Maybe, if the Mississippi cops aren't too thorough with their background check. I'll clear my schedule this morning and head down. This'll cost, you know."

Lazarus laughed. "It always does, but you're worth it. Handle it and get back to me."

Ross sighed as the sound of a door closing could be heard. Then he picked up the phone.

"Janet, how does my day look... Uh-huh... Okay, call Fisher and reschedule him for three this afternoon. Put Tomasino off until tomorrow. I have to go down and see a new client in Tunica. I should be back by one."

He hung up and the recording stopped. The next voices heard were those of Ross and another client. Then the tape ended.

"Oh, brother," I muttered. "And we thought Don was small fry."

Colin shook his head. "He was. My uncle, however, was a first class bastard, that's for sure. But at least we know why he never blackmailed Joey Lazarus."

"We do? Why?"

"Joey obviously had him on retainer and Ross charged him an arm and a leg for the privilege."

"Sounds like blackmail to me."

"Not to someone like Lazarus. Merely the cost of doing business. Wouldn't be surprised if he tried to write it off on his taxes."

"Could this, and maybe other tapes, mean that Joey Lazarus killed Ross to get them?"

Colin shrugged. "Well, my uncle was retiring...and then there's that book deal. It's a possibility he didn't want those damning words falling into the wrong hands." He paused. "I wonder if Ross recommended another attorney for Joey—and who."

I'd never thought about that angle before. Of course, Lazarus would need a new attorney.

He inserted another tape and turned the machine on. We had maybe another five or six to go, but the day was catching up to me. I yawned. Then, near the end, came another revelation. This time in the form of Don Merrick.

"Sit down, Merrick."

"What did you want to see me for, Mr. Patterson?"

It was odd hearing both Ross's and Don's voices again. Kind of like bringing the dead back to life.

"You know, Merrick, if you hadn't been with my stepdaughter and if your boss hadn't asked, I'd have never taken you on as a client."

"I know, and I appreciate all you've done for me. I got a low bail I could cover, and the story we told to the judge was perfect. I'll wash a few cop cars and rake a few leaves for the next couple of months. And I thought my performance about my past indiscretion was heartfelt. That silly twit of a girl took the blame because it was her car and she had a record of drug possession."

"The judge was only interested in the present, and the testimony of the so-called friends you lent the car to was good. Their tale of picking up a couple of hitchhikers put a few more people in the picture— people who could have stashed the drugs in the trunk— worked. It was all a lie, of course. You got real lucky, but then you had me."

"And I'm really grateful you took the case."

"How grateful?"

"Uh, I'm not sure I know what you mean."

"I told you at our first meeting, my fees are quite high. You can't come close to affording me."

"I...I thought...that is, Mr. Lazarus said..."

"I know what he said, but this is between you and me. I think we can work something out on the installment plan. A little private contract, so to speak. I want two hundred dollars a week for the next year to cover my expenses."

"Two hundred dollars a week?" Don's tone rose several decibels.

"That's right. And you're getting the referred customer discount," Ross said with a laugh. "Oh, and it's cash only. Got that?"

"And if I don't pay?" Don's tone changed to belligerent.

"Then I'll be forced to tell Mr. Lazarus the money must come from him. I don't think you want me to do that now, do you?" Silence stretched for several seconds. "No I didn't think so. Here..." The sound of paper being ripped from a notepad came through. "...just put the cash in an envelope and deliver it to this address. Drop it through the mail slot. I'll get it."

"How do I know you won't keep doing this after the year is up?"

"You don't, but I'm a man of my word. Goodbye, Merrick. I expect your first payment next Monday."

We listened as footsteps crossed the room and the door slammed. Then Ross laughed and said, "Sucker."

I wanted to throw up and clapped a hand over my mouth. Here was proof my stepfather was a crook—worse than any of his clients.

"Well, if ever there was a motive for Don Merrick to kill Ross, this is it," I said unable to keep the disgust from my voice. "Wonder where it was delivered."

"Ross owned a lot of property in the city. Could have been some house he was renting, and the renter did this little favor for his landlord as a way to reduce the rent."

"I'll bet he just kept on and on demanding payment, too."

Colin shook his head. "Not according to the financial statements I've seen. The outgo and the input stopped on time. But it does put Merrick right up there on the suspect list. What I can't figure out is why my uncle would tape himself blackmailing someone. It's stupid."

"Ross's ego probably preventing him from thinking he'd ever get caught."

"Or he assumed the attorney/client privilege would come into play if anyone turned him in. If they did, he could simply destroy it say 'what tape'?"

"Obviously, Don didn't lend his car to anybody for a trip to New Orleans. Do you think Ross bribed the witnesses—the guys he supposedly lent the car to?"

"He wouldn't be that careless. Either Merrick did it or Joey Lazarus."

"Then who killed Don and why?"

"I don't know, but let's finish these tapes."

We were on the final tape, dated within the last ten months of Ross's business life when we heard another familiar voice. Jim Price.

"Jim, good to see you. Glad you could come on such short notice."

"I'm glad you finally have some information for me. I thought you'd forgotten."

"No, no, I didn't forget. I just got so busy winding

down things here, I didn't have the time. Here's what you need." Something slid across the desk.

"I'll read it tonight when I get home. So, are you really going to call it quits?"

"Yeah, it's time. I made my bucks and now it's time to see what other avenues are open to me. I'm thinking of writing a book about being the premier defense attorney in the Mid-South. Just wish you could have been along for the ride."

Price sighed. "I tried, Ross, but you dealt with so many unsavory characters, including killers and drug dealers, I had to leave. It was just…"

"I know, I know. And I'm sorry for what happened. How's Martha doing?"

"She still has her moments, but the doctors at the sanitarium say she may be able to finally come home soon. Lord, I hope so."

"So do I. Still, we had a great run. Hope you can put that information to good use."

"I will, and thanks."

The name Martha stuck in my mind, but I couldn't place it. We listened to the end of the tape. I yawned again.

"Is that the last one?" I asked.

"That's it. Wonder why this one's on tape? From what your mother said, Uncle Ross changed to digital a year ago."

"Maybe he ran out of discs and used this as back-up."

"Maybe. I don't know about you, but I'm calling it a night." He rose and slipped the tapes and the recorder into the desk drawer.

"Me, too. I'm beat. See you in the morning." I

paused. "Of course, I'm not that tired."

He grinned. "Your mother, remember?"

"She is in Never-Neverland and likely to be for a long while." I walked over to him and slid my arms around his neck kissing him hard. "I suppose we could go to your place."

"The drive will destroy the mood." He kissed me back harder. "Exactly how sound does she sleep?"

"Very sound," I replied nibbling on his neck. "And her room is not anywhere near mine."

I walked from the room, deliberately swaying my hips in a provocative way. Colin chuckled and followed.

My bed would finally get a workout.

****

I awoke the next morning alone in the bed. The cool sheets told me Colin had been up for a while. My bedside clock read nine-thirty. I stretched like a satiated cat. Hugging a pillow to my chest, I breathed deeply of Colin. Two weeks ago, he'd been the enemy. Now he was my lover, my friend, and maybe a bit more.

No, a lot more. I'm beginning to think he's the one.

Was he? Having never been in love before, I wasn't certain, but it sure as hell felt like it to me.

I threw off the covers and rose, stretching again. A shower was in order, then breakfast, followed by…who knows. I'd go wherever Colin went.

Half an hour later, I barged into the kitchen. Effie stood at the island chopping vegetables. Colin was not in sight.

"Effie! I thought you took the morning off." I poured a cup of coffee and sat at the table.

"I said I'd be late, miss. Got here about eight. Can I

get you something to eat?"

"No thanks. I'll wait for lunch. So, how did it go last night? Is the wedding still on?"

She chuckled. "Yes, miss. Seems Passy wanted to include a former boyfriend on the guest list and Bobby Lee objected. I pointed out a *former* boyfriend is a good sign. After all, Bobby Lee got the girl."

I had to laugh. It made perfect sense.

"Is Colin around? I didn't see him in the study when I passed by."

"No, miss. He was leaving just as I got here. Said he had some places to go and people to talk to. He'll be back for dinner. Sure I can't get you anything?"

"I'm fine. I think I'll head upstairs and do some work on the computer. I'll be in my room if you need me."

I refreshed my coffee and wandered upstairs. A whole day without Colin and investigating sounded boring as hell.

I fired up my laptop and checked my e-mail. Other than a few spam items, I had precious little to answer. I still hadn't heard back from the Lighthouse School of Design. How long did it take to get accepted? Would they deem my work worthy of enrollment?

I sighed and moved on to Facebook. I kept my postings on the light side by reposting funny quotes and photos before switching over to Twitter. I didn't care for tweeting. I found I said the same things as on Facebook. Still I maintained the illusion of my usual self. No mention was made of Ross, Don, or Mother's predicament.

Finished, I sat back totally bored. Now what? Surf the web? For what? Read? I owned a reading device, but rarely used it. It had been years since I'd willingly read a book.

A discreet knock on my door ended my gloomy thoughts.

"Come in."

Effie poked her head around the door. "Mr. Price is here, miss. He wants to see Mrs. Patterson, but she's not up yet. Should I tell him to come back later?"

I rose. "No. Go wake Mother. It's after ten and she should be up anyway. I'll go down to talk to Mr. Price."

Effie had shown Jim into the living room.

"Good morning, Jim. Mother will be down in a few minutes. Can I help?"

"Ah, good morning, Hilary, and no. I just dropped by to discuss some things relating to Ross's will."

I indicated he should have a seat. He chose the sofa. I chose the chair opposite. "Nothing serious, I hope."

He hesitated. "I guess this does involve you, too. Probate has been put on hold until this mess with your mother's arrest is settled."

"Why?"

"Because someone accused and/or convicted of murder cannot inherit anything from the victim."

"Does this mean nobody gets anything until the charges have been dismissed?"

"I'm afraid so, at least until after the trial—if there is one."

Well, nuts. This would hold up everyone. Sam needed the money soon or would have to file for bankruptcy and Bonnie would be doing without alimony. Ian would lose out on his opportunity to develop whatever was on his agenda, and even Effie would be affected. I was sure a part of her share had been earmarked for her niece's wedding.

"Colin's pretty sure it won't go to trial. The evidence is flimsy." Or at least explainable.

"Let's hope so. Speaking of Colin, is he here by any chance? I'd like to talk to him. I know he's helping the family investigate."

"Yes, and so far, it's been interesting, I'll say that. He's not here at the moment."

"Are you helping investigate, too?"

"In a very minor way. He's been nice enough to allow me to tag along to interviews and read some of Ross's old files. Did you know Ross taped a lot of his dealings with clients and with friends?"

"Lawyers often do that, especially from the criminal side of things. It's not unusual and keeps the record straight. Have you listened to any of them?"

"A few. They're really boring. No offense, but you must yawn your way through the day."

He chuckled. "Sometimes. Guess it's all a matter of perspective. As a man, I don't find shopping any fun."

"No man does."

"Where did Colin find the tapes?"

I told him how Ross's secretary had helped. "Should they be turned over to the cops? I mean, they were all old tapes, some going back years."

"No, what's on them constitutes attorney/client privilege. If they want them, they'll have to get a court order and that'll be tough, though not impossible." He checked his watch. "I should have called before dropping by. Maybe I should come back later."

Mother chose that moment to make her

appearance. She wore long, wide legged slacks to hide the ankle monitor, a silk tank top, and sandals. Her hair, while not the usual perfection, was decent. She'd even slapped on a little make-up.

"Jim, how good to see you," she said in a smooth tone. "Sorry I took so long. Have a seat."

"If you'll both excuse me, I'll be upstairs."

Back in my room, I remembered why the name Martha had sounded familiar on the tape from last night. She'd been Jim's wife. A wave of sympathy washed over me. Did he have any other family? For his sake, I hoped so.

Lunch was a tedious affair. Mother was grumpy and complaining.

"Why doesn't Jerry call? He said he was going to talk to the DA about getting the charges dropped and this stupid thing around my ankle off. I can't go anywhere with this on. Suppose someone sees it? And none of my friends have called, texted, or returned any of my calls and texts. Some friends! And now this business with the will!"

I let her rant, not bothering to answer. She needed to vent and I was available. I hoped she'd find someone else to bug after lunch.

"You know, to hell with this ankle monstrosity. I'm going to the mall. Unless someone looks real close, my slacks hide it pretty well. You want to come, too?"

"Do you want the company?"

Mother hesitated. "Actually, I would like someone to talk to. Maybe we could shop, and have a glass of wine or something."

I felt sorry for her. Abandoned by her friends, she was going stir crazy in this house. I didn't blame her. I was on the stir crazy side, too. The fact I was the last choice on her list should have rankled, but that was just Mother.

"That sounds like fun. It's been a long time since we've gone shopping together."

She smiled for the first time today. "Wonderful. Let me do something with my hair and make-up."

We finished lunch and I waited in the den. The doorbell rang and a few minutes later Effie showed Ian into the room.

"Hilary, good to see you. Is Colin here? I've been trying to get him on the phone, but it all goes into voice mail."

"No. He left this morning to do whatever it is he does. Can I help with anything?"

"I just wanted to see if there have been any new developments. I heard Ross mailed a jump drive to you. What was on it?"

I knew Ian had a right to know, but, I didn't completely trust him.

"Just a bunch of case files. Nothing important."

"I also talked to Uncle Sam at the funeral. Things are not going well with him. First he tries to find some kind of recording Ross apparently made of family affairs, and now he and Bonnie are under suspicion of murder, although your mother's arrest may have laid that one to rest. How is she by the way?"

"She's holding up well, considering. It's nonsense, of course. She didn't kill her husband. Did Jim Price talk to you about the will?"

He nodded. "This morning. If this drags out much longer, there's no way I can get in on this new development over in Fayette County."

"How well do you know Jim?" I asked.

"Fairly well. Why?"

I explained about his actions at the cemetery.

"Yes, his daughter died unexpectedly, and his wife had a breakdown as a result. She committed suicide not long after."

"How awful. The poor man."

"Yes, it was tragic, but he seems to be coping. Not sure I could." He glanced at his watch. "Hilary, I can't stay. If Colin shows up, have him call me, Okay?"

He left a few seconds before Mother came downstairs.

"Was that Ian? What did he want?"

"Just to touch base with Colin. He told me about Jim Price's wife and daughter. So sad."

"I kind of remember that. We went to both funerals. The daughter was murdered."

"Murdered!"

"I don't remember the details. Shot, I think. Martha was one of those people who never seem to come to grips with reality. For years, I thought she was just plain stupid, but it was more of a vagueness regarding what was around her. I guess she lived for her family, especially her child. When she died, Martha just gave up. I often wondered why Jim had married her. He's very personable—for a wills and trusts lawyer. Are you ready? I'm rather excited about this trip."

I sighed and followed Mother out the front door. I did not want to go shopping.

What I wanted was for Colin to come home. I had no clue what he was up to today, which hammered home that until Ross's death, my life had been depressingly barren. Thank God, I was taking steps to change that. Once the real killer was arrested, I knew I'd never go back to my old life.

I shivered as we drove to the mall. Something was in the air. And it wasn't a good something. For reasons I couldn't explain, apprehension slithered down my spine.

Chapter Twenty-One

I paced around the den, sipping from a glass of Grey Goose on the rocks in my hand. Where the hell was Colin? I'd had more contact with his voice mail than with him. Had something happened? Worry made me irritable. I paced faster as the creepy feeling from earlier in the day that something was about to occur—or had already occurred—gave me goosebumps.

Finally, the front door opened and closed. I charged into the hallway and heaved a sigh of relief when I saw Colin striding toward me.

"Where the hell have you been? I've been worried sick all afternoon." I knew I sounded bitchy—like a suspicious wife, but couldn't help it.

He kissed the top of my head. "Sorry, but I was actually at my office doing real work today. I ignored the phone unless it was business related."

He dropped off his briefcase in the study before heading for the den. I followed.

"Well, don't do that again. I was looking for you, Ian was looking for you, even Jim Price wanted to know where you were." *Thank God he's safe. Why am I so disgruntled? Get a grip, Hilary.*

"I know. I talked to everyone a while ago."

"You didn't talk to me." My grumpy tone said it all.

He grinned. "Knew I'd be seeing you soon."

"Hmmmph!" Now that he was home and had suffered no harm, my mood improved, but not by much. *This is so high school.*

His grin widened as he poured himself a glass of scotch. "And what did you do all day?"

"I had to go shopping with Mother, at the mall of all places. It was not a fun time."

"The mall? Ah, I get it. She's well-known at those exclusive Moreland boutiques. Too many sales clerks staring at her new ankle jewelry? Will she be joining us for cocktails and dinner?"

"No. Mother talked to Jerricus and apparently he told her she wasn't really under house arrest, but under surveillance, so she made a decision this afternoon. If she had to wear the damned thing, she'd make the most of it. She decided to go out to someplace very crowded every day just to bug the cops, hence the mall. Someone has to monitor her movements. She called a couple of the few friends she has left and is now chowing down at that Brazilian steakhouse in Peabody Place."

He chuckled. "Never piss off a Southern woman. They get even in the most inventive ways."

"I take it Jim Price told you about the hold up with probate."

"I expected that. Not a problem for me. I don't need the money."

"No, but Ian and Sam sure do."

"Ian's finances are in better shape than Sam's. I might as well tell you that he and Bonnie's split is heading for divorce court. He's filing for bankruptcy and the house is going into pre-foreclosure."

"Doesn't surprise me."

Effie entered to announce dinner. I'd told her to

301

keep it simple tonight, and now I leaned over my plate to inhale the Italian spices and garlic of lasagna. A simple salad with breadsticks accompanied it. As usual, the food was delicious. We finished in record time. Where I found room for the cheesecake dessert, I have no clue, but managed.

"Effie, that was wonderful," I said with a moan only a full stomach could create. "Why don't you just stack the dishes and take the rest of the night off?"

"Oh, I can't leave until my work is done, but there isn't much to clean up. I'll go home as soon as I can. It's been a long day."

Back in the den, Colin turned on the TV. "Hope you don't mind, but the basketball playoffs are on. The Grizzlies are playing the Mavericks tonight."

I knew the Grizzlies were the Memphis team, but had no clue as to where the Mavericks called home. I poured a glass of wine and snuggled next to him on the sofa, my good humor restored. I hadn't liked feeling so needy just because Colin wasn't around today. I missed investigating with him. I missed tossing out theories. I missed him.

"Mother told me something disturbing today," I said taking a sip.

"What was that?"

"She said Jim Price's daughter was murdered. I saw her marker at the cemetery. She was so young. And then his wife died about five or six months ago. I think Ian said she killed herself. Really tragic. I feel so sorry for him."

He turned to stare at me. "I know. The recording we listened to last night reminded me."

"He sounded so happy that his wife might be

coming home again."

"His daughter's death hit them both hard."

"Do you know how his daughter was murdered? Mother seemed to think she was shot. Was it like a robbery or a drive-by?"

His forehead furrowed and he rose. "Let's go find out."

"What about the game?"

"Nothing happens until the fourth quarter anyway."

I followed him to the study while he worked his magic on the computer. He found the information quickly.

"The daughter was found with a bullet in her head in an alley in North Memphis."

"What was she doing there? That's an area to be avoided at all costs."

"Drugs would be my guess. She was a mess. Had emotional problems all her life. Alcohol and drugs dominated her teen years. She'd been in and out of rehab facilities since she was thirteen. Finally got her act together her senior year in high school and was enrolled at the University of Memphis."

"How do you know all this?"

"At some point in time, she ran away. Jim contacted me to track her down and gave me the background on the problems they'd had. Finally found her living on the street in Little Rock. Jim and Martha convinced her to come home and into rehab. It seemed to work. I'll bet she started up with the coke again at college."

"You think she went to buy drugs and got killed instead?"

"Not if she was a paying customer. I wonder if she

owed a dealer more than she could pay. Some dealers would cut their losses and off her to send a message."

"How awful! No wonder the mother went nuts." Colin's mention of the tapes and recordings brought back something else that had been bothering me. "You know, I can't help but think that recording conversations is asking for trouble."

He shrugged. "I can see why it's done. If a client comes back and claims his attorney didn't tell him something, the attorney can pull out the recording, play it, and say, 'yes, I did and here it is.' Conversely, the attorney can also use the recording to tell the client, 'no, you never mentioned that.' It's a way of covering their asses if they lose in court."

"That I get, but to record blackmail?"

"My Uncle Ross was so successful at it and had been doing it for so long, he may have gotten sloppy, careless, or arrogant. Pick an adjective. Maybe he used them as reminders if the payments didn't come in a timely manner. I doubt his victims even knew they were being recorded. My guess is he just got a kick out of listening to them over and over—the bastard."

His voice was tinged with bitterness. It must have been hard to come to terms with the fact that a family member—even one you didn't like—was an unethical asshole.

Effie came into the doorway. "I'm all finished, miss. If you don't mind, I'll be heading home for the night."

"Drive carefully. We'll see you in the morning," Colin said with a smile.

She left, but before I could ask Colin another question, his phone rang.

"Blackwood… Did you catch him… I'll be right there… Thanks for calling." He disconnected. "I've gotta go. Someone broke into my house."

"I'm coming with you."

"Of course you are."

The drive to Colin's took less than fifteen minutes. When we arrived, two police cars and a car from the security alarm company were parked out front. An officer stopped us on the front porch. Colin showed his ID, told him I was with him, and we entered.

"What happened?" he asked the security man.

"We got a signal that the power had gone off. We checked the rest of our clients in the neighborhood, but yours was the only one with a problem. Tried calling your landline, but it was also out of order. That's when I called the police, then your cell."

A policeman stood nearby. "Both the alarm and phone lines were cut. Whoever it was smashed the glass in the back door and entered. Worked fast, too. We got here less than five minutes after we were called, but he was already gone. Most of the damage seems to be in one bedroom."

"My office." Colin strode down the hall with me trotting to keep up.

File drawers gaped open and papers littered the floor. The desk drawers had been dumped on the desk. Across the room, the curtains fluttered in the breeze coming in the open window.

"We figure that's how he left. The screen is punched out," the security man said.

"Do you know what he was looking for?" the cop asked.

"I have several open cases at the moment," Colin

said, running a hand through his hair. "But most of my stuff is at my office."

"Where's that?"

"The Higman Building over at Park and Ridgeway, second floor." He stopped abruptly. "I think you may need to send a car over there."

The officer spoke into his radio requesting a car head there immediately.

Colin turned to the security company rep. "I need to get to my office. I'll leave you to deal with repairing the alarm system. I'll call the phone company tomorrow."

The man assured us he'd have the alarm system rewired and working in a few hours. We raced for the office of Blackwood Investigations, Inc. Outside, two patrol cars with lights flashing stood near the front entrance. The nighttime security guard waved us through into the lobby.

"Did he get me?" Colin asked.

"Seems like it, Mr. Blackwood."

Before I could make a pithy comment about the man's efficiency, Colin grasped my elbow and steered me to the elevator.

"How did he get in with a guard in the lobby?" I demanded on the ride up.

"There's a parking garage around back. People come and go all the time."

"At night?"

"There's a CPA firm on the third floor. They've been busy the last few months."

"Tax season is over."

"It's only the end of April. They'd be dealing with extensions and such."

"Then why bother with a guard at all if it's so easy to get in?"

"It looks good," he replied.

The doors slid open and we exited. A cop stood outside the open door to Colin's office. Inside, the mess was ten times worse than at his home.

"It'll take me a couple of days to figure out if anything's missing," he told the policemen on the inside. "Any information from the surveillance tapes?"

"We're reviewing them now. Should know soon." He'd no sooner spoken when his cell rang. He answered and listened for a few seconds. "Mr. Blackwood, could you go to the security office? They have something on tape."

We left and returned to the lobby and an office down a narrow hallway off of it.

"What have you got?" he asked the policeman and another man sitting in front of a bank of monitors.

"Can you identify this person?" he asked.

The image of a man wearing a trench coat and a baseball hat pulled low swam into view. He leaned down at Colin's office door, poked something at the doorknob, then straightened, opened the door, and entered. The time in the lower right hand corner read six-twenty-two. The man exited at six-forty-four.

"I don't have a clue. I left the office around six-fifteen, stopped by my place for a few minutes before heading out to my uncle's house in Moreland."

"Any other tape of this guy?" I asked.

"Nope. This is it."

"Well, he had to leave the building sometime," I objected.

"He's obviously in disguise. All he had to do was

take it off in the stairwell, stuff it into a briefcase, and walk out. I'm not even sure enhancement will help much."

"Let me guess," I drawled. "No cameras in the stairwells."

The security guy shook his head. "Nope. Never needed them before."

"How many people would be in the building at that hour?" I said.

The man shrugged. "There's a CPA firm. Some of them work late. The building also houses a couple of lawyers, five doctors, and several one man offices."

"People who work here would use the parking garage, but I can't think of who from the building would want to get into my files that bad. How about a visitor?"

He switched to another monitor showing the lobby. We watched the tape as it displayed images from six o'clock until seven. During that time a total of seven people either entered or left. Some stared straight ahead, others' faces were hidden as they looked down. None wore a trench coat or a baseball cap. Further identification would be difficult due to the poor quality of the tape.

"That's a lot of people for a Friday night," I pointed out.

"One of the doctors is a shrink. Has some kind of group session from four until six on Fridays. And the accountants come and go at all hours."

Colin ran a hand through his hair. "This could take forever. Make sure my office is locked when you all leave," he told security. "Let's get home, Hilary."

He once again grasped my arm and rushed me from

the building. He shoved me into the car, got behind the wheel, and drove off.

"What's the hurry?"

"Something's not right. I need to go through Ross's stuff again."

"Who knows you have it?"

"It's no secret. Other than the information on the jump drive, I've been open about things. I'm not sure the cops know about the tapes and recordings yet, though."

He drove with a scowl on his face as if trying to solve a complicated puzzle. Not wanting to ruin his concentration, I remained silent. He swiped in at the gate, and a few seconds later pulled into Ross's drive. Mother's car sat off to the side. No lights shone from within.

"Didn't we leave the lights on when we left?" he asked.

"Yes, but Mother's home. She probably turned them off when she went upstairs to bed."

"But she'd leave at least one on when she saw we weren't here."

"I can see light coming from the study," I said pointing to the windows along the side of the house.

"This set up bothers me."

My mind slipped back to the night we caught Sam in the house. "You think someone who shouldn't be is in there?"

"Let's be safe about this." He pulled out his cell and dialed 9-1-1 giving the operator the pertinent information.

"First he hits my office. When he doesn't find what he's looking for, he makes a beeline for my house. Next stop—Ross's."

"What the hell do you have that's so vital?"

"I'm not sure, but it has to have something to do with those recordings or Ross's files."

I made a grab for my door handle. Colin stopped me.

"Stay put until the police arrive."

"Colin, Mother's in there!"

He shot me a look and removed his gun from the console. "You stay here."

"Like hell I will! She might be a pain in the ass, but she's my mother."

I didn't give him a chance to argue further, but opened the door, got out, and closed it softly again. He muttered something profane under his breath and followed.

"Stay behind me, and if something happens, run like hell. Got that?"

"Whoever is in there is going to hear us come in," I said. "Let's just do it. If nothing else, he's got to come out of the study—assuming that's where he is."

"Why do you always argue with me?"

My voice took on an impatient tone. "Why do you argue with me? You go around the back like you did the last time. I'll walk in the front door. Maybe by then the cops will be here."

In the end, he had no choice. Colin left me on the porch counting slowly to fifty while he took off for the back of the house.

"…forty-eight, forty-nine, fifty."

I took a deep breath, grasped the doorknob, walked inside, and slammed the door shut.

"Mother, I'm home."

The light in the study went out throwing the foyer into darkness. Flashing lights swept up the driveway. An instant later, footsteps rushed from the study toward the rear of the house. Someone pounded on the front door.

"Open up, police!"

I flipped on the foyer light, jerked the door open and pointed down the hall. "He went toward the kitchen. Colin's waiting out back."

Four cops raced around the side of the house. Three more pushed past me, guns drawn.

"Go outside and wait on the porch."

Naturally, I didn't. I followed as best I could in the dim light now filtering down the corridor from the entryway. Halfway down the hallway, I stumbled over an object on the floor and fell to my knees. My hand sent something skittering across the hardwood, jingling until it hit the baseboard.

I scrambled to my feet and continued into the kitchen. The lights were on. The back door gaped open and from outside I heard the sounds of a scuffle and shouting.

"Drop the gun."

"Down on the ground, now, both of you."

"Put your hands behind your head."

I reached the door to find Moreland's finest had the situation under control. Colin was laid out next to the intruder, but I knew that wouldn't last long. I whirled and retraced my steps. I had to find Mother.

"Mother, Mother, where are you?"

I flipped the lights on in the den, but it was empty. I didn't bother with the study. In the archway leading to the living room, I spied the object that had caused me to fall—Mother's purse. Her key ring lay near the wall. The living room, however, was also uninhabited.

An edge of panic sawed along my nerves. "Mother, are you all right? Answer me."

Then I heard a thumping sound from the winter coat closet under the stairs. Rushing over, I opened the door.

My mother sat on the floor. A muffler had been used as a gag. Words of what I assumed were rage emanated from behind it. Her hands and feet were bound with some sort of cord. I immediately removed the woolen strip of cloth.

"Get me the fuck out of here!"

The knots on the cord around her lower legs had tightened with her movements.

"Just a minute, I have to get a knife and cut you loose."

"Hurry up, dammit!"

I raced into the kitchen, got a knife from the drawer, and ran back. Effie keeps sharp knives. One slice had her legs free. A moment later her hands were also unbound. I helped her to her feet.

"Mother, what happened?"

"You tell me. I came home from dinner and was headed to the den for a nightcap when suddenly... Hell's bells, I don't remember. Jesus, my head hurts!"

I steered her into the living room and onto the sofa, then felt around her head. A lump the size of a boulder lived just above her right temple.

"Ouch!"

Colin, followed by a policeman, entered the room. Two other cops went upstairs.

"Priscilla, are you all right?"

"No, I'm not all right. My head hurts like hell and I'm scared shitless."

"What happened, ma'am?" the officer asked.

"I assume I interrupted a robbery."

"When did you get home?" Colin said.

"Around ten-thirty, I guess." She told them the same thing she'd just told me.

"Were you unconscious, Priscilla?" Colin asked.

She sent him a withering look. "I must have been, because I don't remember jack shit from after I entered the house until I woke up in the closet."

"Ma'am, you need to get to a hospital. You got slugged pretty hard," the policeman told her.

A stubborn expression crossed her face. Before she could open her mouth to protest, I answered for her.

"I'll see she gets there. Don't bother with an ambulance."

"Can't do that, ma'am. She was injured in the commission of a crime. Just covering ourselves."

"Oh, for Pete's sake, I'm fine."

"Mother, for once in your life just shut up. Head injuries can be deadly hours after the fact. Go and get checked out. I had to after the accident."

"Oh, all right, if you insist." She looked up at Colin and the cop. "With all the activity here, I assume you caught the burglar. Did he steal any of my jewelry?"

For the first time since entering the house, I thought about the identity of the intruder. The last I'd seen, he'd been face down on the back lawn with his hands cuffed behind his back.

I turned my gaze onto Colin. His hair was mussed and his clothing rumpled—like he'd been in a fight. I must have missed a good scuffle.

"Did you recognize the guy? Anyone you know?" I asked as visions of Joey Lazarus and Sam flitted through my mind.

His expression turned grim. "I'll say. It's Jim Price."

Chapter Twenty-Two

My jaw dropped. Even Mother stared at Colin with wide, shock-filled eyes.

"Jim Price! You've got to be kidding. Why?" I asked in stunned disbelief.

"I don't know. He's not a lawyer for nothing. Clammed up immediately and asked to call his attorney—Jerricus Monroe."

"What?" Mother's voice took on a screeching tone. "He can't have the same lawyer as me. I won't allow it!"

Colin shot Mother an exasperated look. "Priscilla, Ross once defended a drug dealer on murder charges while at the same time defending the guy's brother for armed robbery. High-powered defense attorneys will defend anyone who can pay their fees."

I thought that sounded like a conflict of interest *and* unethical. Then I remembered he was talking about Ross.

Another set of lights flashed up the driveway.

"The ambulance is here, Mother. Let's get you checked out." I held up a hand as she opened her mouth. "Just to be on the safe side. Humor me."

I helped her out to the waiting vehicle and assisted her in.

"Can I go with her?"

"No, ma'am," one of the paramedics answered.

"But you're welcome to follow in your car."

"Mother, just go with these men. I'll be along shortly."

She nodded, laid down on the gurney, and smiled at the cute EMT who draped a blanket over her legs. As the doors closed and the ambulance rolled away, I had the feeling Mother enjoyed the attention.

As I headed back to the house, a glance to my left showed Jim Price in the back of a patrol car. He refused to look anywhere except straight ahead.

Inside, I gathered up Mother's purse and keys from the floor, then turned to Colin.

"I suppose the study is a mess."

"It's been searched, but the debris isn't as bad as I expected. The tapes we listened to are on the desk. I'm thinking your mother arrived just a few minutes after Jim. He may have heard her drive up, hid in the living room, and whacked her when she passed the doorway."

"What did he hit her with?"

"A lamp from the end table. I take it she was tied up."

"Trussed like a Thanksgiving turkey," I confirmed.

"Thought so. The cords to the blinds in the kitchen have been cut. Is she on her way to the hospital?"

I nodded. "I'm going along to make sure she's all right. What about you?"

"They'll be transporting Jim to the police station soon. I'll tag along and see what I can find out."

"I hope he has a good explanation for this. I'm confused."

"Join the crowd." He leaned over and kissed me. "Thanks for your help tonight. You did a good job. Flushed him right into my waiting arms."

Heat burned my cheeks at his praise. "Glad I did something right. You coming back here when you're finished?"

"Probably." He kissed me again. "Go tend to Priscilla. I'll see you later."

I wove my way through the remaining police cars and hurried to the hospital. Ten minutes later, I walked through the emergency room doors.

"Mrs. Priscilla Patterson, please. She was brought in by ambulance a few minutes ago. My name is Hilary Watson. I'm her daughter," I said to the receptionist.

"Please have a seat, Miss Watson. Do you have any insurance information you can give me?"

I rummaged in Mother's purse and wallet until finding the proper cards, then handed them to the lady.

"Is she all right. When can I see her?"

"She's back in a treatment room at the moment. The doctor will be out shortly to talk to you. In the meantime, please have a seat."

Doctors, just like lawyers, have their own language. In this case, I understood that "shortly" was a euphemism for "whenever I'm ready." I could be sitting here with the four other people in the room for three minutes or three hours. I picked up an ancient magazine on home decorating and prepared to wait it out.

I waited a long time. I was now alone in the room. Finally, at three-thirty, a doctor breezed through the double doors leading to the patient cubicles.

"Miss Watson? I'm Doctor Richardson."

I put my sixth magazine down on the table next to me and rose. "Yes. Is Mother all right?"

He smiled. "She's going to be fine. We sent her down for a CAT scan and did an MRI just to make sure.

She's got a mild concussion. We'll keep her overnight for observation."

A relieved breath escaped from between my lips. I hadn't realized how worried I'd really been about her.

"Thank goodness. Can I see her?"

"We're getting her settled in a private room at the moment. If you'll follow me, I'll take you to her."

I entered the room to witness Mother fussing with the blankets and fluffing the pillows. She smiled at the doctor as I walked up. I didn't blame her. He was good looking. Then, she noticed me.

"Oh hi, dear. I'm going to be fine, but they want me to stay overnight."

"I know. Can I get you anything?"

"No, I don't think so. If I need anything, I'll just ring for it. Right now, I'm looking forward to getting some sleep."

Ring for it. I had visions of the nurses ganging up and beating her into silence.

"Well, I'm glad you're feeling better. Get a good night's sleep and I'll see you tomorrow."

"Yes, dear. Tomorrow."

She fussed with the blanket some more in an attempt to bunch the folds around the ankle monitor. I wondered if the doctor had noticed Mother's strange choice in jewelry.

I arrived home at four. The cops were gone with the exception of one patrol car still in the driveway. As I parked, the policeman got out.

"Miss Watson? Everything's quiet. I'll be running by every couple of hours just to make sure."

"Thank you, officer. I appreciate that." I didn't see Colin's car. "Is Mr. Blackwood around?"

"No, ma'am. He followed the other officers to the police station several hours ago."

I let myself into the house and trudged upstairs. All I wanted was my bed and to sleep until noon.

It had been a helluva night.

****

I came downstairs shortly before eleven the next day. Exhaustion is better than a sleeping pill. I'd slept through the night. I peeked into the study and found Colin at the desk working on his laptop.

He smiled, but looked like hell. His hair was mussed, as if he'd run his hands through it, and hard lines grooved around his mouth. His eyes looked puffy from lack of sleep and his slumped shoulders suggested he was more exhausted than I. A five o'clock shadow had lengthened into stubble.

"Hi there. You look awful. When did you get home?" I asked.

He rubbed a hand over his chin. "About seven."

"Were you at the police station all that time? Did Price say why he broke in?"

"Jim said nothing. They booked him and locked him up. Jerricus showed up around midnight and left around one. I asked to speak with Jim, but he refused to talk to me, so I left and headed for my office."

"Did he take anything from there?"

He shook his head. "Messed things up a lot, but nothing's missing. Same at the house. Took me hours to clean up."

"Why don't you go up and crash for a while?"

"Can't. If Jim Price won't talk to me, then I'll have to research his past."

I sat in a chair. "I don't understand any of this. We

heard that recording. There wasn't anything on it to warrant breaking and entering."

"No, but it does confirm that my uncle gave him some sort of report, maybe on a former client."

"Is that ethical?"

"The report might not have been about the client's activities while Ross was his counsel. It's a murky area."

"And Ross was in his element with murky." I paused. "How did he get into your office? I don't recall seeing him on those surveillance tapes."

"The tape quality wasn't all that great, but I reviewed them again while I was there and saw him. He came in the front entrance about an hour before we started looking the first time. He was wearing khakis and a polo shirt, and carried a large briefcase. He also had his cell phone plastered to his ear and kept his head down so there wasn't a clear shot of his face. He then walked to the stairwell and disappeared. He left pretty much the same way. We weren't looking for someone entering that early."

"Okay, so your office building doesn't have the greatest surveillance equipment, but my question is how the hell did he get in here? This is a gated community. There's a guard house and swipe cards."

"Just because it's gated doesn't mean it's impregnable. If you'll notice, the neighborhood is surrounded by a six-foot high stone wall. Wrought iron spikes project from the top. A determined thief can make it over."

"And that's what happened?"

He nodded. "The cops found Jim's car parked about two blocks from the back wall. The area's under construction and no one lives there yet who would have seen him. They also found a rope device hanging from one of those spikes."

"A rope device?"

"Yep. Jim's five-ten or so. He looped a length of rope over one of the spikes, tightened it with a slip knot, fashioned a stirrup from the other end, and just hoisted himself over."

I heaved a deep breath. "God, I'll bet the residents don't know about this. They paid a premium for this so-called secure neighborhood."

"You're only as safe as you think you are."

"So, what have you found out about Jim Price so far?"

"Just the usual. I need to dig deeper. I already left a message with his brother, Carl. He might be able to fill in the holes."

"Do you think he killed Ross? I mean, Ross would certainly have let him in. Would the guard at the gate keep a log on whoever came and went? After all, it was a party. Lots of people on the guest list. I don't remember seeing Jim that night, but that doesn't mean he wasn't here. He could have arrived after I left."

Colin shook his head. "I'm trying to figure out a motive and can't—at least not yet. And then there's that damned frying pan thing again. Oh, and here's one other thing—Jim is left-handed."

"Maybe he'll talk to us when he makes bail."

"He won't be arraigned until Monday unless they can find a judge and an assistant DA willing to work weekends."

"Breaking and entering is pretty serious. What's going to happen to him?"

"Plus there'll be an assault charge. He clobbered your mother over the head. Knowing your mother, I'm sure she'll press charges. It's his first foray into the criminal world, so I'm betting he'll plead guilty. The judge will take his past into consideration and likely give him a light sentence at a minimum security prison and a hefty fine. The bar association may or may not disbar him."

I'd almost forgotten about Mother. As if on cue, my cell rang. I dug the instrument out of my jeans pocket.

"Hello, Mother."

"Get me the hell out of here."

"I take that to mean the doctor has released you?"

"Yes. Now come and get me. This place is worse than jail."

I sighed. Mother was back to being Mother. "I'm on my way."

"Mother is demanding transportation," I said to Colin.

He grinned. "I guessed. What? No good-looking doctors around?"

"Actually, there was. Maybe he wasn't impressed with her ankle accessory." I heaved another sigh and rose. "Guess I'd better go spring her. Is Effie here?"

"Came in about the same time I did. Very shocked and upset at what happened."

"Not enough to give notice, I hope."

"Not Effie Tollivar. She's tough. It would take more than this to scare her."

I started to leave the room, and then paused in the doorway. "By the way, did you hear anything yet from the people down on Parchman about that prisoner who was killed? You know, the one from the letter?"

"Not yet. If it comes via e-mail, I'll forward it to you, but I don't think that one has legs. Everybody concerned is dead and has been for years." His phone rang. He answered and listened for a moment.

"Thanks for getting back with me... Mrs. Patterson is who you'll be dealing with on that... She's fine. In fact, I understand she's being released from the hospital this morning... Give me thirty minutes to shower and shave. What's your address?" He wrote on a notepad. "Thanks. How's Jim doing... I see... Yes, I'm sorry this happened, too. Always liked Jim. I'll see you shortly."

"The brother?" I asked as he hung up.

"Yeah. He's agreed to see me. Full of apologies and hopes your mother won't press charges."

"Fat chance on that. I'll talk to you later."

The drive to the hospital took less than ten minutes. I found Mother sitting in a wheelchair in her room.

"Where have you been? It's been ages since I called."

"You called less than half an hour ago. Are all the papers signed?"

"Just about. They won't let me go until you sign that you picked me up or something. Go tell those pesky nurses you're here. I want out of this hell hole."

"I take it you didn't have a good night."

"Those damned nurses came in every few hours to take my temperature and blood pressure. Some mumbo-jumbo about head injuries. And the food! It looked and tasted like one of those microwaveable breakfasts from the frozen section in the grocery store. I hope Effie's making a decent lunch."

"I'm sure she is. I'll go sign whatever they want, and then we can go."

I signed what needed to be signed, and within minutes an orderly was pushing a protesting and complaining Mother down the corridor. No one said goodbye. I figured the nurses were glad to see her go. I didn't ask about the good-looking doctor.

"Oh, thank goodness," she exclaimed when she walked into the foyer. "Home at last. I'm going to take a long hot bath, and then sleep forever. Tell Effie to send up a tray."

She disappeared upstairs while I conveyed her message to Effie.

"Very well, miss. I'm so glad Mrs. Patterson is all right. I can't tell you how shocked I am about this whole thing. Why Mr. Price was almost a member of the family."

"I know. I'm not sure how much more of this any of us can take. Was Mr. Price here the night of the party?"

Effie frowned as she wrinkled her forehead in thought. "Seems I do remember him in the living room, but I could be thinking about another party. No, it was the last one. He was talking to that publisher person. Do the police think he killed Mr. Patterson?"

I shrugged. "I don't know. Colin doesn't see a motive."

"Motive—the reason for killing him." She shook her head. "Sometimes things can fester in someone's mind and soul for years. They can't let go, if you know what I mean. Perhaps their business breakup produced bad feelings. It was long before I came to work here. I don't recall hearing about any bad words or anything, although I do remember a time not too long ago where I heard raised voices behind the closed door. It was right before Mrs. Patterson moved out."

"Hopefully, Mr. Price will talk to Colin and give us all an explanation. Effie, make up a second tray. I'll eat upstairs with Mother. And keep dinner simple tonight. No need to go to extremes for the three of us. I'm sure you have your hands full with your niece's wedding. When is it?"

"In a month. The guest list is small and I'll have help from family. The cake is the only big thing on the menu, but I still have lots of time to make it. I don't imagine I'll be here much longer."

I stared in alarm. "You're leaving?"

"Well, miss, I can't see Mrs. Patterson staying on by herself. I know Mr. Colin is ready to sleep in his own bed. Told me so this morning. And you have a home, too. Besides, I think your mother is going to sell the place. A real estate agent stopped by last week."

"What? I didn't know this. When?"

"I believe it was the day you and Mr. Colin went to Hot Springs, miss. With all that's happened since, I clean forgot about it."

I supposed this had been inevitable. Mother had said she planned to sell. I just hadn't expected the wheels to turn so quickly. Of course, with probate stalled the process would take longer. Which brought up another question—who would deal with the family legal problems now that Jim Price was out of the picture? That was for Mother to decide with help from Sam, Ian, and Colin.

I helped Effie make up the trays. We carted them up to Mother's room. It was a tedious lunch, but I stuck it out listening to Mother's rants against the hospital, the police, Jim Price, and the rest of the family. An hour later, I stacked the dirty dishes and took both trays back to the kitchen, leaving Mother to snooze away the afternoon.

I also hunkered down in my room and fired up my laptop. It had been over twenty-four hours since I'd checked my e-mail or social media accounts. I kept my fingers crossed a message from the design school would be there. My heartbeat accelerated when I saw the first one was from Lighthouse School of Design. I was almost afraid to open it. I had fifteen other e-mails and opened them first. Most dealt with the great bargains I could find at various shops I frequented. I deleted them. In my reduced financial circumstances, I wouldn't be indulging for a long while.

That left two messages—one from Colin, a forward, and the one I was scared to open. I heaved a deep breath. Colin could wait a moment.

I clicked on the Lighthouse School of Design and read it. A moment later, I clapped a hand over my mouth as tears filled my eyes. I'd been accepted.

For the first time in years, I had a sense of purpose. Someone must have liked my portfolio, slim as it was, or seen potential.

Or maybe they just take anybody that comes down the pike. At any rate, it didn't matter. I was in. I jumped up and did a happy dance around the room. Visions of my own business ran through my head. I'd be overwhelmed with clients, all clamoring for my services. I'd be respected and honored as the best interior designer in Memphis.

It took several minutes for the fantasy to fade. Of

course, all that wasn't likely to happen, but dreams are what keep us going. And Lord knows I needed those dreams.

Calmer now, I opened Colin's forward e-mail. It was from the Mississippi State Penitentiary. His message was above it. "Hilary, this came through just as I was leaving for my appointment with Carl Price. I haven't read it yet. I don't think we'll find anything of interest, but can talk when I get home. Love, Colin."

Love? Oh, wow. Did he mean that in the usual sense? I hoped with all my heart he did. For years I'd wanted his approval and attention. The approval never showed up, so I encouraged the attention with bad behavior. I saw it all so clearly now. I'd been in love with him forever. I just hadn't admitted it to myself. *Well, this is a kick in the pants. Do I dare tell him or will he laugh me into next week?*

I didn't want to dwell on the possibility, so quickly clicked on the attachment.

The report was lengthy and I had to wade through a lot of nonsense until getting to the news that no prisoner by the name of Edward, Ed, or Eddie Haskins had died violently or otherwise while in custody during the years in question.

I sat back and scratched my head. That didn't make any sense. The hate letter had been specific. I needed to reread that letter again. Something just wasn't right. Instead of logging out of the report, I read on to the last page. "The only inmate to die violently during that time was a young man from Senatobia named Eddie Jack Smith. He was killed by another inmate in the shower when he refused to give up his soap to said inmate. The man was already doing a life sentence for murder.

Another life sentence was added for Mr. Smith's murder. Since then, the prisoner has also died of natural causes."

I logged out and sat thinking. This tallied more with the letter, and even though the details hadn't been in print, the manner of death rang true. Yet the letter pre-dated the tapes we'd recovered from Janet's safety deposit box.

Eddie Jack Smith. The name sounded kind of familiar. Had I read it in one of Ross's files? I wasn't sure.

I held my head in my hands. Too much was swirling through my mind. Eddie Jack Smith. The name pounded in my brain. Did it mean anything? If not in Ross's files had I seen it somewhere else? Like on a guest list at a party? But where and when would I have seen that? And there was still that frying pan angle that so perplexed Colin. I wanted to scream.

But I'm forgetting the drugged scotch. I suddenly sat up straight. *Oh my God, of course. With Ross drugged, he might not notice when someone walked in carrying a frying pan. Anyone could have done it.*

I thought of Mother upstairs. Of Sam. Of Bonnie. Even Carlotta ran through my mind. And then there was Joey Lazarus *and* Jim Price.

A thought crossed my mind. Guests weren't the only people at that party. I called Colin. His voice mail answered.

"Colin, it's Hilary. I just read the report from Parchman. The name Eddie Jack Smith sounds familiar, but I just can't place it. Also, I think there's an angle no one has explored. I need to talk to Effie. We can talk more tonight. Love ya."

I hung up and went downstairs to the den where I poured a glass of wine to steady my nerves. I then hurried into the kitchen.

Effie may hold the key to this after all.

Chapter Twenty-Three

I sat at the kitchen table sipping my wine while Effie chopped vegetables at the chopping block on the island. My thoughts were a bit jumbled and I needed to get them straight before making accusations.

"So, what's for dinner tonight?"

"I'm starting with vegetable soup, and then I'll make meatloaf with mashed potatoes and gravy along with a simple salad." She looked up from her task. "Is that all right, miss? You said to keep it simple."

I waved a hand. "That's fine. Sounds delicious. Uh, Effie, the night of Ross's party you said you hired in extra help."

She resumed chopping carrots. A shiver rolled down my spine as she neatly sliced off the green tops. It reminded me of a beheading.

"Yes, miss, that's right."

"Did you go through an agency?"

"Yes, miss. Whenever I need more people I contact Gray's Temp Service. Why? Don't tell me something is missing?"

"Oh no—at least, not to my knowledge. I was wondering if you personally knew the crew that showed up."

"I remember having worked with one of the girls before, but the rest—not that I recall. Most of the temps are in their twenties and do this kind of thing for extra money. The turnover rate is quite high, I believe."

As we'd talked, Effie had peeled the carrots and now proceeded to chop them with a smooth rocking motion of the chef's knife. The blade flashed in the light coming through the window.

"And how many people showed up for work that night?"

"Oh, goodness, let me think." She paused, her brow wrinkled in thought, and then swept the carrot slices into a large pot on the stove behind her. "Seems to me there were five or six of them. They arrived around noon to help Keisha clean and me with the prep work. A bartender came later, near six o'clock, if I'm not mistaken."

"And they all left when the party was over?"

She glanced up from her task of slicing onions. "Why yes. At least, I think so. I mean they didn't leave as a group, but one by one. Why would any of them stay?" She sucked in a deep breath. "Oh! You think one of them…"

"It's the one avenue we never explored. Somehow one of the maids, or the bartender, doesn't leave. Maybe one of them was related or friends with one of Ross's clients. Plus being here all evening, they'd certainly know where you kept the skillets. If they were here early to clean and set up, then doctoring Ross's scotch with Xanax would be easy. Was Ross in his study the entire time that afternoon?"

"No. He left the house around three-thirty, four o'clock. Said he had to run a couple of errands. I'm not sure when he returned. I was busy."

"So one of the hires slips into the study, dumps the anxiety medication—perhaps found in Mother's room—into the booze, and then after the party hides until he's sure Ross is drugged up good, and wham! Nails him with a frying pan stolen from the kitchen."

"I suppose that's possible."

I sipped more of my wine. It sort of made sense, although how a temp determined to kill my stepfather would find out about the party was a long shot.

"Effie, when did you contact the temp agency?"

"Oh, I'd say three or four days before the party. Wanted to give them plenty of time to get the workers."

So, that could have given a temp a few days to hear about the assignment—perhaps even request to work it. My mind was still fumbling for the lost pieces of the puzzle. After reading the prison report, I was certain the answer lay in the hate letter that had so stuck in my head.

"Pascagoula Haskins," I murmured.

Effie ceased her food prep. "Miss?"

"That was the name on one of the hate letters Ross received. The woman called Ross a whole bunch of names because he didn't take her son's case. He went to Parchman and ended up getting killed by another inmate. Colin researched the name. She and her husband died several years ago. An inmate was murdered, only the name was different—Eddie Jack Smith. Maybe she had been married before Mr. Haskins. Pascagoula—can you imagine naming a child after a city in Mississippi? Especially one that odd? I wonder if she had a nickname. People with odd names often shorten them. When the police came to tell me about Ross's death, they said they'd gotten my name from Ephemia Tollivar. I had no idea who they were talking about at first."

I wanted to laugh when suddenly the name of the murdered prisoner clicked into place. It didn't fit precisely, but it led me down an avenue none of us had explored.

Pascagoula—Passy for short?

My niece Passy is getting married...

My gaze slowly lifted to Effie's face. It was totally devoid of expression, but the eyes held anger.

"The night of Ross's funeral, you told Colin and me about how you and your sister married brothers. One of the brothers was named Jackson. Smith was the last name. Is your niece...?"

"My older brother's youngest daughter. Passy Mae Webber. Named after her aunt, my late sister."

My breath halted somewhere in my chest.

"Passy—Pascagoula. Odd names must run in your family." It was a silly thing to say, but the only words that came to mind.

"Passy's daddy is named Kissimmee, after the town in Florida. Can you imagine the fun poked at him when he was a kid? We call him Sim. My younger brother is named Birmingham. Ephemia is a small town in Georgia. My grandmother was born there."

Her gaze never wavered from mine. It was so obvious, I couldn't believe no one had seen it.

"You...you killed Ross." My voice came out as a croak from a suddenly dry throat. I gulped the rest of my wine.

"He was an evil man who destroyed people's lives. My sister loved Jackson Smith very much. When he died, she transferred all that love to her son Eddie. Don't get me wrong, she was fond of Joe Haskins— they had two more children together, but when Eddie was killed, she just came apart. Had no will to live."

Her gaze shifted to the wall behind me. "Joe went first about a year after the death. Heart attack from stress, according to the doctor. Passy lived another six months. The family agreed they'd all be alive today if Ross Patterson had taken the case. He was the best, and Eddie deserved the best. But they had no money, so he didn't."

She frowned and continued staring at nothing. "Joe and Passy begged him to let them pay it off a little at a time. He still said no. Claimed they could never work long enough to cover the expenses. He treated them like trash. They weren't trash. Just uneducated. My sister and brother-in-law were dirt poor, but decent, God-fearing folks. Broke all our hearts when Joe and Passy died. Public defender did what he could, however the entire family blamed Ross Patterson. Money really is the root of all evil. He deserved to die."

Her voice remained soft, but her eyes took on a glazed look. She reversed her grip on the chef's knife, grasping the hilt, blade pointed down, in a white-knuckled hand.

I leaped to my feet. God, how stupid could I get? I'd just unmasked and confronted a killer who minutes before had been chopping vegetables. I didn't know if she meant to kill me, too, but took no chances. I screamed, then turned, and ran through the swinging door into the hallway.

Footsteps echoed behind me. I screamed again. I was younger and faster. Surely I could make it to the front door. I made it to the staircase when the door opened and Colin walked in.

"Run!" I said gasping for breath.

He stopped my flight and shoved me behind him. From over his shoulder, I viewed Effie ten feet away. Damn, for a woman her age, she moved fast. I panted like an overheated dog.

"It's over, Effie. Put the knife down," he said in a gentle tone.

She didn't reply, just stared at us with a blank expression.

"I've already called the police. They'll be here any second. Why don't you give me the knife? You don't really want to hurt anybody else, do you?" The silence lengthened. "Please, Effie."

She broke eye contact, looked at the knife, and then back to us again. With a groan, she dropped it and sank to her knees, then sat sobbing with her face in her hands. Colin moved quickly to retrieve the weapon, whipped out his cell phone, and called the cops.

"What the hell is going on down there?" Mother's voice called from the top of the stairs. "What's all the screaming about? Knock it off. I'm trying to sleep."

Laughter bubbled in my chest. Laughter with a hint of panic. I'd never given in to hysterics before, but now I laughed and cried at the same time. I staggered to the staircase and clutching the newel post, collapsed on the lower step. I couldn't help it.

****

The rest of the afternoon and evening passed in a blur. The cops came and arrested Effie for Ross's murder. Colin and I trooped down to the police station to give our statements. This time, Detective Hamilton's smile was real. Didn't make me like her any better.

After we returned home, Colin and I packed our bags. Mother came with us claiming she couldn't and wouldn't stay in that house another minute. Nor would she consider moving in with me. That, too, was a house of death.

We ended up at Colin's, ordered in Chinese, and discussed the case as we knew it.

"Effie didn't hold back once she was in custody," he said. "Said she didn't want a lawyer. Justice had been served and she for one was glad."

"I still don't get it," Mother said, forking a hunk of General Tsao's Chicken into her mouth. "I mean how did she know Rosie would quit as cook?"

"Effie had this planned down to the last detail after her sister died. She got a job as a temp-maid at one of the homes in the neighborhood, and after work, she would stake out Ross's place. She followed Rosie home from there one night. She had an address and a name. More careful tailing and it wasn't long until she knew which church Rosie attended. Effie started attending, too, struck up a friendship. Rosie leaving for Florida was like a gift from God—Effie's words." Colin shook his head. "She'd have made a pretty good private investigator."

"And I hired her on the spot," Mother said with a groan.

"Why did it take five years to finally kill Ross?" I asked, scarfing down spicy garlic chicken.

"Opportunity. With Priscilla living there, her options were scarce. She had to be patient and watch. Sooner or later, a chance would present itself. She had it all planned. If nothing else, Effie was tenacious, not to mention patient. Then when the wife moved out, it was game on." He shook his head. "Her vengeance ran deep. Most people would have given up after that length of time."

"And the party set the stage," I commented. "How ironic. Ross engineered his own murder. How did she do it?"

"She lifted three or four Xanax from your mother's bottle before she moved out. She took a chance, but overheard enough telephone conversations to know Ross was fooling around with another woman and that the marriage was in trouble. She figured Priscilla was likely to leave soon. When Ross left to run his errands Friday afternoon, she slipped them into the scotch."

Mother shook her head. "And who was going to question where she went? She was the housekeeper."

"As soon as everyone was gone, she finished cleaning up, and then headed for the study. She said it was close to one o'clock. He was sitting behind the desk, nodding off. All she had to do was sidle around his chair and whack him. According to her statement, the first blow wasn't too hard. He merely slumped over. She nailed him again hard enough to crush his skull. When he still showed signs of life, she hit him again two more times. And for the record, Effie is left-handed."

"Then she went home, and came back the next day to discover the body," I said in wonder. "On the surface, it's so simple, it's scary."

"Too simple," Colin replied. "We chased every theory regarding party goers and former clients. The book deal thing threw us off."

"What about our accident? Was it just that? An accident?"

"No. If you remember, we were discussing the case and going to Hot Springs during lunch. Effie heard it all and got scared. She knew we were investigating and feared that sooner or later the pieces would fall into place. She had a friend of a friend send us a little message."

"You were in the interrogation room with her?" Mother asked. "They wouldn't let anybody other than Jerricus in with me."

Mother's decorative anklet had been removed earlier by an emergency court order. Once Effie was in custody and spilling her guts, Jerricus had ridden to the rescue.

Colin shook his head. "No, but I was observing from a two way mirror. Her exact words were, 'I didn't want them hurt, mind you, just scared enough to not think straight.'"

"Well, she succeeded in that. I was terrified."

"Is my attorney going to represent *her*, too?"

"Effie said no lawyers in a strong tone. She hates lawyers."

"I don't blame her," I said taking a sip of wine from my glass.

"The court will insist she have some sort of representation at the arraignment. Public defender, no doubt. She'll plead guilty, make a statement, and a judge will sentence her."

"Hope she finds a lenient judge," I muttered.

"She shows no signs of remorse and isn't likely to see freedom again."

We ate in silence for a while before I asked, "You didn't seem too surprised at the scenario when you walked in the door this afternoon."

"I was at the office and had stepped out for a moment when your call came through. The name Smith rang a bell with me, too. So, I called the prison and spoke with someone about Eddie Jack Smith. Turns out Ross wasn't the only one his mother wrote. She also sent a nasty letter to the prison authorities. They kept it as routine. It was in an old archive file on their computer. The minute I heard the name Pascagoula Haskins, I knew we were on to something. Too much of a coincidence. And then I remembered listening to Effie talk about her past the night of my uncle's funeral. She didn't have a lot of brandy, but what she did loosened her tongue. Smith, the most common of names, struck a chord and suddenly, the frying pan made all the sense in the world."

"I know. I made the same connection, only thought one of the maids or the bartender from the temp agency had done it."

"I tried calling you as I raced to Ross's, but got your voice mail. That scared the crap out of me."

"I'd left my phone in my room. Never suspected for a moment that I was in danger when I went downstairs."

Mother pushed her plate away and sipped a glass of wine. "Well, all I can say is, I'm glad it's over."

I finished my wine and set the glass down on the dining room table.

"Actually, it isn't. Why did Effie kill Don Merrick?"

Colin got up, opened each of us another bottle of beer, and poured Mother a glass of wine, then resumed his seat.

"She didn't. There's nothing official—no confession or even investigation yet—but I think Jim Price killed him."

"What?"

Mother's jaw dropped. "Why the hell would he kill one of Hilary's friends?"

"I had a long talk with his brother, Carl, today. It all goes back to Jim and Martha's daughter, Caroline, and her drug addiction. The girl cleaned up her act and enrolled at the University of Memphis. Her parents ponied up for rent on a small apartment near campus. Things were looking good." He stopped and raised the bottle to his lips, taking a long drink.

"What happened?" I asked, pretty sure I already knew the answer.

"She met up with her old supplier one night at a local bar."

"Don Merrick."

He nodded. "It wasn't long before she was using again. Crack this time. When Jim found out, he practiced tough love. Refused to pay her bills. She flunked out, began turning tricks to pay for the apartment and the drugs. According to Carl, not even that was enough to cover her habit. She was eventually evicted and got another apartment in a less desirable part of town."

"Was Joey Lazarus involved? Doesn't he run some working girls?"

"Probably. Merrick and Lazarus were hooked up in the drug scene. Since Caroline owed money to Merrick, it's possible he shoved her in Lazarus's direction to help pay off the debt with her body services."

"Didn't you say the daughter was murdered? Random or…"

"Nothing random about it. Her body was found in an alley near her run-down apartment with two bullets to the head."

I heaved a sigh, glad I had always steered clear of drugs. I'd seen too many of my friends get hooked on both booze and coke. I shuddered to think how close I might have come with the liquor. It was ironic that Ross's death turned my life in a different direction.

"Why kill her if she was working it off?"

"Ever seen someone addicted to crack? Their looks go downhill fast. I doubt she brought in enough to come close to covering what she owed."

"Did Don kill her?"

He shook his head. "Don't know for sure, but I doubt it. She owed Merrick, which meant she owed Lazarus. My guess is Lazarus had her taken out as a warning to others. No way to prove it, though."

"Oh God, what a nightmare. How do you suppose Jim made the connection between his daughter and Don?"

"Who knows? He may have had Caroline followed, seen her with Merrick, and asked around until he got a name."

Mother, following our conversation with wide eyes, now piped up. "Wonderful. My cook kills my husband, and my family attorney kills some drug dealer in my daughter's house. Boy, can I ever pick 'em."

"So after the daughter's death, Jim's wife ends up in Happy Acres for a while before committing suicide," I added.

"Jim came home from work one night and found her hanging from a beam in the living room."

Mother grimaced. "If I was going to kill myself, I'd take pills or something."

"Carl said that after Caroline's death, Jim became

obsessed with finding the dealer responsible for getting Caroline hooked again."

"The recording," I said. "The recording had him getting a report from Ross. On Don?"

"Most likely. Jim was a lawyer, but Ross was a *criminal* attorney. He had resources. Once Jim had that report, it wouldn't take long to find the man. He made it his business to know every move Merrick made, especially after Martha died. Now, this is only conjecture, but my guess is Jim staked out Merrick as often as possible. One night he follows him to your place."

"How did he know it was my place?" I interrupted.

"I don't think he did. He was just tracking his prey, saw him park, sneak around to the back of your house, and break in. Jim followed, found the letter opener on the desk, went upstairs, and killed him."

"I'll bet he damn near had a heart attack when he found out I lived there."

"His actions had inadvertently put you in the hot seat."

"Colin, you say none of this is on record," Mother said. "Will it ever come out?"

"Hard to say, but I don't think Jim cares much about anything anymore."

"Did Jim's brother know about Don? And if so, didn't the name Merrick ring a bell?" I asked.

"I don't think Carl Price knew specifics. He and his wife were on a cruise. When they got back, the media was full of Ross Patterson. Don Merrick didn't rate page one or the lead off story. By the time they got home, he was old news."

"Think Jerricus Monroe can get him off?"

"No reason for any of this to come out. Unless he confesses, Jim will be charged with breaking and entering, and assault—period."

"And I'm still left in the hot seat," I said.

"I don't think so. I commented to Detective Parker that Merrick had ties to the drug world through Lazarus, as did Price's daughter. Merrick is still an open case. They'll investigate further."

Mother shook her head, a serious expression on her face. "In a way, I understand what he did. I know I'm selfish and self-centered, but if someone harmed Hilary, I'd go after them."

I looked up in surprise. Mother and I had always had a distant relationship. Maybe she did care after all. Her sudden maternal instincts put a warm glow in the pit of my stomach.

I reached over and placed my hand on her arm. "Maybe the two of us should take a trip together soon. You talked about the Bahamas a few weeks ago."

She smiled. "Maybe. I do know I won't be returning to Jackson for a while. Bitches. Not a one of my so-called closest sorority sisters called to offer support. They can eat shit and die."

It was Mother at her redneck best with a touch of cultured Memphis socialite thrown in, and while time with me might be viewed as any port in a storm, it was a beginning. I'd take that.

She drained her glass and yawned. "If the two of you will excuse me, I'm going to bed. I take it the spare room is set up for guests."

"It is, Priscilla, and you are welcome to stay until you find a new place."

"I'll be quick about it. You two need your

privacy."

"Mother…"

She stood and waved her hand. "Oh, don't be coy. I know the lay of the land. I'm not stupid—or blind. Colin could have come back here anytime, but he didn't. That told me he found a reason to stay at Ross's." She winked and exited.

"And here I thought we were being so discreet," I murmured.

Colin chuckled. "It appears I held back for nothing."

The murders had been solved. At least Ross's had. Don's would remain open until heading for the cold files. I'd have liked to have Jim's confession, if for no other reason than to exonerate me. But time had a way of making people forget. It would be out of sight, and out of mind. My old friends would go on their merry way without me. New friends wouldn't connect me to any of this. New friends had become a priority.

And then there was Colin. I loved him. I knew that without a doubt, but did he feel the same about me? All those fears and insecurities resurfaced. *What'll I do if he says, 'So long, Hilary?'*

I wasn't sure how I'd react. I was so afraid of failure, and this would be the biggest failure of them all. Had his words at Mother's knowledge that we were lovers been just that—words? Sex is one thing, but love?

While I was hesitating, we'd cleaned up the kitchen and wandered back into the living room. Colin pulled me into his arms and kissed my breath away.

"Wow," I murmured when he finally lifted his head.

"Hilary, we need to talk."

My heart rate shot up several beats. "All right."

It was a lame reply, but for the life of me, I couldn't come up with anything else.

"I have a confession to make," he said in a serious tone. "The past two weeks has brought something into focus I kept hidden for years. I care about you. I more than care. I realized how much the day you called me for help when you found Merrick's body in your townhouse. You were scared, you were vulnerable, and you needed me."

I heaved a ragged sigh. "In spite of our past verbal jousting, I knew you'd come. I not only needed you, I wanted you. I wanted you to hold me and tell me everything would be all right. You did. That day made me realize how important you were in my life. I know it sounds crazy, but suddenly my lifestyle choices seemed shallow and callous. I wanted your approval. I guess I always did. I just didn't know how to do it."

Tears choked my words and I sniffed. This was so damned important and I was certain I was screwing it up.

He smiled and pulled me back into his arms. "Oh, Hilary, you have no idea how much I wanted to approve." He backed off and cupped my face in his hands. "You're intelligent, talented, and I love you."

My heart almost stopped beating. The tears overflowed. I laid my head on his shoulder.

"Oh God, Colin are you sure? Because I love you, too. When Mother married Ross, you were the only one of my new relatives I looked up to and liked. And then, somehow, I blew it. I couldn't admit I'd fallen for a man who didn't seem to like—or respect—me at all.

I...I...Are you sure?"

His arms tightened. "I'm thirty-five years old and know what I want. I want you, Hilary. I want you in my life forever." He stepped back and took a deep breath. "This is it. The moment of truth. The total commitment. Will you marry me?"

Oh my God, he had just asked the question I'd been waiting to hear most of my adult life. The fact that it was coming from the man I couldn't live without made my heart pound even harder.

"In a heartbeat," I cried. I threw my arms around his neck and kissed him hard. "Oh God, Colin, I love you and promise you'll never regret this."

"If I thought I'd regret it, I wouldn't have asked. Honey, you've got to build up that self-confidence. No more fears. No more dwelling on failure. You can do anything you want and succeed." He kissed me again. "Should we set the date?"

"As soon as possible. I've waited ten long years for this moment. I refuse to wait any longer. Can I move in here until we say, 'I do'?"

He grinned. "As you say, the sooner, the better."

I paused, looked around the living room, and then let my gaze wander down the hall toward the bedroom.

"I vote we find Mother new digs starting tomorrow."

Colin laughed. "I second the motion, but for now, I hope she has earplugs!"

I laughed along with him. He picked me up and carried me to the bedroom.

My life was complete.

Chapter Twenty-Four

Our plan for a quick wedding was thwarted by Mother who went into full mother-of-the-bride mode.

"But, darling, you can't just run off and tie the knot. How would that look? Besides, I want to see you in a ball gown with lots of beading and such. Oh, you'll look just like a princess."

Was she kidding? A ball gown? A princess? I leaned more toward simple with clean lines, and form fitting to show off the few curves I possessed. I could see we'd have a hard time reconciling our tastes.

To my surprise, she'd capitulated when I stood my ground. I bought a sleek, strapless satin, fit and flare dress that suited me to a "T." I wore Colin's wedding gift to me—a dazzling forty-carat, heart-shaped blue topaz pendant necklace—as my only "bling."

"Okay, I guess I can live with this look," she said. "It's a good thing Colin has such wonderful taste in jewelry. But, Hilary, I really must insist you get married here. Eloping off to Nevada sounds like you have something to hide."

I gave in on location and scrapped the Las Vegas idea. We were married a month ago in Memphis. The guest list was small. Ross's family was invited and actually showed up. Bonnie and Mother were civil to each other for a change.

None of my former friends were invited, but I did

extend a hand to several of my sorority sisters. Mother, while still not talking to the Jackson contingent, sent invitations anyway. Only Chynna Delaney showed up sans husband, who was once again on an extended golf outing. Mother was civil to her, too.

The past month wasn't so hot for Effie or Jim. Colin attended both court hearings.

"Things went pretty much as expected," he reported after returning from Effie's allocution. "She pled guilty, told the judge why she'd done it, but had no remorse. She was sentenced to twenty-five years to life in the Tennessee Prison for Women near Nashville. She may come up for parole, but I doubt if she'll ever be released. She's sixty years old, after all."

"In a way, I'm sorry Effie didn't get away with it. If Mother hadn't been arrested, I just may have told her it would be our little secret. I wish she could have seen her niece get married. I'll bet her cake would have been dynamite."

A week later, Colin also attended Jim Price's hearing.

"Jerricus had him primed on just what to say. He admitted he was looking for a tape that may have put him in the uncomfortable position of having discussed a client with Ross thereby violating the attorney/client privilege. He didn't admit to searching my office or house, just Ross's. Said he panicked when Priscilla came home, and he was sorry he hit her. He pled guilty. Case closed. Judge sentenced him to two years minus time served at a nearby minimum security facility. With good behavior, he could be out in as little as ten months."

"Will he be disbarred?"

Colin shrugged. "Hard to tell. Lawyers don't like sitting judgment on other lawyers. And the name Merrick never crossed his lips."

"Would the police have reason to look into the background on his daughter's problems?" I asked. I still hoped to eradicate my name from the police files.

"Caroline's death was a cold case and with my information on Jim and Merrick, the police are reopening it. I spoke with Detectives Parker and Hamilton after Jim's sentencing. They said you were exonerated from any involvement with Merrick's murder. Your alibi of being at Ross's and your actions when finding the body led them to believe you told the truth."

"Thank goodness," I said.

Ross's house sold three days after being put on the market. Mother immediately bought a three-bedroom condo on the riverfront with a spectacular view.

My townhouse also sold quickly. I put the proceeds toward my continuing education.

"Did I tell you how proud I am of you?" Colin said when I told him the good news about being accepted at the design school. "Why don't you build on your portfolio by redoing my house?"

"Our house," I corrected him.

"Our house," he said with a grin.

We're both easing into married life, and even discussed starting a family. I'd like that. A couple of little Colins running around sounded like fun. I wouldn't mind a Hilary or two either.

Any way I looked at it, life was good. Damned good.

A word from the author...

I was born in Indianapolis, Indiana, but lived for many years in Memphis, Tennessee, which I now consider home. I have two adult children and seven grandchildren. At present, I reside in Ft. Lauderdale, Florida, with my husband, Bruce.

I've been a serious writer since 2002 and belong to Romance Writers of America and River City Romance Writers. I'm also a member of Mystery Writers of America.

I love writing and hope readers enjoy the journey along with me.

Thank you for purchasing
this publication of The Wild Rose Press, Inc.

If you enjoyed the story, we would appreciate your
letting others know by leaving a review.

For other wonderful stories,
please visit our on-line bookstore at
www.thewildrosepress.com.

For questions or more information
contact us at
info@thewildrosepress.com.

The Wild Rose Press, Inc.
www.thewildrosepress.com

Stay current with The Wild Rose Press, Inc.

Like us on Facebook

https://www.facebook.com/TheWildRosePress

And Follow us on Twitter
https://twitter.com/WildRosePress